I0665140

other lives
for the
desert

Steve Nahaj

ISBN-13: 978-0-692-66042-3
ISBN-10: 0-692-66042-9

For the road, land, and people on it

summer

1

I HADN'T SHAT MY PANTS since the third grade, but somehow it happened on the drive home from work that day. It wasn't much, but enough to make me uncomfortable as I waited in the dry heat, hovering above the seat cushion of my hatchback, packed in traffic on the 405. It was the flu, I thought. Or worse: food poisoning. I remembered being seven years old with a horrible case of food poisoning—hooked to an IV—possibly when I first became aware of death. And now with the AC on full blast and my ass in the air, I would wait three more exits before finding clean relief.

The fuel gauge blinked red while my red face blinked. LA is no fun when you're poor. It's like living under a circling mobile—shiny things hanging from strings, sparkling and circling, but never lowering. A vacation you can't be part of. Palm tree you can't climb. And then there was the sun, tantalizing with its godly rays, showering me in gold, a sick display for cheap sunglasses. I was so broke that I didn't even own a pair. But that's only part of the reason that I was preparing to abandon my California crib.

I ran up the stairs of my apartment as quickly as possible, trying not to leave evidence. Sprinting down the hallway, I landed on the cold commode and exploded. It wasn't pretty. Luckily my roommate was away. I sat there for half an hour, head hanging, hunched, hungry for lunch, knowing it wouldn't happen with my bellowing bowels. Pacific winds blew through the bathroom and I thought about the big ocean outside and wished I was surfing something other than the toilet seat.

Before long I was back on my feet at the sink, hand washing my jeans and hang-drying them in that beautiful air. I lived in Santa Monica at the time, and when you live in Santa Monica you feel it all around—everything, right there, waiting. And so I doubled up on underwear, put on a fresh pair of khakis, and left to walk the neighborhood.

Old palm trees on Sixth
Took a left on Washington towards the beach
Middle-aged women in trendy jogging suits
pushing strollers with brilliant, bright-eyed babies
Exotic plants, groping
Spitting pollen
Sea foam green garage
Homeless man with wet hair - sweat?
Geo Metro
Bugatti

My pocket vibrated. It was Francine, my girlfriend.

"Hello?"
"Heyyyyy babe!"
She was bubbly as ever.
"Hey there," I said. "What's going on?"
"Just getting some errands done. I opened the sunroof in my car and I'm staring up at the sky. How are you?"
"Well, I shat my pants."
"Ha-ha. Hey, I thought we could get together later and watch the second half of that movie we fell asleep to. I can make a rice dish with eggs and—"
"No. Babe. I shat my pants."
"Oh."

—

I HAD no friends.

Twenty-five years old, wrapped in soggy sheets with my soggy thoughts, distanced from the world. But there it was next to me on the wall—two poster maps: America and a sprawled-out planet earth. They were starting to fray at the edges. I'd purchased them years earlier, promising that I would travel once I had the money. Once Francine and I were in a good spot. Once I was in good enough shape.

Once I had read the guidebooks and studied the languages. Once I proved myself to everyone around me.

Well, there I was anyway. Staring at it with salty eyes.

And that rotten sunlight continued to pour through the window, despite the fact that my blinds were shut. Even when I closed my eyes sunlight streamed through my ears—bird chirps, scooter wheels, hushed talking.

That's the world, I thought.

There are people out there, pressing sweaty palms onto those steering wheels, bending joints, tying laces, kissing faces. There's a wave crashing onto the shore right now, and someone—something—is watching while I'm here thinking about it. Short snaps of electricity whipping through the pebble brains of blue jays, impelling their beaks to open.

I wanted to be part of it all.

Didn't want to miss one beat, one whisper—What was that? Oh.

Thought you said something.

The maps taunted me, climbed under the covers and slept with me. I woke up next to at least thirty states. Cradled by the Bible Belt, spooning with Colorado, noogied by Alaska. On the map, each state had a different color and I wondered about the real colors. Surely Michigan wasn't purple. But I wanted to see, had to see, needed to see.

Kept telling myself to stop. 'There's nothing out there, go back to work. Go back to Francine. Slurp soup, cough cigarettes, make money. That's the plan!'

"You're trying to sabotage me, self."

How dare you! I'm trying to protect you!

"From what?"

Scary stuff.

"Like what?"

You know. Stuff that's out there, which isn't good for you.

"Like what?"

AAaaarrrrrrgggghhhh!!! Just listen to me, dammit! I'm your protector.

—

DAYS LATER there was no doorbell.

Multi-million dollar house and no doorbell.

But there was a handle-knocker in the shape of a lion's head; peep-hole in his mouth. I gave it a few hard thumps. Something stirred. Blinds cracked, then snapped shut. A dog barked somewhere in the back yard. Getting closer. I prepared to kick it with my boot, should it charge at me with open jaws.

KNOCK KNOCK

I felt like a stain on a magazine ad. The entire neighborhood a photograph, developing in the brightening sky. Lighter, lighter, lighter—the disappearing marine layer that always began the day on a somber note. But this wasn't LA, this was the Palisades. This is where LA moved when it could afford to.

KNOCK KNOCK KNOCK

"Not interested!" came a woman's voice from inside.

"Sorry to disturb you, ma'am," I said, "but I'm from the U.S. Census Bureau, here to gather some information."

"Not interested!!"

"Ma'am, I don't think you understand. I'm not here to *sell* anything. This information is required by the government. It's a simple survey that only takes a couple of minutes."

Nothing.

"Okay, thanks anyway. I'll be back."

I'd been talking to Simba the whole time.

—

OTHER HOUSES were easier.

The older and lonelier, the more welcoming. Fifty-year-olds gave me two minutes, eighty-year-olds gave me life stories, and forty-something single mothers liked to play with their hair a lot. And cookies. One balmy Sunday I ate Oreos, with milk, next to a busty Persian, while her frenetic children ran circles around us. Her skin was gold and glowing like the ornaments adorning the room.

—

OL' ARMY had no Oreos to offer, but plenty of tasty bebop jazz. He was frail, scooting across his floors with fluffy slippers. The music seemed to emanate from his evaporating irises, but I soon saw the old radio buried under newspaper.

"Arman. That's my real name," he said. "But they called me Army for short, see. Funny thing is, I went into the *Navy*. So the joke always was 'Army went to the Navy, how 'bout that?'"

He gave his finger a good lick and flipped through a stack of papers, pulling out a black and white 8x10".

"That's me," he nodded.

It was a picture of a man on a surfboard—slick black hair, muscular, riding the expansive ocean, healthy smile. I turned it over.

ARMY, HERMOSA BEACH. 1961.

"Like jazz?" he asked.
"'Course."
He fished through a bowl of cassette tapes.
I wanted to give him a hug.

I CAN'T REMEMBER when or how I came up with the idea of traveling the country in a big truck. I think it was around the time that Francine and I took a trip up PCH to Big Sur. It was morning—hot July—with windows down and Francine's hair dancing. She looked like a beautiful sea creature that grew legs and climbed into my car. Her smile, however, a conundrum. It was like a child's, but a child who is slightly unhappy. Birthday party canceled; cake still available.

An odd morning. We didn't talk much.

All that blue sky and beautiful coast, and naked bodies on the beach. And the cars with children in the back seats, screaming for something. Something outside of the car, something within themselves, something that hadn't even happened yet. And the parents screaming back at them. Screaming through their heads, fallen hairs, and beneath the skin—sprawled spider vein screams. Screams for their dreams, which were directly ahead past that bend. No, not that one! The one past the next, just around the corner from the end.

I turned on the radio and people were screaming on it.

I turned it off and we listened to the screams of silence.

"When do you think we'll arrive?" asked Francine.

"Few hours."

"Oh, babe!" she perked up. "A picnic."

"What?"

"We can have a picnic in the park. It'll save us some money and, besides, when's the last time you had *real* barbecue?"

"Yeah . . . sure."

"Well don't look so thrilled about it."

"C'mon babe," I said, putting my hand on her thigh. "You know I'm happy to be with you."

She brushed me away.

It was strange to be surrounded by so much beauty outside but little within.

While trying to focus on the existing outer beauty, I saw a bright orange semi-truck in the lane next to us. Chrome bumper and exhaust pipes running up the sides, bellowing black smoke laughter. Beautiful and noxious it was!

"Hey babe, check out that truck," I said.

She looked up and stared for a while. One of the things I admired about Francine was that she appreciated beauty in all forms. Still, she feigned indifference.

"It's a *truck*."

"Yeah, but it's a sexy truck."

"Sexy?"

I shrugged and downshifted into third, keeping the beast in sight. The driver's arm was perched on the ledge of the window, tan and thick, and I imagined its little hairs dancing in the wind. What kind of human was that arm attached to? Where did he come from? What has he seen?

"They live in them, you know," I said, pointing at the back of the long cab.

"Are we still talking about the truck?"

"Don't you find that interesting? These men—and women—live inside their trucks. It's like living in your office. Wake up and BOOM! There you are at work."

She rolled her eyes. "You think that would be fun?"

For all that went unsaid, yes, I did. But I dropped the subject and kept cruising along, past the farmlands of Oxnard, up the twisty cliffside roads, hairpin turns, steadily climbing California's crust. The sun was starting to set and now the water was right next to us, five hundred feet down; and when I saw a sign for SCENIC OVERLOOK I immediately pulled into the dirt lot, dashing through a gap in oncoming traffic, which made Francine gasp.

"Babe, I swear!" she yelled.

"What? C'mon, let's go take a look."

It was windy. Francine zipped into her white hooded sweatshirt that was a tad baggy and puffed up with the wind. I thought she looked like a big pillow.

"You look like a big pillow."

She frowned.

"But a really *sexy* one."

I pulled her in for a kiss and when I opened my eyes I finally saw the smile that I'd been missing. We approached the cliff hand in hand and peered down at the foamy shoreline, sprinkled with rocks and white seagulls. It made me sick to stare down without any fencing or barrier. I wondered if it was due to distrust in myself. I tended to imagine how it might feel to jump. And with the thought came little squirts of adrenaline. They reminded me that I was alive, and that there was a soft hand inside of mine. And my heart pumped blood down into my long legs which reminded them of the ground, and across the ground, my car, and the tall trees waiting for us in the forest, and all that would follow above and beyond.

"I love you, babe," she said.

"I love you too."

A truck rattled past and I tried not to look, for the urge to jump was still there.

2

THE WHOLE WEEKEND I thought about trucks.

There was plenty to do in the flowering forest, but my mind was focused on the greener pastures of piss-stained parking lots. I saw myself bobbing along the highway, maybe with a cheap ten-buck cowboy hat plucked from a spinning rack in the Deep South. Maybe I'd keep an acoustic guitar in the back of the cab and pull it out whenever I decided to stop for a swig of scenery. Maybe I'd learn the chords to every Johnny Cash song in existence. Maybe I'd meet a sexy cowgirl wearing her cheap ten-buck hat and thigh-high somethings.

"Babe?"

Maybe I'd—

"Babe?"

Francine was nudging me with her naked body.

"Yeah?" I turned to her.

"I'm really horny."

"We just had sex."

"I know, but can we do it again? Something about being surrounded by nature makes me horny."

We had one those cabins, the kind you see in snow globes. Except there was no snow, and it was so warm that the fireplace and jacuzzi were practically worthless. But it was certainly cute and, best of all, wasn't in the city.

"Okay," I said. "Just give my dick a moment to wake up."

"It went back to sleep?"

"Yes, even dicks have to sleep."

"You know, babe," she said, "Sometimes I get the feeling that you don't *like* having sex."

"What are you talking about?"

"You just seem to be doing it, like a chore, or bored about the idea. Do you think we have different sex drives?"

"Possibly. Everyone's different, right?"

"I guess."

We began making out, then had sweaty sex, and afterwards ate pancakes with real maple syrup, which I liked to imagine I'd extracted from the trees outside. And suddenly I was reminded of another dream I once had, which was to move to the mountains and become a lumberjack while leading a simple existence. Maybe with a dog who had a strong name but was very sweet. Maybe with a garden in the backyard where I could grow things like potatoes and avocados and marijuana. And I would brew my own beer and wave to all the neighbors. Maybe I'd have an old typewriter that I could punch away on during the night. Maybe with—

"Babe?"

Maybe with—

"Babe?"

And then, looking at Francine, I realized that she wasn't in any of my dreams.

I wondered why I kept dreaming about everything but her, and why I kept dreaming in general.

"Yes?" I responded.

"What do you want to do today?"

As if by instinct, I looked across the room to my poor wallet.

"I don't have much money, babe."

"We don't have to do anything crazy," she said, finishing her last bite of pancake. "How about my picnic idea?"

—

AND SO WE WALKED with bags of picnic supplies slung over shoulders, listening to the birds sing, feeling the day poke through webs of branches to say hello. I watched Francine, smiling with every step—she seemed happy to exist with me. Just to *exist!* I continued to feel guilty for being only half present.

We stopped at a campsite with barbecue grills and wooden tables. It was nice and cool in the shade, and we laid everything out—buns, hot dogs, chips, beer.

Look at all that condensation dripping

Franks ready for charring

And the potato chips, already crunching

beneath teeth

There were children running around with other families and I closed my eyes and imagined them my own. Was that something I wanted?

Nah.

Was it?

Nah.

I opened my eyes and saw Francine watching them, too.

—

LATER, full stomachs, we hiked a trail deep into the woods, tossing a foam football back and forth. Then we sat down on a narrow bridge constructed from two logs and let our feet dip into the rushing river. We were the only ones there and it felt like we owned the entire plot of land, the water, the sky, life itself. Everything pure. In that moment we were married with children, and a house, and steady incomes with savings, and a 401k, and health insurance, and life insurance, and assurance insurance, and three-hundred-sixty-five channels of cable TV—one for each day of the year.

We had it all because we were happy.

Suddenly, Francine's football slipped from my hands and into the water.

"Babe!" she cried. "NOOOO!"

She moaned as though the entire sum of our joy was contained inside that foam, and that it would be forever lost if I didn't save it.

"Shit."

I leapt up and ran down a trail that paralleled the water, watching the football bounce along like a soggy heart. When I finally got ahead of it, I rolled up my pants and trudged across to rescue the poor thing. I scooped it up and saw that I was standing smack-dab in the middle of the river. Francine in the distance, a happy speck, waving from the log bridge.

I held the football in the air and waited for lightning to strike.

—

ON OUR WAY back to LA we drove through Ventura, a beach town with young people wandering about carrying surfboards. Blond hair and freckles just like the blond-freckled faces I'd seen on advertisements from the 1950s, and suddenly I was thinking of Army sitting in his gloomy kitchen back in the Palisades and that photo he showed me of the wave he once surfed. And then I thought about the bumpy canyon roads we had just driven down and how I felt the car surfing the land. And the way Francine's fingers surfed the curls of her hair.

It was a hot day. I wanted to be out on those waves. I thought surfboards made everyone look younger somehow. I couldn't tell who was twenty and who was forty. Possibly due to the accompanying tan. Francine was looking out the windows alongside me, commenting on things like cute bakeries and pastel-painted bungalows and rosy children skipping down sidewalks. Despite this, I continued to feel separated from everything outside the windows; chained to my lovely sea creature but barred from the bigger picture. I turned off the AC and rolled down the windows.

"What are you doing, babe?" asked Francine.

"Just want to smell the air. I like the smell of saltwater."

"It's hot," she said.

"Just wait 'til we get through town."

She dug in her handbag and pulled out a Chinese fan.

It was quiet again.

Maybe I should move to Ventura, I thought. Or some beach town in Hawaii. If these people were having fun in Ventura, I'd be on cloud nine in Honolulu. Maybe with a pair of really good-looking swim trunks. Maybe with a pair of sunglasses that had excellent UV protection so that I could see the sky without having to worry about the pesky sun. Maybe with—

HOOOOOOOONNNNNNNKKKKK
HOONNNNNNNNNNKKKKKKKK

"Babe!!!!"

I looked to my left and saw the gigantic rotating tires of a semi-truck. Swerved back into my lane.

"Oops," I muttered.
"Pull over," commanded Francine.
"Why?"
"I can't do this anymore."
"Do what?"
"PULL OVER!"

I took the next exit ramp and parked outside a convenience store. Francine pushed open the door and went inside, and I watched her disappear behind swinging glass.

I could feel that she sensed a change in me—the beast. Clawing, balling up my soul like a straw wrapper and jamming it into my arteries; pumping it into my brain, where it exploded and fogged up my thoughts with these damn dreams. *Dreams!* Why were they there? Maybe I'd understand on my deathbed when the puzzle is complete and I can see each piece. Maybe then the beast will emerge and tell me a final bedtime story.

—

I KEPT WORKING the Census job.
    One day a man opened the door wearing a silk bathrobe.
    "Hello, sir, I'm with the U.S. Cen—
    "GO AWAY!"

I sat in my Honda and wondered what the hell I was doing with my life. I wanted to be a filmmaker, not a trucker. It's why I moved three-thousand miles from home. It's why I put up with these bathrobe assholes and scraped the belly of the porcelain pig each week. I'd spent three years in this sprawling city and all I had to show for it was a short resume of Reality TV gigs.

You aren't cut out for this world. Why'd you choose such an unstable career anyway? Why don't you get a real job? Stop all this foolin' around.

'Course, this is all before I understood the Abyss or knew how to recognize it. I took these thoughts to heart, where they wrestled with the artery beast, further fogging my brain.

I opened my glove box and pulled out a pen and notepad. In fat letters, scrawled out:

LIFE IS BIGGER

It's exactly how I felt. That despite LA being my dreamland three years earlier, the dream had moved, like a butterfly, fluttering on some crooked path that I was forced to blindly trust or sit and ignore. I looked around in the stale heat. Surely the latter wasn't working. I stuck the paper to my dashboard and drove off.

Why trucking? That's a job for people without an education.

LIFE IS BIGGER

What makes you think you could even handle that kind of work?

LIFE IS BIGGER

You're just a wannabe.

LIFE IS BIGGER

I grew tired of looking back and forth at the paper, but found it necessary to maintain sanity and keep my Honda centered on the freeway. I wondered where the nastiness came from. I'd never considered myself a destructive person until now when I finally gave myself permission to do something I wanted.

This will be the end of you and Francine. She'll hate you forever.

Oh yeah, your family will think you're nuts and also hate you.

Eventually I stopped looking at the paper and let the blackness wash over me.

Chocolate blood.

Yes, that's what it tasted of.

3

"YOU'RE GONNA do what!?!"

She nearly fell off the bed.

"I'm going to attend a school to learn how to drive big rigs. Then I'm gonna drive one for awhile."

"You're joking."

I sat up and held her hand. She winced, as if already smelling the grease that was soon to glaze my skin.

"Don't you remember when we were driving up the coast a few weeks ago," I said, "When I pointed out the big orange truck and mused about the idea of living as a trucker?"

"Yeah, I remember you *musing* about it, but didn't realize you were serious."

"Well, I am."

"Why would you want to drive a truck?"

"Because why not? I need some stimulation. C'mon, it's not so bad. You could even join me for my adventures."

"Adventures," she scoffed, standing up. "That's why you're doing this. You have some crazy fantasy like always. What about us?"

"I still love you, babe. But I'm losing my head here. I'm unhappy."

"You're unhappy with *me*?"

"I'm unhappy in general."

"And your fantasy is going to make you happier than us being together?"

"We can still be together! And if you love me you'll understand that this is important for my well-being. This is to save our relationship."

She paced around her tiny studio while I plopped on the bed and stared at the ceiling fan. Sweltering August. Outside the window a Mexican man hummed around with a weed-whacker, and as he came closer I could see his brown cheeks squeezed behind a dust mask. I wondered if there were words of wisdom behind that mask, and whether if he removed it, they would pour out like an opened tap—ancient mantras passed down from Mayan prophets.

No. Just kept buzzing around.

The ceiling fan must've been on high power. Its chains clinked in the breeze. Somehow I didn't feel it.

"Are you falling asleep?" asked Francine.

I propped up on my elbow. "No."

"Then why aren't you moving?"

"It's fucking hot."

—

I WAS emotionally exhausted by the time I got back to my apartment. Francine and I had run the same circle of dialogue about ten times, remixed on each roundabout so that it seemed like we were making progress. But we always came back to the same checkpoint: "I'm leaving to drive a truck." And eventually I left her crying into a pillow—the saddest sight a man should ever have to witness—someone so dear crying into a pillow, and feeling as though he couldn't do anything about it because he was already crying into the pillow of himself.

My roommate, Georgina, was sitting at her table in the kitchen, sniffling as though she had some kind of cold; but I thought maybe it was a cocaine cold because she seemed perfectly fine otherwise and always tended to sniffle and rub her nostrils with a quick pinch. I did not dwell on the minor mystery. Besides, she was kind and respectful and we'd never really had an argument.

I approached with a piece of paper in hand. It was my thirty-day notice to move out. Georgina took a gander and then looked at me naturally large eyes—I couldn't tell if she was surprised or apathetic.

"So you're moving out," she said.

"Yep."

"Cool. Find a new place?"

"Not quite. I've decided to become a truck driver for awhile."

"A trucker!? You?"

"Yep."

"Do you have any experience? Won't that be hard work?"

"No, and probably."

"Right on," she said. "Kudos for takin' the leap. Wish I could get back out there. Used to travel a lot, y'know."

Georgina motioned to a series of framed photos on the wall. I went over to take a look and, as with Army, saw her vibrant face surfing elephants in Africa, yoga cushions in Nepal, guitar strings in Barcelona.

"You don't travel anymore?" I asked.

"Nah. I'm gettin' up there, you know."

"Can't be much older than me."

"Thirty-three."

"So what's the big deal?"

"You just hit a point. Can't explain it. Things become more serious."

"Looks like something you really enjoyed though. What if it's your purpose to travel?"

She laughed, sniffled again, and then just stared at me as if allowing me to glimpse her soul and read the answers for myself. I couldn't.

—

IN THE COMING WEEKS I spent most of my time preparing to leave town. I'd already registered for a driving academy in Phoenix. My bus ticket was booked, and I'd have free lodging at a hotel for the entire duration of the three-week program. Just needed to pack my bags and of course tell my family about the whole plan. I saved that for last because frankly I didn't want to be discouraged by mentions of practicality or snide comments. My brain had to remain fog-free up until the date of departure—already quite the feat amid my bouts with Francine.

One of the last meals we shared was at a Thai restaurant in Culver City, somewhere along Venice Blvd, with modern architecture shaping the place like a half dome, and bold meals that cooks brought out still blazing—flames that shot up like spicy fireworks and made the faces of fat white men and hipster teens glow in the dim interior.

"So, you all packed?" asked Francine, flipping through the menu.

"Just about."

"Cool. When are you *leaving*?"

"Are you trying to provoke another argument?" I asked. "You know the answers to these questions. I'm leaving this weekend."

She sighed and continued flipping.

"I've been thinking," she said. "I don't know if I want to be in a relationship with someone who lives this kind of trucker lifestyle."

"Okay. So you wanna break up?"

"Maybe. I don't know yet."

"Well, you'll have three weeks to decide while I'm gone at the academy. Then I'll return for a week and we can reassess. How's that sound?"

"Good, I guess," she said.

I reached across the table for that elusive hand of hers. She made a sour face before meeting me in the middle. My stomach swirled. I was trying to remain calm about the whole thing, but I was shitting the pants of my gut. What was I doing? Francine glowed like the rest of these beautiful Angelinos. But there I was, running off into the dirt to drive a truck. In that moment I couldn't recall the bathrobe assholes or maps on the wall, or bickering up the coast, or bright orange truck.

I just saw Francine and felt weak.

It's fear, I thought.

There's a reason I wanted to take this adventure. And I felt it on the night that I handed Georgina my thirty-day notice. A sense that things were possible, and that they would be just as cool as my ten-buck cowboy hat dream.

"Everything'll be fine, babe."

—

"YOU'RE GONNA do what!?!"

I held the phone away from my ear for a moment and thought about telling my dad it was a joke, and quitting the whole plan right then and there.

"I'm leaving for an academy in Phoenix this weekend, to learn a new skill so that I can have steady work for the next year."

It was as dry and sensible as I could've presented the idea, which for my father, an inherently analytical engineer, was crucial.

"Why trucking? Can't you find another job in LA?"

"I need a break from LA, dad."

"Okay. But...*trucking*? What am I gonna tell my co-workers when they ask what my son does for a living?"

"You tell them that I'm on my big adventure."

Silence.

I could almost feel his finger push through the phone, into my eyeball.

"Dad?"

"Yep, still here."

"Okay."

"So do you need any money for this...thing you're doing?" he asked.

"Nope. Got it all covered. Academy takes care of housing and the training is free, so long as I agree to work for the company afterwards."

"How do you know you'll still want to drive a truck after training? You do realize it's hard work, right?"

"I understand that it's a risk, but this is something I'm enthusiastic about and therefore confident I'll push through."

"Alright."

—

"YOU'RE GONNA do what!?!"

"I'm going to be a trucker, mom."

"Well, I think that's *wonderful*. I'm so proud of you!"

"Yeah? Really think so?"

"'Course I do. That's an interesting job. Always thought it'd be cool to drive a big rig. 'Member when you were a kid and we had to hitch a ride with that trucker when my car broke down?"

"How could I forget?"

"Truckers are good people, and so are you. So good for you. My son, a *truck driver*."

—

"HOW MUCH stuff you got, hon?"

"Four boxes, three bags of clothes, and two rolled up maps."

"Well that's specific. So you don't need much storage?"

"Nope. What's the smallest unit you've got?"

The thin black clerk anchored a pen on her lip. I looked at her hair. It was short and trim and made her eyes glow like two almond pearls.

"We've got a four-by-four unit. That work?"

"That'll do."

I went to the parking lot and started pulling my belongings from the hatchback. There really wasn't much, having sold most of it online during previous weeks. I noticed that one of the cardboard boxes was cracked open and I peered inside to find scattered photos of me and Francine. They were happy photos from happier times. My stomach churned. I started to doubt everything again and thought I must finally be going insane.

The elevator creaked and hummed as I was carried up a shaft to the top floor of the warehouse. Dark, dusty corridors led me past lockers and lighted buttons. I stopped and let out a sigh that felt like my soul running for its life. A rat scampered across the floor and halted in the middle of one of the corridors, propping on its hind legs. I could see its little paws making some kind of gesture. If only I understood rodent sign language. Tell me something, Great Warehouse Rat!

I located my dwarfish locker and began cramming things inside.

Then I paused.

Technically, this was home for the moment.

Still feeling insane, I crawled inside my humble abode, finding that the only way I could fit was by assuming the fetal position. And with that, I closed the door and everything went black. Despite my cramped knees and ankles, I was strangely comfortable. The deprivation of senses brought me back to breathing—it was the only thing I could hear save for the occasional rise and fall of the elevator.

Concrete womb.

It was just like my bed and maps and when I'd shat my pants. All of these experiences were moving me forward and reverting me back to infancy simultaneously. Maybe a rebirth had to occur for me to take this journey and everything began right here, in this box.

My breathing changed pace. I was excited. I was ready again.

I went to open the door, but it wouldn't budge. Leaned against it with as much force as I could muster given my awkward positioning, but still there was no give. Trapped. Shit. I started huffing and puffing, banging on the door, screaming, "LET ME OUT!!!"

THUMP THUMP THUMP

"Somebody help!! I'm stuck in the locker!!!"

THUMP THUMP

Then I heard something outside. Rustling. My rat friend. I imagined his paws prying at the door. No, I thought. He's not trying to save me. He's chewing through my possessions, some of which still remained on the cart in the hallway.

I banged on the door even harder to scare him away.

My legs were going numb below the knees, and my kneecaps were fiery little peaks. Not knowing whether or not the door was sealed, I rationed oxygen and began limiting my screams to every other minute.

—

DON'T KNOW how long I was in there.

Along with sensory deprivation came the loss of time perception. My eyes welled up. All I could think about were those cardboard boxes and the photos I saw, and suddenly I could remember the details of each one. I saw Stearns Wharf in Santa Barbara. Francine and I sitting on a bench with ice cream cones and the scintillating sea behind us. And the hotel room where I held a coat hanger in victory, having improvised to open our bottle of wine. Soon I started to see things that weren't even in the photos, like Francine's smile behind the camera as she took them.

Footsteps.

"Hello? Somebody help!! I'm stuck in here!"

They quickened and neared.

"Where?" came a muffled male voice. "Which one?"

"The square-shaped one."

"Do you know the locker number?"

"No. It's the CUBE. I'm in the CUBE!"

I heard keys singing, then jiggling. The latch caught with a click and the door flew open.

Light blinded me as I plopped onto the floor.

Sticky, mute, and unable to walk.

4

THE BABY was going to cry the whole way.

All I wanted was an hour of sleep, but the tiny passenger kept on as we barreled into the rolling suburbs of San Bernardino. It was dawn and I felt like I was still lying in bed, except now it had been converted into a dusty bus seat where my dreams unfolded beyond smudgy glass windows; and in smudgy brown faces, where the dreams actually were all along—the strangers surrounding me—cacophonies that opened my mind only to be cauterized by Ego . . .

No, this isn't the dream you imagined. It won't be the dream until you have your ten-buck hat and Johnny Cash.

The sun began rising over purple mountains and it looked like something from a Ridley Scott movie—lone, red, absent of rays—the burning iris of a fiery god welcoming me into the unknown. Or the yoke of the egg of the universe welcoming breakfast, which sadly was nowhere in sight . . .

WAAAAAAAHHHHHH
WAAAAAAAAAAAAHHHH – AH – AH – A - AAAAAAAAA

I recalled Francine back at the Greyhound station earlier that morning. She stayed with me 'til the end, and I could feel her tugging my shirt, stapling it to the floor, staking it to her body. I must still be dragging her down the highway, I thought. Smiles evaporating with fumes and hues.

I tried looking around the cabin for reassurance—maybe Cash himself—but kept finding screaming babies and jaded faces with nowhere to look but down in their laps; or out the window at dilapidated shacks, drooping clotheslines, and sleeping dirt-lot dogs.

A truck passed our bus and I watched it scoot along, the driver droning behind the windshield, lifting a giant coffee mug to his lips. Again, it looked nothing like my fantasy and I had to continually remind myself that this was what I wanted!

This—*this moment*—was It!

—

EVENTUALLY the baby dozed, I think, because eventually I dozed, only to get awoken by the sound of squealing brakes ten minutes later. A sign read BLYTHE and outside there was nothing but asphalt and sand, and a little greasy oasis of tacos.

"Alrighty, folks" said the driver. "We've got to do a routine check real quick. Please stay seated."

Three uniformed men equipped with guns and batons stepped onto the bus and began questioning some of the Hispanic passengers, demanding papers and passports and such. Those who didn't have anything to show were promptly escorted off the bus and thrown into squad cars. It was strange, I thought, walking to the taco stand, considering how the officers themselves were Mexican.

I slopped
        down
           the
                  street   with   my   taco,
spilling pieces of beef and wincing at the minced losses. It was so warm that I could've sworn I saw it sizzling on the sidewalk. Within minutes, covered in flies, frying right along with their meal. At the edge of the highway, I looked eastward down the 10. What lie ahead in Phoenix? What oasis, if any, was to be found there?

—

I SLEPT the rest of the way.

The baby was ejected from the bus with his mother and I tried not to feel sorry for sleeping. Mostly I just wanted to enter this new situation with a fresh mind. Occasionally I'd be rattled awake to some new scenery. The addition of cacti into my lost Mojave.

> Or the dirt devils in the distance
> Spinning dust just because
> Shopping plazas packed with cars
> Roadside carts, paper scraps
> Sun-bleached, Bud-drenched ink
> quivering fingers

—

THE TERMINAL was bright, and as with all bright places I looked for the darkest corner. Mainly because it was easiest to observe from and allowed me to absorb all the brightness I needed in moments of uncertainty. I set my bags down and waited for the phone call I was to receive from the driver of a shuttle van that would transport me to the hotel.

What the fuck are you doing here, man? Trucking?

"Shut up."

Seriously, why?

"It's an adventure."

Who do you think you are to be taking an adventure? What kind of adventure is this anyway? Look around. It's a dirty bus station with gypsies and lost souls.

"Well maybe that's who I am."

Well I don't like that. I don't like who you are.

"That's too bad. 'Cause you are me."

—

WHEN THE SHUTTLE finally arrived, I climbed into the back of the long van with my luggage. The driver was a black man, mid-forties, sunglasses. He wore a shirt that read STRIKE TRANSPORTATION. The letters were cracked and faded, and the shirt itself frayed at the edges. I wondered how long he'd been with the company.

"Name's James," he said.

"Sorry?"

"Name's James. My name. Is James."

"Oh. Sorry. I'm tired."

"Nice to meet you, Tired," he said with a chuckle.

"No, I mean Johan…is my name."

"'S'alright. Heat gets the best of us out here. And you picked a hell of a time of year to learn how to drive a truck, lemme tell you."

"Is there really a perfect time to learn how to drive an eighteen-wheeler?"

"There is in Phoenix!"

He sucked on the straw of a large soda, which was so big that it wouldn't fit in the cup holder, then motioned towards me with it.

"Thirsty? You can drink off the side, I don't have cooties or nothin'."

"I'm alright, thanks."

He shrugged and crammed the cup between his legs.

I looked around the empty van and bright white parking lot, and the flat land beyond the road. I wanted to know when and where it would take me to the sky. When it would twist and turn cold. When cliffs would transform into smiling faces, dripping gravel from their lips. When the map's colored squares would pop up in front of me like those books I used to read as a child, raising to wide-eyed retribution.

"So, is anyone else coming along with us?" I asked.

"Guess not!"

He took another sip and put the van in gear.

I was quiet most of the way. Only because my head was so loud and James kept layering more words on top of mine. I hadn't heard from anyone on my cell phone—not even Francine—and was mostly glad, as more voices would only add to the whirlwind. James stuck to the highways which disappointed me because I wanted to see downtown Phoenix and its people and character. And maybe pieces of Old Phoenix with eagles rising through Adobe architecture— some flaming bird-god to tuck me under its wing reassuringly. But no. Only more highway and James talking about how he hasn't smoked a cigarette in three days.

—

WHEN WE ARRIVED at the apartment complex, James circled around the parking lot. He wasn't sure which unit was mine. On a tiny square lawn in front of one of the buildings, a group of mangy men stood at a barbecue grill wearing sleeveless t-shirts and snarls.

"Who's zat you got in there?" they asked, lumbering forward and peering into the bus.

I leaned forward to say hello to the three faces and they looked at me with furrowed brows as though I were a mistake. I tried to blend. My face wasn't exactly baby-fresh. I had a beard, jeans, steel-toe boots. Still they stared, and I wondered about scents and intonations and other culturalisms. What a picky little world.

When I had finally climbed the stairs and reached my hotel room, I took a deep breath before turning the lock. I knew that I had roommates, but did not know whether I would survive them. Who was behind the door?

ROOM 203.

Click.

5

TERRY WAS FUNNY.

That's how I would distinguish him years later.

But now was *now*, and in the moment I could only laugh.

He was rosy-faced and had a rosy disposition, squeezing little jokes between serious sentences. His complexion seemed entwined with his emotions, alternating shades of red. A stalky sixty-year-old, Terry wore a shirt that stretched across his stomach, khaki cargo shorts, and sandals.

"I always wear shorts," he snickered. "I'm from Manhattan Beach."

I was suddenly happy to be in the company of another Californian.

"So what brought you to trucking?" I asked.

"The wife."

"Oh? It was her suggestion?"

"No," he said with a pause. "It was *her!*"

Terry chuckled and cracked open a soda, offering me one.

"Yeah," he continued, "Were thinkin' about getting a divorce, but this was the cheaper option."

I nodded, tight-lipped, not wanting to stoke any fires.

"And you?" he asked.

"Looking for new experience."

"Cheers to that."

I glanced around. The hotel room was like an apartment. Spacious, with large kitchen and two bedrooms on each side of the main living area. Best of all: working AC. But those white walls taunted me. I had an urge to plaster something onto them. Newspaper clippings, flattened cereal boxes. Anything. Maybe I'd rip open a few pillows and knit a tapestry.

Suddenly the front door flung open and the white Phoenix heat rushed in, followed by a young man wearing a bucket hat—something a fisherman might don on a lazy Sunday. He had a round, stubbly face and beady eyes.

"Hot damn it's hot out there!" said the newcomer, dropping his bags on the floor and crashing onto the couch. "Nice to meet y'all. I'm Boyd."

We all shook hands.

"Where you coming from, Boyd?" I asked.

"Crescent City."

"Never heard of it," said Terry.

"All the way up north in California. 'Bout fifteen minutes from the Oregon state line."

He pulled a can of Skoal from his pocket and tucked a wad of tobacco along his gum line.

"Y'all got a cup I can spit this shit in?"

"Check the cupboards. Should have dishware."

"Hot damn."

Boyd loved to say hot damn. Everything was hot damn.

Hot damn hot outside.

Hot damn hot women.

Hot damn hot dogs for dinner.

It was strange. He had all the mannerisms of a country boy, but I'd never seen a California country boy before. Only the tan skins with their surfboards and salty smiles. And the Midwestern transplants with sunglasses and glossy headshots.

"Yessir we got the plates, now we just need the food," said Boyd.

"And beer," chimed Terry. "Not that we're allowed to have any."

"There's a grocery store down the road," I suggested.

———

AND SO we locked up and walked out into the evening; the heat still lingering in the pale blue air. It was the beginnings of a trio. Terry and his shorts. Boyd and his floppy hat. His sunglasses that served no purpose in the dusk. But hot damn he looked cool. I thought of Tarantino's *Reservoir Dogs*, except we were the schleppy would-be truckers from different mothers. It was a trio I didn't mind being part of because suddenly it was the only family I had. They were warmhearted guys from California, and I thought maybe I'd been grouped with them for a reason, whether cosmic or administrative.

I pulled my phone from my pocket and thought about Francine back in LA. I hadn't heard from her and knew she was waiting for me to call. But I stalled. Felt that I hadn't let the experience breathe, and hearing her voice would only serve as a wet blanket, much as I loved its sweet pitch. Even the awkward octaves were sought then.

"So Boyd," I asked, walking along. "What brought you to trucking?"

"Bored," he said with a smirk and spit.

"That's it?"

"Welp . . . been workin' for the fire department for the past five years. Already got some experience driving fire trucks. Figured it was only natural."

Spit.

"I see."

Terry remained quiet. I think he was hungry.

We kept on down the street.

Gas station buzz
Beams electric love
Mutes shadows, nostalgia
A time I could remember
Like this
When I walked just to see
All the things
that were watching me

—

"THERE'S NO WAY," I said, laughing hysterically.

Boyd and Garrett were trying to lift a shopping cart up the hotel stairwell so that they could unload three weeks' worth of beverages and food. (Garrett was another trucking student we bumped into at the grocery store. Somehow we could sense that he was one of us. He had the same lost look—like a child's. All the faces of the students, I'd come to find, were those of children. I thought new experiences must be one of the ways to recapture feelings of childhood.)

"She's gonna make it!" he grunted, lifting the ass-end of the cart while juice and soda sloshed around. Garrett was a hundred pounds heavier than me, but shorter by a few inches. He had a goatee. Always wore a hat. Everyone wore hats. I thought they were preparing to be truckers by wearing hats.

"She's gonna make it!"

"Sounds like you guys are giving birth," giggled Terry.

The old cart bulged.

"If anything's giving birth, it's that cart," I said.

Boyd was standing in front of the growing heap—"Fuck, fuck, fuck."

"Just another three steps!"

Finally, they arrived at the top and Garrett dropped the cart with a thud, walking away to nurse sore hands. Boyd wiped his face with his shirt—"So much for the idea of it being easier to *push* everything home."

"Couldn't we have just unloaded from the bottom of the staircase?" I asked.

"Where's the fun in that?" said Garrett.

They continued, shoving the cart into the hotel room where we unloaded everything into the fridge, cupboards, etc. I had purchased quite a bit myself, including snacks for our daily lessons on the tarmac. Anything with fiber or protein took precedence, and a metal thermos to keep my water cool when my head got hot. Everything would be hot, I knew. And later that night I'd scold myself for bringing so much black clothing.

My pocket vibrated.

I pulled out my cell expecting to see Francine's name on the display; but instead a low battery warning. Nonetheless, it reminded me of her and I nodded to the guys and left the room.

—

OUTSIDE it was dark, but the heat remained. Must've been ninety degrees. Still, I was thankful that we were in the dry desert where mosquitoes had no place (they tended to suck me dry). "Too much iron in your blood" I was once told.

"H—hello?" came a sweet voice.

"Babe?"

"Babe! I've been thinking about you all day. How is trucking school? Drive any trucks yet?"

"It's the first night, babe. No trucks 'til later this week. They've got to teach us the basics first."

"Oh."

"Yeah."

"How are you?"

"I'm okay. Miss you."

"Miss you, too."

". . ."

"There are no mosquitoes here," I mentioned.

"That's nice."

"Well, gotta sleep soon. Have to wake up at four a.m."

"Okay."

"Goodnight."

"'Night."

6

SHE THINKS MY TRACTOR'S SEXY!

"Huh?"

PLOWING THESE FIELDS IN THE HOT SUMMER SUN

I was staring into the blackness and apparently there was a tractor somewhere out there.

And it was sexy.

I'd never seen a sexy tractor before. Always thought of them as dust-covered, green-colored hunks of steel.

It was four a.m. and I was far too pensive.

"Sorry, man," said Boyd, turning off his country-music alarm and rolling over.

"All good," I mumbled, falling back to sleep.

SHE THINKS MY TRACTOR'S SEXY!

"Huh?"

"Ugggghhhhh…wakey wakey," groaned Boyd.

Within minutes I was standing and showering.

And the shower was a slap in the face, hitting me in the stomach first

Cold

Jumped out

Linoleum's cold

Turned the knob

Change! Change, dammit!!

34

I want to know I came to the desert.

—

THE BUS picked us up outside the hotel at 4:45. Easy to recall because I started wearing a watch for the first time since childhood. It was a simple black Casio, and I made a habit of turning my wrist and illuminating its face on those dim mornings. Paired with Boyd's wacky alarm, it ensured that I made it to the curb.

Our shuttle crawled forward and stopped with a squeal.

Terry, Boyd, Garrett, and a group of others stood patiently with their bulletproof thermoses and paper bags. A driver named Harper stepped down. He looked like a wild west gunslinger, wearing a cowboy hat and mustache that curled past his cheeks and summoned infinity.

"Top o' the morning," I joked with him.

"And the rest o' the day to you," he said.

"Huh?"

"That's the proper response," he assured.

"Oh. Are you Irish?"

"No. I just know. That's what it is."

I found a seat at the back of the bus, next to Boyd, across from Terry. We bobbed along like Jello molds in a warm, dead fridge. Not many spoke. I locked eyes on the silhouette of Harper's hat. It was a good focal point when I wasn't looking out the windows. Wasn't much to see outside anyway. Cornfields and warehouses. Power lines. One thing I do remember: Just before reaching a set of train tracks, a rank smell permeated the air.

"What the hell is *that?*" someone asked, sniffing around.

"Cat food," crackled Harper. "See that building over yonder with the big smoke stacks?"

"Yeah?"

"'Swhere they make cat food."

And every morning, that's where I officially woke up.

—

THE CLASSROOM was just as I remembered classrooms being: bland. They'd always been bland, and I wondered if there was some conspiracy to prepare us for bleakness. Looking around, I noticed that I was one of the youngest students. Most were beyond forty, searching for a mid-life crisis career it seemed. Or post-recession career.

There was Charlie from Wyoming. He had a square head and military cut, and large-lensed glasses that complimented his proportions. During breaks he pulled out beefy science fiction books and buried his long nose in them.

Then Big Ed from Dallas.

Big Ed looked like a Big Ed. Round as the Michelin Man, bristly-chinned, and a voice that made it feel like he was vomiting on you during conversation.

Who else? Oh! Ricardo from Escondido—shaved head, Hispanic, tattoos up and down each arm and chest muscle. Always a bandana tied to his jeans.

Corey. Local out of Phoenix. White kid about my age with mustache and buzz cut. Of the punk variety, he was usually seen rolling his own cigarettes and zoning out with neatly tucked ear buds.

In the very front of the room sat three ladies—the only women in the classroom who had banded together and formed some kind of alliance. One of them was a Bolivian, Teresa, with long dark hair. Always blushing at me. I found her attractive and might've blushed back.

In walked Professor Jake.

Jake was about sixty with a thinning head of white hair and bronze skin. Voice like a rusty bike chain.

"Hello everybody," he coughed, gently placing his coffee mug on the desk.

Written on the mug:

I'M NOT MEAN.
THIS IS THE FACE I WAS BORN WITH.

"So y'all wanna be truckers, huh?"

The room shuffled.

"Let's start with the basics."

He pointed at the big mug.

"Been drinking thirteen cups a day for the past twenty years. Now I'm not suggesting you do the same and neither would my doctor, but it will One) Help you wake up for these hellishly boring texts we'll be reading and Two) Help you wake up for those hellishly boring roads you'll be chugging along."

One of the women raised her hand.

"Thirteen cups?" she asked.

Professor Jake extended his arm and held his palm flat.

"See any shake there?"

"No."

"Body adjusts. We're adaptive creatures. Now pass these worksheets around."

He didn't really have a mean face, Jake. It was calm with steel blue eyes, and his movements windless and mindful, as though his time on the road had taught him to put the brakes on everything he did. Written on the worksheets were basic descriptions of what an articulated truck was, complete with illustrations showing how the truck had two parts, tractor and trailer, which moved independently.

"This is the reason you're enduring three weeks of my voice," said Professor Jake. "A tractor-trailer is not a normal vehicle. It's a tractor *and* a trailer, and *all* that you're carrying with it. Usually between twenty and sixty thousand pounds."

He went on explaining the particulars and eventually handed out more worksheets, scribbling facts on the board, ashing chalk everywhere. My hand was cramping as I'd already filled half a notebook, determined to learn everything there was and do the whole plan justice.

—

THE FIRST few days were like that. Waking up to Boyd's country music, cold linoleum, skinny Harper and caffeinated

Jake. The lessons, routine and similar. We were taught everything there was to know without actually stepping foot inside a truck. Mostly safety. Safety was a boring thing to listen to, and I think Professor Jake knew this because eventually he started showing us clips of trucking accidents. The poor TV fluttered with images of char and smoke, split metal and skin, and last words—"Oh shit, OH SHIT!! CLIFF!! TURN THE WHEEL!! GOD ALMIGHTY!!!" When it was over and done, the three women were digging in their handbags for Kleenex and the men scratched various parts of their faces.

Professor Jake continued, lecturing about 'blind hills' and how he once nearly killed two little girls because he was barreling down an old country road and came roaring over one of those hills, only to see a car full of passengers stopped in his lane waiting to make a turn.

"I'll never forget their faces looking through the back windshield," he said. "Luckily there was enough room for me to pass on the shoulder. Otherwise they would have been flattened to my bumper. I pulled into a parking lot after that and puked all over the dash."

Just then, a stalky bald man danced through the door—

"Woohoooooo! Y'all ready to be truckers!?!"

He was there to tell us that we were about to begin training on the blacktop, and that we had three days to decide whether we still wanted to commit to the academy contract or leave without having to pay for the school.

I thought about it. Wasn't too late.

—

I STAYED.

One evening, while shuffling around the parking lot of our hotel and talking to Francine—still toiling over our relationship—a Buick full of young thugs pulled up next to me, one of them hanging out the window.

"Ayyyo!" he hollered.

"Hold on, babe. Yes?" I asked.

"You like cologne?"

"Sorry?"

He showed me a blue glass bottle.

"Come smell this shit, dawg," he said.

"Not interested, thanks."

"Twenty bones for the whole thang. Your girl will appreciate you for it."

"I'm good, man. Can't you see I'm on the phone?"

Now I could hear the car shifting into park, and the door opening, and saw the kid jogging over to me.

I hung up, irritated.

"What's up man? Do I look like I have cash for perfume right now?"

"It's not *perfume*," he insisted, brandishing the bottle. "Smell it."

"Okay. Spray."

He pointed the bottle towards the air and I leaned in, ready to take a whiff of the concoction. Then, at the last second, he turned the nozzle and squeezed a cloud into my face. It felt like fire.

The Buick rocked with laughter.

"Jack that motherfucker, Manny!"

And so the cologne salesman began frisking me, patting down the pockets of my shorts, pushing me into bushes. Everything blurred. I only saw the brown square of his head and a silver-colored tooth reflecting the remainder of daylight.

"I *know* you got some money, punk ass white boy."

"I've got nothing. Told you!"

I wrestled around with him for a bit, eventually landing a boot to his gut, kicking him off me.

"Awww shittttt!!" yelled the driver of the car, mocking Manny, which only served to further rile him up.

Manny slammed the bottle on the ground and picked up a sizeable piece of glass. I couldn't tell exactly how large it was; I just knew it was sharp.

"You like to kick people?"

"C'mon, man, chill out. No need for that."

I was backing away towards the hotel while the car paralleled me, trying to block me.

"All this for some perfume?" I yelled.

"It's *cologne!*"

He charged at me.

Suddenly, a white blur slid across the hood of the Buick. It was Ricardo from class. He tackled Manny to the ground and squeezed the shard from his hand.

"Five-O's on the way," he barked, tossing the weapon aside. "Get the hell out of here."

Manny jumped back into the car, staring me down.

"Lucky," he muttered.

Bass rattled as they peeled off.

Ricardo ran over to me.

"You alright?"

I squinted at him. "Yeah. Thanks for that. I owe you."

"Don't worry 'bout it. Let's get you cleaned up."

—

I NEVER did pay Ricardo back. At least not in the way I would have liked—a meal or cold beer. We did however share many conversations in the nearby gym. Mostly about his wife back in LA, and how he didn't really want to be a trucker but had to pay the bills. How he wasn't into thuggin' anymore and the bandana was just to keep the sweat out of his eyes.

"Gotta get swoll for your lady," he said, lifting a set of barbells. "Pump them arms up. Never know how often you're gonna get to see her workin' a job like this. Go home and treat her right."

He did a few curls, then stopped and turned to me.

"What are you doing here anyway, man?"

"What do you mean?"

"What I mean is that you don't look like a trucker."

"What do I look like?"

"Like a damn…computer nerd or something."

7

THAT BOLIVIAN was a fox.

It was at least 110 degrees and everyone was shiny with sweat.

Her legs! Smooth and long and unblemished. I felt like a horny preteen hiding hard-ons from his science teacher (true story). Imagined myself in the back of a truck with her, enraptured, unwrapping her, parked somewhere on top of a mountain with her lips inside of mine and—

"Nivens!"

"Hm?"

"NIVENS!"

It was O'Sullivan, one of our field instructors—a stocky Arizonian with eyes like portholes back to Old Ireland. And I knew that's where his heart was. Maybe he'd visited Ireland in his younger days, or maybe his Grandmother used to drag him to his steaming plate of shepherd's pie each night. The reason for all my conjecturing was because O'Sullivan embraced Ireland with every action—ones that he believed were most Irish. Like cursing. And exposing veins on command.

"Yes?" I answered.

"What the hell are you looking at? Wouldn't be Miss Pretty's legs, would it?"

"Nope."

"'Cause we're talking about *couplers* right now, and it's *pretty* important stuff. Know what happens if your coupler is loose on, say, the red brake line?"

"I don't."

"Well. Let's say you're easin' on down Donner Pass sometime in January, eatin' your chicken sammich, when suddenly you notice a major drop in air pressure. That's your main brake line, right? Okay. You set down your grub and try your emergency brakes—this red line here—and what's gonna happen?"

"They won't work."

"Bingo bingo! And what the fuck's gon' happen to you?"

"Going off a cliff?"

"Metal burrito."

—

O'SULLIVAN was joined by two other instructors. One named Rick who looked kind of like a rat. Unkempt mustache; always wearing a NASCAR hat. Human cigarette. He reminded me of the barflies I grew up around. The ones I'd met in the smoke-filled Fleet Reserve my mother took us to, when my sister and I played pool and bought candy bars from machines. And the barfly men were always interested in what we were doing—

"Got a pack of basketball cards there, do ya?"

Or

"Model airplane, huh? Wanna know how these bad boys take off?"

Or

"NASCAR? You like NASCAR?!?"

I didn't. But after staring at the tube all day, you start to get absorbed. I liked seeing Dale Earnhardt rip around the track. Started smelling the fumes, feeling the thunder in the bleachers of the soles of my shoes. It was all exciting because I was a kid after all, and everything was exciting then.

Even the mustache—look at that!
All those hairs growing under that nose
And from the nose comes smoke

He's a creature of himself
An alien of Adult
They were once kids you know,
my mother turns to say
Cocktail and beer
Clink to the day
Clink, clink, clink! goes the fear
Washed away

But this is all beside the point.

There were two instructors: One named Rick, and the other was Bear. I can't remember his real name, but he looked like a bear.

More on Bear later.

—

THE FIRST FEW DAYS in the field were all about using the mirrors, proper technique of climbing into the cab, and learning how to keep the truck straight or maneuver the trailer left and right.

I remember my first big mistake.

Mainly because it involved O'Sullivan.

I was driving one of the student trucks around an obstacle course that looped the vast parking lot we practiced on. Orange cones marked a path and simulated the experience of driving on an actual road—complete with twists and turns. The goal was to swing wide on the turns so that the back tires of the trailer wouldn't crumple the cones. I'd never towed a trailer before and wasn't used to swinging wide. Therefore, when I went to make my first loop around the course, I immediately took a turn as I would in my little Honda and sure enough flattened a few cones, which I caught glimpse of in the side mirror.

"HHEEEEEYYYYY—GRRAAAHHGG—!!!!"

Fire and brimstone.

"SHUT 'ER DOWN RIGHT NOW AND CLIMB YOUR ASS DOWN!!!"

I set the brakes and stepped onto the boiling pavement, which instantly turned my boots into an oven. Roasted foot was always on the menu. So was Chapstick stew. O'Sullivan was standing at the end of the trailer next to one of the plastic victims.

"NOW," he said, placing a bronzed hand on my shoulder. "What in God's name do you call that? Driving?"

"I didn't see the cone."

"Did you use your mirrors?" he asked.

"Thought I did."

"You *thought*. Is that what you're gonna tell the mother of the two children you just smushed?"

"It won't happen again."

"I pray. Pray for your whole God-forsaken generation. Now get back in there and SHOW ME HOW THE SHIT'S DONE!"

I did as he said, walking back to the cab, tail tucked between legs. Meanwhile the rest of the gang was performing spectacularly. Boyd, perched behind his windshield like a fleshy extension of the truck. Even Terry and that cigarette-rolling hipster were double clutching like champs.

Told you this was a bad idea.

—

IN THE EVENINGS I kept to myself. Honestly couldn't remember what I did with my spare time. What do any of us do with spare time? What's spare time good for if we can't remember any of it?

Surprises cropped up in odd places.

Once, I came across a woman inside the laundromat who was drinking Pepsi and looked as though she was about to pass out. Her hair was wet and matted to her forehead like exposed veins. Dirt-smeared shirt. Shoes, maybe.

"You okay?" I asked, pulling shorts from the washer.

"Just need sugar," she stammered. "Sugar. Blood sugar's low."

"Is your Pepsi not helping? That's sugar."

"Don't know."

She laid her head onto one of the dryers and stayed there for a long time, draped over the machine.

I called hotel security.

"Oh, that's just Vicki," they scoffed.

—

THEN there was the Waffle House.

I remember the Waffle House because we went there to eat after visiting a sex shop. Boyd, myself, Margaret (one of the women from class), Garrett. Terry stayed home to chat with his wife. Said he'd meet us right after.

The sex shop was a haven for horndogs in Phoenix's dry industrial outskirts. A Megamall. Wall-to-wall shelves of books, DVDs, toys, greeting cards, racks of t-shirts and hats. Dildos, lubes, substitutes. The employees were two busty women of about forty with black hair. Tan teeth, white skin. Or was it white skin, tan teeth? Spare time is not for the details anyway. It's for the bigger picture. And the bigger picture here was that I was spending time in the company of good friends, laughing and eating a stack of waffles that towered over me like a tasty totem pole. It was all nipples and syrup and nobody got hurt.

—

THERE WAS a jacuzzi, too.

The guys would invite me to sit with them sometimes. After standing in triple digit heat all day, the last thing I wanted to do was boil like a lobster, but *c'est la vie* said the old Frenchman.

On this particular day I sat at the far end of the jacuzzi with Garrett and Boyd opposite. They were slathered in sunscreen, guts floating freely, belching words across to me. Children ran around the nearby pool, screaming, yelling profanity—"Fucking this and that"—and I was surprised as they couldn't have been more than eight or nine years old.

"So Johan," asked Garrett. "You married? Girlfriend?"

"Girlfriend. Yourself?"

"Wife."

"And you, Boyd?"

"Free agent," he said with a smirk.

"How long you been with your wife?" I asked Garrett.

"Well," he began, sinking further into the bubbles, "Seventeen years. But we're about to be divorced."

"How come?"

"Conflict of interest. Caught her in bed with a sushi chef."

"That's crazy."

"You're tellin' me."

"Really? A sushi chef?" asked Boyd.

"Couldn't write this shit," said Garrett. "You're a filmmaker, right, Johan? Wanna make a movie about my life?"

Just then, we were blinded as the water exploded in front of us. A young boy surfaced from the foam.

"Could have at least called 'cannonball'," Garrett snapped.

"What are you guys talking about?" asked the rascal.

"Stuff you shouldn't be hearing."

"What? How come? I'm old enough."

"No, you're not," continued Garrett. "Where's your mother?"

"Somewhere," he said, flicking water. "Probably getting high."

"Are those your brothers and sisters over there running around?"

"Some of them, yeah."

"And your parents aren't nearby?"

"They're around. Just don't know where. They live here. We live in these hotel rooms."

"I see."

"So what are you fuckers talking about? Like I said, I know stuff."

"Okay then," Garrett started. "I'd just turned twenty-one and somehow woke up in Tijuana with an empty bottle of tequila in one hand and some hot little mama's tit in the other. Nivens, you taking notes for our film?"

—

GARRETT DISAPPEARED a few days later. The kid went home and told his father everything, and sure enough the guy knew Garrett from the gym and had him evicted from the hotel. Once the academy found out, it was all over.

—

THE HEAT CONTINUED.

I squinted through sunglasses and sweat to see every nut and bolt on those trucks. I'd never studied so hard for anything in my life. Notebooks filled front to back, scribbles and scrawls, and the occasional doodle. Photos that I took to memorize gauges, shifting patterns, pre-trip inspection procedure. Rules, rules, rules to remember and always an instructor peering over my shoulder to make sure I got it down pat.

One afternoon, we moved lessons from the training course to the highway.

It was our first day in real conditions. Bear took us out.

Bear's real name was never disclosed. He was thick as steak with hands that looked permanently swollen. We drove into the desert—Bear, Boyd, myself, and one of the women from class, Sarah, who was a chubby twentysomething with eyeglasses and black lipstick. She seemed to be at the tail end of a gothic trend, and I pictured her blogging about things like acrylic paint and tarot cards.

The highway was an old two-lane road that cut through nothingness—cacti, scattering crows—and the tarmac cracked from extreme temperatures, patched over the years so that the double yellow lines were crisscrossed several times.

"Women first!" said Bear, and Sarah hopped behind the wheel.

She was hesitant, inching out from the dirt patch we'd parked on.

"I can't see," she said, peering over the dash, nearly swerving into the opposite lane. Bear reached across and yanked a lever, pushing her upward.

"That's something you wanna adjust *before* putting the truck into gear," he growled.

"Sawwwwwrrrrryyyy," said Sarah with a cute little frown.

"It's alright," he calmly replied. "You're *learning*."

It was a cute frown, I had to admit.

She continued on down the road while Boyd and I sat on the bed in the sleeper berth just behind the opened curtains. Boyd was wearing his best floppy hat. I could barely see his eyes.

"Can I tug the horn?" asked Sarah.

"Sure," said Bear.

BBRRRROOOMMMMPPP
BROOOOOOOOOOOOOMMMMPP

"Hehe. Always wanted to do that."

Bear gave a slow nod and looked out the window, probably thinking of his next beer. He seemed to always be lost in thought, pausing in the middle of a lecture and then swallowing the ellipses. After the three of us finished our straight road practice, Bear decided we had proven ourselves enough to attempt city driving. Since I was already in the driver seat at this point, Bear instructed me to continue on from the dusty road and take a right, left, left, and a right which led us toward that smelly cat factory, and beyond that, the town of Tolleson.

Along the way Bear fell asleep and I looked back and shrugged at Boyd and Sarah. He seemed to have timed his two-minute nap perfectly because he woke up just before we hit our first stoplight.

"Okay," he said, emerging from hibernation, "I want you to practice turning. This will be on the final driving exam next week."

I fixed my posture, focusing ahead. As much as I had practiced on the lot back at the academy, I quickly became unsure of myself. My hands clenched the wheel as though rigor mortis were setting in, and I let out a long sigh.

What's all this trucking business? You think you're a real trucker now just because you're driving on real roads with real people?

"Shut up."
"What?" asked Bear.
"Nothing. Trying to focus is all."

Red light

You're going to mess up, you know.

Red light

I slammed the brakes.
Bear cringed.
"You know," he leaned over, "a student once did that at a slightly higher speed, and there was an old lady behind us who didn't realize we had stopped. Plowed right into the trailer. We hardly felt it. Hardly realized she hit us until people ran over and banged on our truck."

Gulp
Green light
Go

I crawled along at a much slower pace now, watching cars zoom around like marbles kicked across a basement floor.

"Speed it up, Miss Daisy!" said Bear. "Driving too slow can be dangerous, too."

We passed a few more traffic lights and shopping plazas; Boyd and Sarah quietly observing from the safety of their cushy bed.

"Alright now," Bear continued. "I want you to downshift into second and make a right turn at the third traffic light ahead."

I couldn't tell which one he was referring to since we were cruising along more quickly now.

"This light?" I pointed, aiming for one of the series.

"Yep."

It was coming really fast and I slowed down as much as possible, but didn't have time to downshift. I swung wide and took the turn in a relatively high gear, tilting the trailer, causing Boyd and Sarah to slide across the bed. I held my breath, knowing how badly I'd fucked up. At the same time, I was utterly surprised that I pulled off the maneuver, and for a moment, with confidence.

After I straightened out the truck, Bear turned to me, bowled over, eyes like golf balls. Thorlike, he raised his hand and slammed it onto the dash—

"Don't EVER do that again! That was the STUPIDEST, most DANGEROUS thing I've seen in ALL MY YEARS! I don't even know what GEAR you were in!"

My heart sank.

Boyd and Sarah had somehow made themselves completely invisible.

Bear was redder than Terry had ever been.

I puckered my lips best I could.
"Sawwwwwwrrrrrryyyy."

8

SHE THINKS MY TRACTOR'S SEXY!

"Wha? Oh."

I dragged myself from shower to kitchen.

Terry was rummaging through the fridge. Pulled out a bottle of eye drops.
"They're better cold," he said, tilting his head back. "Refreshing."
Boyd was singing in the shower.
I filled up my water bottle.
Someone watching TV next door.

"In other news . . ."
"Congress met in Washington . . ."
"Another scorcher ahead of us . . ."
"Now back to Cindy. Cindy?"
"Thanks, Todd. In other news . . ."

—

WE WERE back on the lot again.

It was the last practice session before our big test the next morning. Everyone on edge. Passing the test meant that we would receive our official Learner's Permits, laminated by the local DMV. It also meant that we could hit the road with a mentor and begin the 250 hours of on-the-job training required before we could fly solo.

Professor Jake showed up to give us some last minute pointers. He was double-fisting cups of coffee when he arrived. I thought maybe he'd brought one for someone until

I saw him throw one cup away and start swigging from the other.

"Feel like truckers yet?" he asked.

We grumbled.

Slurp

"Now look," he continued, "It's going to be a little bit cooler tomorrow morning, but still hot as a dog in heat in hell. Drink plenty of water and get lots of sleep. You already know everything there is to know; it's just a matter of committing to memory."

Slurp

"There's something else you can do, too. Any of you ever tried meditation?"

We looked at each other.

"I know what you're thinking."

Slurp

"Hippie stuff, right?"

Slurp

"Can someone run and get me a refill, please? Listen— I'm not here to recruit you to into becoming monks or anything. I'm just saying that it's good therapy, it's free, and it's worked for me. Whattaya say we all sit down and give it a go?"

A few guys walked off. Others stayed.

Most of us stayed. The ground was already hot and we sat down and crossed ourselves into Lotus-legged pretzels.

"Is this going to be on the test?" someone asked.

"It's going to help you *pass* the test," replied Jake. "Now get as comfortable a possible and close your eyes."

Boyd and I closed our eyes last, snickering.

"Shhhhhhhhhh," whispered Jake.

"Shhhhhhhhhhhhhhhhhhhhhhh."

Air brakes in the distance

Idling

Crow

Nervous ruffle

Wind eardrum

Cough (or sneeze)

"Can you hear your thoughts?" asked Jake.

This is stupid.
Actually it's amazing. Who would've thought Jake could be so spiritual?
You forgot to buy shampoo. You're almost out.
Ack…it's gonna be hot today.
I'll fail the test tomorrow. I'm not prepared. They should've made the course longer.
Francine is probably fucking some other guy right now.

"Well, can you? Notice how clogged up our brains might be."

Jake's voice is raspy. I wonder how many packs of cigarettes he smokes per day. How could he be into meditation with that lifestyle?
Save 20% on all blue jeans when you sign up for a Star membership card—

"Open the dam and let them flow away. Notice each thought and let it go. Just let them pass, like so many angry drivers you'll encounter on the highway."

Before long, I realized the technique had begun to work. I felt calmer than I had in weeks. Months.

"Finally, when you feel clear and ready, focus on your breath—the rise and fall of your chest. The rhythm of it.

When a thought washes back through the dam, just breathe it out."

Fuzzy
Floating
Breathing

Slurp

—

IT WAS LUNCH by the time we finished our practice rounds. I had pleased Bear by making cautious maneuvers, conscious of his swelling blood pressure. He finally agreed that I was ready for the test, shaking my hand and cracking a few bones in the process. Anyhow, after practice, everyone gathered inside the cafeteria.

Hair nets, flies

White light raining onto plates of dull-colored crap (food)

Cutlery

And the cute cashier who seemed misplaced. Like she woke up one morning and found herself in an apron and was too tired to question it, and got stuck in a vortex of veal patties. I just hoped that one of her long lashes would fall into my food and I'd have a reason to complain and get her fired to freedom.

Trays loaded, we all sat down at tables, chatting, trying to ease tension. I sat with Stefan, a German who looked like Vanilla Ice, with a gold chain and swirly design shaved onto his head. He was shoveling mashed potatoes into his mouth like the end of the world, stopping once in awhile to take a breath. I thought it was peculiar that he came to America and decided to drive a big rig; but then again, I didn't know his story.

"What's your story?" I asked.

"I'm sorry?"

"I said what's your story. Where are you from?"

"Germany."

"Wow. How long you been in the U.S.?"

"Five years now."

"Do you like it?"

"Yes. But why are you asking so many questions?"

"Just curious."

He kept eating.

"Five years," he repeated. "Met my wife in Berlin while she was on vacation. She's from Ohio. Three years later we had twins. Bought a house. Now we have lots of bills to pay."

"I see," I said. "What do you miss most about Germany?"

"The food. My mother cooks amazing *buletten*— meatballs. I've always wanted to learn how to make them like she does, with the spices and everything."

"You like to cook, too?"

"Of course . . ."

His eyes lit up and he began rattling off recipes.

I told him he should become a cook.

His eyes dimmed and he began talking about baby rattles.

It was sad, I thought, the things that we come alive for— how obvious, and how easily they're lost.

Cook your buletten, Stefan!

Climb that mountain of potatoes and seize the spice of your life!

> If ever there were a time to act
> it is now
> If ever there were a time to act
> it is now
>
> If ever were now, it is time.

—

LATER THAT NIGHT, I sat around in the hotel room studying my guidebooks when Francine called. She wanted to wish me luck before my big test. Somehow it only served to upset me. I thought maybe it was hearing her sweet voice and wanting to have my ear next to it and not being able to. Or maybe it was because every time I spoke to her I felt guilty—

Damn you! Why would you leave such a beautiful sea creature?

"Because I had to. Following my heart, remember?"

Go stick your head in a microwave.

"Where did you come from?"

Francine and I spoke for a long time.

She often wanted a scene-by-scene synopsis of my day, even when I was dead tired. This would become an issue as I progressed in my journey. As usual, once I finished speaking, she would take the baton and go on for twenty minutes about her day while I remained completely silent. Any words that I uttered were like speed bumps. Slipping in a full sentence was like trying to stop a freight train.

I hardly remember anything that was said during our hundreds of conversations. Work stuff, life stuff, joke stuff. The stuff of days. Stuff we use as evidence to justify a day well spent. Receipt stuff.

I miss you, she said.

I miss you, too.

Maybe I can join you on one of your trucking adventures, she said.

Sure can, I said.

—

IT WAS a scorching hot day again.

My ass stuck to a plastic bench.

Today was the big test. The hipster cat with pencil mustache was far too immersed in his cigarette-rolling to care like I did. Boyd shrugged and spit like always. I thought maybe he had driven trucks all his life, and that he was enrolled for some kind of sick ego boost. I knew why Terry was there. I could imagine his wife, sitting at her kitchen table, eating a whole pot roast by herself; long nails tapping table while the clock ticked.

Gong, gong, gong
All those ticks gone
There goes Terry
Singin' his song
He don't care
She don't care
Look at the sky, it's blue!
Look in the mirror, it's you!
What are you gonna do?
What you gonna do?

—

BEAR, O'SULLIVAN, AND RICK lined up in front of us. They looked like washed up pirates who were forced to shave and wear collared shirts. I felt prepared enough, but those buccaneers stared us down as though we were the scum of the sea, unworthy of their greasy vessels. Everyone took turns on the course, in groups of three, while the rest of us stood in the shade and sipped from the fat water cooler. Some students had to wait longer than others, and in fact I tested last. I waited so long that I ate my lunch while watching everyone else return gleefully.

Eventually Rick cut the tension, ushering me into the high cab; watching as I made my way over to the first and easiest section of the exam: the straight line test. The exercise is as simple as it sounds. A spread of pavement defined by two sets of cones, in which you begin with the truck parked at the very front and then must back up . . . in a straight line.

Rick stood outside the truck and evaluated. I focused on his face; the dry hair sprouting from the top of his head down to his back, and the tan, tobacco-tinged skin. His eyes weren't visible through his sunglasses, but I knew what they looked like, too.

I was more curious about Rick than I was about the straight line, and there he was moving his arms up and down, signaling for me to begin.

The sun started to set and I felt rushed. Wasn't going to finish in time. Everything would turn black, and I'd be left in this cab, and everyone would laugh and run off to enjoy a pint of beer and talk about the great failure of the day, Johan Nivens.

Damn straight they will.

Beads of sweat trickled down my cheeks, mocking each pore. Mocking my mouth for breathing and attempting to survive.

"Back 'er up!" Rick hollered.

He looked beat and I felt pressure for being his last student. Even the truck was starting to grumble at me, and in the distance I saw everyone congregating in the shade; cackling like schoolgirls.

I released the brakes, put the gearshift in reverse, and let off the clutch, steadying the wheel as much as possible. Rick kept motioning with his hands, squinting to see, lathered in sunlight. The cones looked like dunce caps waiting to be tried on. Back and back I went, watching the mirrors, until I caught sight of the edge of my trailer veering off to one side. Shit. I corrected by turning the wheel, but mistakenly turned it in the wrong direction, which only worsened the offset, pushing the trailer closer to the cones. Rick continued motioning with his hands—"Straight, straight!" Yes, I know. Straight.

Over and over I tried correcting, but couldn't remember which way to turn the wheel anymore, and wished I could become a giant hand, like the hand of my five-year-old self playing with toys on the carpet. Then I could straighten her out! I'd nudge the trailer back into alignment with the truck and pick up G.I. Rick and place him into the Dale Earnhardt #3 stock car. Goodyear was the sponsor. I remember. Black.

TV. Lipstick. 'Nother round for the kid's mother. That's one goddamn good driver, innit?

—

NEEDLESS TO SAY, I crushed those cones.

And when I returned to the shaded haven, my classmates raised hands for high fives that never connected.

"What's up, buddy?" asked Terry. "You passed, right?"

"Failed. Straight line test."

Laughter.

"Sure," said Boyd with a nudge. "Hey, we're all gonna celebrate later at the Waffle House. Wanna join?"

"No. Boyd. I failed."

"Oh."

—

SOON everyone went to get their licenses, and not long after they were gone. I was alone in my hotel room, studying late into the night; practicing through the day like a gray lot goof. Deep down I knew none of it mattered. Didn't matter that I was left behind or that it required extra time. It was all part of the bigger plan, and it would happen as it had to. It would happen in due time. I thought about the surface of the world ballooning over fiery core and layers of rock. And then I thought about the endless void and all the other rocks. Waffles seemed silly in the spectrum of our syrup.

—

AFTER the long weekend of practicing, I took my test again and passed. There isn't much more to say. It was a peaceful morning of mowed lawns and donuts, and my instructor was a calm man of patience. We even got to talking about Pennsylvania and mothers and the stuff of life, which kept my brain in low gear when I shifted to high.

When it was all said and done, he sent me over to have my face laminated at the local DMV, and then off I went on a bus back to Los Angeles where I would meet with Francine somewhere in the grit of downtown.

I didn't want to leave just as I hadn't wanted to come.

I was getting used to the hotel room and its nuances. O'Sullivan and his shouting red face, and Professor Jake and his Buddhist ways. I even missed the punishing heat and blacktop skillet, perfume gangster, and catfood bus rides. It was strange. Always strange, feelings like these. Always the same process each time: resisting, attempting, adapting.

autumn

9

I WAS BACK in Culver City again, waking up next to scents of Francine.

Everything as it should be.

LA still brimming with exotic plants and stray cats. The bums were begging and staggering into mid-day traffic with paper-bagged glass and busted lips. Big-breasted waitresses who had their own fat lips to worry about—that is, concerns of how to make them fatter, plumper, and their hair silky and smooth like the leaves of Palm Springs.

O LA! You've teased and tickled me with your crusty Highland fantasy. You've made me look the other way because I've exposed the underbelly and frowned at the mechanics below. Maybe I should've never seen it. Maybe I shouldn't have gone looking. The only thing that mattered in that moment was the brown beauty in my arms—the waterfall of black hair and radiant skin against mine. And hands on my chest. And my hands under her face, thumbs on cheeks, iris to iris—there's the locking mechanism! Expose that!

"Still, why do you have to drive a truck?" she continued to ask, even as we got down to it.

This would not work. Not with those eyes. Give her another pair. Then I can lie to her and shrug it all off like Bogart: "Let's not spoil a good time with sour talk, baby."

Anything but those exotic gems!

I could swim in those pupils. I could build a tent within them.

Black pool, consume me.

Black pool, soothe me.

Black pool, show me the back door boonies.

—

I HAD A MERE WEEK before I needed to report back to Strike for company orientation, where I would be assigned to a mentor and given a truck. There would be 250 hours of training required at that point. Me and another human being bunkered in a truck for 250 hours. I was not looking forward to it. Mostly I just prayed that it would be someone who understood me.

Francine and I spent our days together, moving about town as usual, and for the time it seemed that everything was back to normal. We went to buy groceries and joked about the vegetables looking like faces, and the stale cracked pies; dancing down aisles like figure skaters on a shopping spree.

We manufactured moments out of nothing.

Everything a moment.

Spaghetti dinner moment, feed the fish moment, wash the dish moment, sneeze moment, football that we've never watched until today moment. Shrink wrapped moments sold in display cases behind glass eyes. Already bought and consumed. Leftovers for dull hues.

—

ON THE SUNDAY before my orientation, Francine and I made our way to the local Catholic church. It was the same as any mass, save for the air of anxiety circling over us. Anxiety like vultures, pecking our scalps while the preacher went on about something or other. He was a good preacher, and what I remember most was that, towards the end of his sermon, he said "Wake up, my child!!"

"WAKE UP, MY CHILD!!!!"

It shook me because what he really meant (I thought) was "Go out and live!" or "Wake up to your inner truth!" or possibly "Get your ass in that truck!"

I squeezed Francine's hand when he said this. I'm not sure exactly why, but I thought maybe she'd better understand how I felt if it came from the voicebox of this beautifully robed man. Or maybe I thought she herself would wake up. But no. She only looked at me with that look she used to give after telling one of my bad jokes.

—

WHEN I RETURNED to Strike, I was assigned a room in a motel with an African man. He was about forty, dark as leather. Could have been older because his skin was a shiny, unwrinkled leather that reflected the world. Or was it the TV? He was watching *Dancing With The Stars* and quite entertained, laughing, while I stood in the bathroom trimming excess hair off my beard—all those stray ends that went rogue from the pore up. Hardly anything but stubble remaining and felt weird, but prepared to present myself to a company that wouldn't care anyway.

"Wow! You look very much younger," the African told me as I wiped my face clean.

"Yeah? Am I ready to hit the town?"

And I did a little dance in the mirror and was the dancing star of the room.

The dancing star of the moon!

It certainly was a bright night when I stepped outside into the air, which smelled of musty tires and overcooked hot dogs. The hotel outskirts of A Town I'd Come To Know Only From The Seat Of My Truck.

Others knew it more simply as Ontario, California.

I was hungry and so I walked to the convenience store where I caught glimpse of a pretty Latina behind the counter with glittering black hair and eyes. She'd be the first of many enchanting women I'd meet along my journey. But that comes later.

While wandering the store in search of something cheap and sustainable, a group of four teenagers walked inside, sporting leather jackets and buzz cuts. I noticed that they were chatting with the pretty clerk, eyeing me suspiciously—

the alpha apes of today. Sensing their toxic energy, I grabbed a few cans of microwaveable stew and paid the dove.

Sure enough the guys followed me out of the store, smoking cigarettes and spitting sunflower seeds.

"Hey faggot!" one of them yelled. "You like my sister? Why would a faggot wanna fuck my sister?"

I pretended not to hear him, although his words latched onto me; plastic shopping bags slicing through my knuckles.

"Why don't you go back to San Francisco?" another one yelled.

"Yeah! Wanna suck my dick, Frisco boy?"

I wasn't sure where they got the idea that I was from San Francisco. Perhaps they saw the laptop case slung over my shoulder and fresh trimmed face and drew assumption. Perhaps they saw me as competition for the clerk. Perhaps they had a bad experience when they were younger. Perhaps they themselves were attracted to me and threatened by their own feelings. Perhaps they were afraid of death. Perhaps there's no answer for these questions and we're paying psychiatrists too much money.

Whatever the case, I escaped unharmed with a small piece of me wanting to give up the whole trucking thing, figuring that I'd run into more people of this disposition down the line.

No, I thought.

I came to drive.

—

THE NEXT DAY I showed up at orientation and shook hands with the African man, attentive and shiny, and other people I'd never seen before. All truckers. Already developing the trucker grumble and shift—squirming in their seats as though they were never comfortable, searching for the sweet spot, anchoring flesh on five-dollar folding chairs. It's a habit that would follow many of them into the cushions of their trucks during the next ten or twenty years. Shifting bodies, eyes, gears, mirrors. Shifting and shitting. Yes indeed, I was once told about a driver who was so hellbent on miles and money that he donned daily diapers.

I took a seat and tried not to shift. But it was difficult because there were so many new faces, and I kept looking around, trying to hear everyone's stories without parting lips. Directly behind me, I noticed a peculiar face. It was white and intent; the face of an intellectual, ogling me as if I were a distant cousin of his. He wouldn't stop burning holes into the back of my head and so I turned around and introduced myself with a firm handshake. His name was Simon, he said. Then he asked—

"So, why are *you* here?"

"What do you mean?" I answered.

"I mean…you don't look like a trucker. I'm willing to bet we're here for similar reasons. Do you have a college degree?"

The other guys leaned in to hear my response.

"I went to film school," I said.

"Yeah, but was it at a university?"

"Yes."

"So you have a degree."

"Sure."

"Listen," Simon said, whispering now. "I get it. I studied philosophy at UNC. You're out for something pure. Richer. Am I right?"

"Pretty much."

"What is it, though? What do you seek specifically?" he questioned.

"Exactly what you just said: new experience. Truth maybe."

"Truth! Thought so. What kind of truth?"

"Well, I feel there's a lot of anger in the world. So maybe something about suffering; how to cope with it."

"Why do you think we suffer?" Simon pried.

"We want to prolong the good and erase the bad, not accepting impermanence."

"See, I disagree," Simon argued.

"Why?"

"I think it's just the opposite. We cling to the bad and shoo away the good."

"Doesn't it all trace back to the idea of acceptance and what we choose to hold or relinquish?"

Simon's face began to change colors as the orientation leader cleared his throat to commence our initiation process. More paperwork passed around.

"Listen," prodded Simon. "Let's talk more at lunch. We've got work to do."

—

"SO, what's our work?" I asked.

"Ah. Come with me to my car."

Simon still had a piece of turkey hanging from his mouth as he stood up from our lunch table. He was quick on his feet, like a child running to the Christmas tree; some kind of gift to be unwrapped behind the rolled up glass of his car, which turned out to be heaps of books and journals scattered throughout the back seat. A rickety old Chevy with North Carolina plates, splashed with dirt, and the graphic of the Wright Brother's airplane imprinted on them. The Wright Brothers who had the same energy of Simon, seeking something in the sky. I can see their eyes now, stretched and bulging beneath skin. I can feel their heart beats in my chest. I can see their toes tangled in all that pedal work, tasting the celebratory—

"See all this?"

Simon flipped through one of the journals, hardly legible.

"Yeah. What about it?"

"I've been keeping entries on everyone I meet. This guy George, for example. He works at a post office in Wheeling, West Virginia. Read it."

GEORGE SANDERS. POSTAL CLERK. ABOUT 45 YEARS OLD. BAD BREATH, CLEAN TEETH. HAS ESTRANGED DAUGHTER. SULLEN WHEN HE SPEAKS TO HER. WANTS TO

SEE HER. LOVE AS MOTIVE? LONELINESS? SEEMS TO ENJOY
WORK AS MEANS OF DISTRACTION.

IF GRANTED ONE WISH: SEE DAUGHTER AGAIN.

"Okay," I said, handing back the journal. "So you're psychoanalyzing strangers?"

"In a sense, yes, but really they're just presumptions. I like to believe most are accurate. Usually I buy these people a beer or meal just to get them comfortable enough to open up. It's all part of a larger project. Kind of like a mirror for society. Here, check this one out . . ."

JEANETTE WILSON. STAY-AT-HOME MOM. GREAT BODY
FOR MOTHER OF THREE. BORED OUT OF SKULL.
SHOPLIFTS IN HER SPARE TIME BUT WON'T TELL ANYONE.
FEARS SHE'LL BE WORTHLESS ONCE KIDS ARE GROWN.

IF GRANTED ONE WISH: PUNK BAND VOCALIST.

"I see. And how do I fit into this project?" I asked.

"Well, essentially I'm setting out to continue my work while driving these trucks across the country. But having met a kindred spirit, I thought we could collaborate and double the research. Figure out this mad world together."

I drew a long breath.

"It looks great, Simon. Really. You're onto something here. But I honestly feel that your work will hold more credibility if it remains uniquely yours."

He clasped the journal and tossed it back into the car.

"Thought you might say that. Maybe our paths are too similar."

"That, too."

He scrunched his eyes at the sun and seemed, for a moment, to fall into a trance. I thought maybe he was allowing me to document him.

"Keep in touch at least?"

"'Course."

10

PACO WAS HIS NAME. My mentor.

When I met him he was wearing a black long-sleeved shirt with hair combed back and wet like motor oil. Mustache. A Hispanic man, but I couldn't quite place him because his eyes resembled those of an Asian, and he used them to smile. Anyway, I immediately knew that I had gotten lucky because Paco was my age and full of enthusiasm. I'd been speaking to the stars for weeks, wishing for a mentor of lively disposition rather than the crabby old truckers who grunted half-witted remarks about their pay, and health, and their wives who wouldn't shave their legs; although now we're getting off the subject of Paco.

"There she is," he pointed, as we strolled through the sea of trucks in the big gray lot.

The truck stood before us, tall and proud, begging to be driven. I climbed inside and looked around—clusters of chrome gauges sunk into the wood grain dashboard. There it all is! There's the shifter! There's the windshield, clean and crystal clear like a wide high-definition screen for life itself. What great scenes were to debut beyond it?

"Not bad considering some of the junkers these other guys get," said Paco. "Only 280,000 on the odometer."

I looked behind me into the sleeper berth, which had two sets of bunk beds. There were also cupboards and drawers, outlets, and two windows on either side of the bed, which could be propped open for fresh air. I felt giddy.

Paco stood outside of the truck, inspecting it, kicking tires and tightening bolts—the ol' pre-trip inspection routine I was taught so thoroughly at the academy.

"I have a confession to make," Paco said, suddenly appearing next to me.

"Yes?"

He revealed a burning cigarette in his hand.

"I'm a smoker."

"Okay."

"Just wanted to let you know because Human Resources told me that you prefer a non-smoker."

"Oh. Yeah. Guess I just didn't want someone who smelled up the cab."

"No problem. I always smoke outside the truck."

Paco continued puffing and told me to log onto a computer that was attached via thick cord to the dashboard. It was bulky and mostly looked like a keyboard except for a narrow piss-yellow display with blocky text. This device was used as a punch-in clock as well as a means of accepting new jobs when they were offered to us. When loads became available, it would emit a shrill, high-pitched beep; one that penetrated the brain and shot through the back of the skull. It also beeped when you exceeded the sixty-five miles per hour speed limit.

Soon after signing in, we got a beep.

PICKUP: 18:00 TUESDAY   PAROWAN, UT
DROP OFF: 11:00 THURSDAY   CHEYENNE, WY

—

PACO DROVE the first hundred miles.

It was mid-day Monday and could've been Anyday, Someday. The road was finally unfolding, straight down the 10—the same stretch I'd traveled to Phoenix in that God-forsaken Greyhound, except now we veered north towards Vegas up I-15. The truck rumbled along and I kept looking around at all the suburbia; cul-de-sacs carved into Mother Earth's dry throat. The sun was beating down, bouncing through the windows, and ohhh don't you know what I mean? When the sun does that *thing*? That shiny warm something? The back porch thing. The sunglasses in snow thing. The sunkissed kiss! The lips

on straw

on beach
The . . . the . . .

—

PACO DROVE the first hundred miles.

We'd just gotten through the mountains and dipped into Apple Valley—Hesperia to be specific—when Paco pulled into a truckstop parking lot to take a break. He yanked out his pack of cigarettes and offered me one, but this is all before I took to the habit; when I was content to inhale imagery.

Off I went into the convenience store, bombarded by shelves of sugar and salt. I craved a solid meal. I was nervous about driving. But no. Only rotating hot dogs that had been spinning for ages and radioactive-green slushies.

One of my goals was to remain a healthy young trucker, dammit! I knew it was possible, but also knew that I'd be stuck in wild places with limited options. Today was the beginning of the health test and I settled for a protein bar and OJ . . .

And there was Paco sitting on the curb with his cigarette, watching the sun set behind a span of turbines. I calmly approached, not wanting to disturb his nicotine nirvana. He seemed content to simply sit, and I was impressed by his poise amid the parking lot bustle.

"What do you think of all this?" he asked.

I took a seat next to him.

"Still soaking it in I guess."

"It's cakework," he said, taking a drag. "Once you get the hang of driving, making your deliveries on time . . ."

"Yeah?"

"Mhmm. No bossman lingering over your shoulder. That's the best part. Just gotta deal with the nagging computer."

"Seems that could get annoying."

"Shit, man. Know what I did before this? Cleaned the inside of sewage tanks."

"Serious?"

"As a heart attack. Every day, suited up head to toe and jumped inside. And before that, concrete construction. Trust me. Cakework!"

And with that, he hopped to his feet and threw me the keys.

"Thought you were driving to Vegas?" I stammered.

"You're ready now, dawg! No better time. Still got some daylight to work with."

I climbed into the cab and tried to remember all the things I'd learned.

There's the steering wheel. Okay, that's important.

And the pedals.

And this big stick helps move the thing forward.

Oh c'mon. Trust yourself, dammit! You know this!

No, you don't.

"Comfortable?" asked Paco.

I squirmed in my seat, trying to carve a nook.

"Yeah."

Then I fired up the truck and took a deep breath. This would be more than orange cones. First gear, gently let off the clutch and she started to move forward. I watched my side mirrors to see when the end of my trailer would clear the other two trucks we'd parked next to. Then I turned straight out of the lot onto a narrow road, which would lead us back to the highway.

Second, third, fourth. And by fifth gear I was taking the ramp onto Interstate 15 towards Mile Marker 44, holding steady at the governed 65. One could obsess about numbers in a profession like this.

Few miles down the road, I noticed a sharp pain in my left hand and realized it was due to tension from gripping the steering wheel so tightly. And when Paco noticed, he told me to relax, and I let out a prolonged sigh that mimicked the truck's air brakes—Pffffffffffffffffftttt—and made Paco and I both laugh at once.

"Gotta relax, man. Can't drive all clenched up like that."

Truly, it was silly. There was nothing but land and straight road. Nothing to get tense about. Not yet at least.

And the sun still burned
But as we rumbled north the sky grew dark
I remembered that it was the season of autumn
The season forgotten in Tinseltown
Where the only indication was the thinning of traffic
Los Angeles!
Somehow missing it already
NO! I couldn't. Mustn't. I had committed.
And dammit, in this life we must commit to something
if only for the season
day

moment

I began to veer off the road.

"Easy, man! Watch where you're goin'!" Paco yelled.

"Shit, sorry."

"Don't be sorry. Just keep your eyes open. Whatcha thinking about over there anyway?"

"Nothing."

"Alright, well that reminds me. You can get tired as hell on highways like this, 'specially at night."

He reached behind us into the sleeper berth and yanked open a drawer, revealing at least twenty bottles of Mojo Max—a concoction of caffeine, B vitamins, and ginseng concentrated into two swigs of liquid. He grabbed a couple and tossed them into one of the cup holders in front of me. "Sleep is always best, of course," he added, unbuckling his seatbelt. "And I'm pretty damn tired. Girlfriend kept me up all night, yapping about how I need to marry her. Stories for the long journey ahead, my friend."

He moseyed into the sleeper.

"Wait. You're not going to leave me up here, are you?"

"Is there a problem?" asked Paco.

"Well, I don't know where I'm going."

"Sure you do. Vegas."

You don't know what you're doing.

"I don't know what I'm doing."

"Sure you do," my mentor assured, "You're driving."

You're not good at it.

"I'm not good at it."

"Doin' just fine," said Paco.

And on that note he closed the curtains and I was left with my widescreen movie. Terrified. All those little cars zipping around, BABY ON BOARD, Paco snoozing away. The lethal left hand grip kicked in (Pffffffffffffffffffftttt) and I confided in the truck itself; my comrade of the Mojave soon to be moonlit, but for now a dreamscape of cherry and lavender. I wanted to be absorbed by it. I wanted to become a color. What would it feel like to exist as a color?

"HEY MAN, WATCH IT!!"

—

IT WAS QUIET AND DARK by the time I reached the Nevada state line, which is when I retreated inward, remembering a trip that Francine and I took to Sin City years earlier. We arrived with approximately $71.53 in our pockets, intending to accomplish the feat of not spending a dime more in the adrenalized land of temptation. When we got to our hotel, we laid around on the bed for a couple of hours wasting our youth because there was nothing better to do. She'd packed a bag of plastic utensils and tupperware meals—rice, eggs, and cold chopped Spam. Outside, the streets were empty save for puddles of rain reflecting neons and bulbs. We made our way into a casino and I played a single round of blackjack for five bucks and lost, but made out with a free cocktail from the painted waitress. Mostly we just wandered around and joked about the great big show of life unfolding before us. This was the best part of youth (and still was) I thought, sitting high in the truck cab, being able to watch everything before becoming it. Yes, the curtains were open that night in Vegas! The night was forever. The Ferrari was okay to stand beside solely for photos because it was a hunk of polished metal and fluids, and we were sacks of free-moving bones, and it was all explainable and pretty to watch.

I thought about that jaunt all the way through California, rolling over the milky desert; trying to peer into nothingness without veering into it. Paco was fast asleep and I wondered how he could trust me so easily. Wanted to know more about him. He was a man of mystery—the only kind of people I enjoyed company with because small talk was unnecessary and there were always more interesting conversations to be had.

As we approached Vegas I began to freak out because traffic was increasing, surrounding the truck on all sides with little following distance between us. I was tired and bleary-eyed, and the sudden onset of urban lighting felt dangerous.

"Uhhh, Paco?"

I reached behind with my hand and opened the curtains.

"Paco?"

He must've become mummified back there. Maybe he escaped through some trap door and fled back to LA on a collapsible scooter. Traffic swarmed the truck on all sides. I couldn't even remember the correct exit ramp to take.

"PACO!!!!"

He jumped up.

"WHAT? WHAT? Everything okay?"

"Yeah. Just need some guidance through the city."

He sat down next to me and rubbed his eyes.

"You're doing fine. What's the problem?"

"Where are we going?" I asked.

"Goin' to the truckstop. Exit 57."

"To do what?"

"Sleep."

—

PACO HELPED ME reverse our truck between two others, requiring three or four tries. And thus began a ritual between us, in which Paco would jump out of the truck whenever I'd prepare to back up, pop a cigarette in his mouth, and direct me. Once in Montana, he jumped outside with nothing but a sleeveless undershirt and shorts when it was zero degrees.

"Aren't you cold?" I asked.

"Nawwww, dawg. I'm used to this shit."

Anyhow, after successfully parking, I went inside the truckstop to use the restroom and clean up, placing my toiletry bag on the counter; pulling out facial cleanser, toothpaste, dental floss. I began brushing my teeth first, looking into the smeared glass and trying not to get distracted by its stains. A scraggly man walked past—a fellow trucker I presumed—and stopped in his tracks upon seeing me, staring with slack jaw.

"Brushin' ya teeth?" he asked.

"Yep."

He let out a chuckle, shook his head, and slipped into a stall.

Meanwhile I did some flossing and washed my face, drying it, noticing a slight rash on my cheeks. Sunburn maybe. Yes, I would need sunscreen in this profession. As I stood there examining my face, the man reappeared next to me.

"Keeps gettin' better every day, don't it?!" he asked.

I turned and stared into his eyes. This driver had been on the road a long time. He was chalky, greasy, twisted. Did he want to befriend or antagonize me? Was I humored or irked? The lines were unclear.

"Depends on the day," I said.

11

THIS WAS MY BIG ADVENTURE.

And when I awoke the next day Paco and I ate McDonald's, and it felt like my five-year-old adventures sans ball pit. Yes, this was my big adventure and today we would scoot along with sausage biscuits. We would bury farts into our seat cushions and casually roll down windows; coolly commenting on the fresh plateau air. We'd cross the Utah state line and see purple mountains and yellow fields.

"But first," said Paco, "We drive through my favorite part: Virgin River Gorge."

The gorge was a large canyon that cut through Southern Utah and Northwestern Arizona. A scar carved by a so-called virgin. It was a sunny day, and the canyon was colored like brick—layered, majestic—and I instantly wanted to be climbing its walls, bare back to the sun.

"Amazing!" I yipped.

Paco snickered as though he'd already seen the entirety of the universe. The road snaked, offering a different view with each curve.

"Water cut through all this fuckin' rock. Can you believe that shit?" Paco marveled.

Once we hit the state line, Paco parked at a truckstop to use the toilet, and I climbed down and stood in awe at the grasslands and snow-capped pimples of Miss Utah.

My pocket vibrated.

"Hello?"
"Hey babe."
"Hey. What's up?"
"Not much. Just lying in bed, thinking about you," said Francine.

"Oh yeah?"

"Yeah. Are you thinking about me?" she wondered.

"Absolutely. I miss you, babe."

"How's trucking?"

"It's great. Learning something new every day."

"Yeah? Where are you right now?"

"Southern Utah."

"Oh okay. Is it nice?"

"It's wild. The kind of place you'd picture prospectors roaming back in the 1800's."

"Cool."

"Yeah."

"Hey," she continued, "So there's a bunch of new employees at work and they're really funny. One guy was reminiscing about *Ninja Turtles* today and asked which character was my favorite. We both said Donatello. Which one's your favorite, babe?"

"Hmm. Don't know. Can't remember the cartoon too well."

"Oh."

"Yeah."

"Well he wants me to go with him to see a movie next week. Some kind of 3D thing. Would it be okay with you if we went together?"

"Uh, not completely comfortable with that. But you can go if you want."

"What? Not comfortable with it?"

"Seems like an impromptu date with a random guy. Dark room. Cozy seats."

"First of all, he's not *random*. Secondly, it's not just *him*. His friend is going."

"So there's a buffer."

"You're so dramatic," she said. "Completely exaggerating this. He's just a co-worker."

"Listen, my mentor is returning to the truck. I've got to go."

—

THE CONVERSATION haunted me for the next hour. Through the Red Cliffs of St. George, Cedar City, straight into Parowan. The landscape radiated crimson and my mind was diving for black. Every time I spoke to Francine, I felt as though I were doing something dubiously wrong. It was confusing because I loved and respected her, and occasionally thought she was right.

I was the crazy one.

You're the crazy one.

—

I CONTINUED DRIVING, getting in as much practice as possible. The season changed rapidly as we went, gradually climbing in elevation; vegetation turned tumbleweed. This was the West that I had never known, for Los Angeles was not the West. It's LA, or the West Coast. And now it seemed that we were really in the mix of it, nearing Salt Lake City, passing silos and the faraway farmlands that fed so many Americans.

Paco nodding off.

Head dropping and jerking as if hearing tiny bombs exploding into fireworks of pillows. He once spasmed awake with such force that his back cracked and made me laugh. I told him to go in the bunk to sleep, but he seemed determined to fight the Z's for some reason or another.

"So, let me ask you something," he started. "Why'd you decide to become a driver?"

"Well, it looked like an interesting job that paid decent money. Wasn't getting much work in Hollywood."

"Wait a second, man. No one jumps into trucking just 'cause they need cash. There are plenty of day jobs in the city. Don't bullshit me."

I froze up, not knowing what to say.

"Got a lot of miles ahead of us," he continued. "Gonna need some stories. Tell me a story, man! Why are you out here? Not gonna laugh or nothin'."

"That's mostly it. I've never seen the country and was curious," I asserted.

"And you just woke up and thought trucking was the best way?"

"Yeah. I like to drive."

Passing through Salt Lake City I was taken aback, as everything truly was salty. It was in the air, the clouds. Buildings covered with it. There was a Morton factory with the "umbrella girl" emblazoned across a barn. There was the lake—vast and lustrous—and then it was east on 80 toward the Wyoming border. Everything brilliant. The colors were appearing just as they had on the map, and the sky closed in. I rolled down the window and dipped my hand into the atmosphere. It danced with my fingers.

—

IN THE MORNING we arrived at our drop-off location in Cheyenne. Thankfully we didn't need to wait for anyone to unload our trailer. It was what they called a "drop and hook," meaning that we dropped the trailer and immediately hooked to another one pre-loaded with merchandise. Before leaving, however, we had to run into the Shipping & Receiving office to pick up the Bill of Lading (BOL)— standard paperwork that accompanied the trailer. Paco and I met with the clerk, a short Mexican man who immediately started speaking Spanish upon seeing Paco—

"*Adónde vas?*"

"Sorry," said Paco, "I don't speak Spanish."

"You don't?!"

"Nah."

"Why not? You're Hispanic, right?"

"Yeah, just wasn't ever taught it."

"Damn. Where you from?"

"LA."

"And you don't know *Spanish*?"

Paco reddened.

"Got a problem with that, man?"

"Just find it strange. Anyway, here's your paperwork. Denver Walmart. Good to go."

—

LATER IN THE TRUCK, blaring south into Colorado, I asked Paco about the language thing and of course he still didn't want to talk about it; only divulging minor details about his childhood. He had been raised in tattered suburbia, where he spent his youth with skaters, punks, and stoners while trying to steer clear of the bangers.

"Why don't you hit the hay?" he advised. "I got this."

We were cruising along 80 towards I-25, straight into the mouth of Colorado. Or the anus. I had no clue. I just knew we were going to Colorado and it was another colored square I hadn't seen. Glancing at the map, it actually appeared rectangular. But then I saw Kansas and realized it was all relative.

I crawled into the sleeper berth and closed the curtains, which clicked with a snap; sealed by magnetic strips, blocking all daylight. Lying down, I pulled a blanket to my chin and buckled myself in using the security harness—a seatbelt for my body, should the truck come to a screeching halt (or worse).

I tried.

Closed my eyes but couldn't doze.

Thoughts of Francine danced in my head. Thoughts of crashing waves and irises. Let's talk geometry and rainbows, yes! There I was, barreling through Colorful Squarado with a mind encircled by brown.

Funny.

I recalled a conversation with an NFL player backstage during a TV production. Hall of Famer. Had everything. Pretty wife, adoration, houses. Yet, on the day of our filming, the athlete's co-star mentioned Ukraine and his eyes lit up.

"Ukraine?" he said. "Ain't ever been to Ukraine. Maybe once, but I can't be sure. Let's go to Ukraine! Damn. For some reason I wanna be in *Ukraine* right now."

Then he turned to me.

"Hey, man. Why do we always want what we don't have?"

—

I WAS BEING kidnapped and taken somewhere.

That's what I thought when I woke up, or tried to pretend, listening to the engine brake kick on—BRRRAAAAPPPPP-PAP-PA-PA-PAAAA. Hearing the wind and feeling it jostle our cab. The sensation of a constant earthquake. Movement. And no idea which direction.

I'm being kidnapped and now someone has to pay the ransom. What was I worth?

Nothing, motherfucker!

Hey now. Worth something.

—

DENVER was great.

I saw it for about sixty seconds as we passed through after picking up a new load, headed back up north to Butte, Montana. It was night. Buildings glowed as we passed under them on the highway. I tried to imagine humans inside, wearing ties, pressing keys and smiling at co-workers, microwaves beeping in break rooms . . .

I wasn't sure what we were hauling, but it was heavy.

"Sometimes they don't tell you what's in the trailer," said Paco, now riding passenger while I struggled to find the correct gear.

"One time I picked up a load from an office building in Philly. Could barely maneuver the trailer out of the lot because it was made for cars and there was no room to swing wide turns. The BOL listed the trailer's weight as *sixteen ounces!* When me and my student finally got to the drop-off location, I broke the lock, opened the doors, and a cop jumped inside and pulled out a padded envelope. Some top secret shit, right?"

I didn't know whether to believe Paco sometimes. He had a knack for making everything sound fantastic, even his construction work. Tanks and drain pipes seemed like a hot idea in his presence. I thought maybe he should become a recruiter of some sort. Anyhow, we continued onward. I was fresh off eight hours of sleep but still tired, so I opened the drawer where Paco kept his Mojo Max and drank one down. It was like sucking on a wall outlet.

The truck hummed along. Cars zipping around.

Where are they going?

Paco stared out the window. What's he looking at?

What is all this?

12

GOD'S COUNTRY they called it.

I just called it Montana.

But there was something of God in it.

As I drove along swallowing lines, the landscape turned colors yet again—hills and mountains popping up like those books I used to read, indeed! I was right! This is no phenomenon! I am no myth-sayer! I may be a dreamer, but it's only because I've dreamt things that have dreamt back at me.

And there I was in the dream of reality.

Fishermen standing in roadside rivers
Evergreens left to pine alone
Blond, sandy wheat grass
You remind of me of Utah, Montana
Your air, clean
Reminds me of the me before I was me

That rotten sunlight looks better without the blinds
Wish I had a second set of eyes
O Francine! She could provide them
She could speak through hers and I would live the words
We could all use a second set of love

But back to brakes and gasoline
My sword is the pen is the gearshift selector!
Take me to fifth, take me to sixth

"Take a left up here," barked Paco, aggravated at something.

He had been sullen since the state line.

"What's going on, man? You alright?" I asked.

"Yeah. Lady drama."

"What?"

"Girlfriend's been all over me this morning. Pissed about some text messages she read last time I was home."

"Texts from who?"

"From a girl I used to date. Listen man, it's not important. Let's get to our drop-off location and find some grub."

—

MONTANA WAS COLD. Paco and I meandered across the truckstop parking lot and I felt like a cattle rancher by simply existing on the land. Imagined little spurs on the backs of my boots, straw tucked between teeth, horseshoe in hand. I loved the weather because it nipped of November, and I was ready to move forward with my adventure. Having not seen Francine in a couple of weeks, I was also itching to get back to her, worried that she might have taken off to a permanent movie theater with her Ninja Turtle companion. Anyhow, this was an interesting truckstop because it had a wooden facade and looked more like a lodge or country inn, complete with sprawling lounge upstairs, couches, TV. Paco went to take a shower while I sat and watched The Home Shopping Network. A clean-cut man and bedazzled woman were pitching a blender . . .

"For just three installments of $29.95, you too can purée your way out of *any* cooking conundrum. Smoothies, vegetables, ice cubes, milkshakes for summer—can you imagine the possibilities?"

"That's right, Melanie. Let me tell you: I haven't spent this much time in the kitchen since I was eight years old, reaching for the cookie jar."

"Ha, that's right. And don't delay. We've only got two hundred of these left."

"Only two hundred."

"Act now."

—

I AWOKE LATER, still in the lounge. Paco hovered over me with a kind of homemade Q-tip—"This is how they make 'em in prison"—and then digging in his ears while flipping channels. My stomach yelled at me and so I went downstairs for food; trying to remain faithful to my health diet (turkey sandwich, OJ, pack of peanuts for the road). Every wall was wood-paneled, and the stench of grandma's attic gathered in the air. I glanced around to see if there were actual grandmas lingering about. No. It was just the old walls and their old stench. And camouflage thermoses for the big-cheeked, big-bearded men coughing their way down aisles; colossal limbs wrapped in cowhide.

Munching on my sandwich, I stumbled upon a gift shop littered with glittering crystals and faux love. There was a rack of greeting cards and I spun through it, locating the perfect one for charming Francine. It had a cartoon illustration on the front—a woman in polka dot dress with pig tails, holding onto a clothesline as the wind blew her sideways.

Inside: HANG IN THERE!

Perfect.

I scrawled some sentiments, then signed, sealed, and shipped it off with a kiss.

—

HOW WE GOT to the strip club I don't remember, but I do remember calling Francine just before and sweet-talking her, and feeling as though she knew that I was up to something. Really, I wasn't up to anything. It was Paco's proposal; I just happened to accept with enthusiasm. Thing is, he was having a rough day with his girlfriend and we both felt camaraderie of frustration with women as many truckers do. It's part of the wacky gypsy world, and I was starting to understand what Paco meant about holding high hopes.

Anyhow, we'd been sent to Missoula to wait for another pickup and had nothing to do in the meantime.

Missoula.

Missoula was picture perfect. Most impressive was the smoky sky, as if Mr. and Mrs. Montana projected their scenery onto its canvas—a simulacrum of our solar system fashioned from brown houses and hills, brick churches and steeples, and those fishermen who remained knee-deep in roadside waters.

But the strip club was not Missoula. The strip club was its own bubble of blonds and brunettes, and they too were part of this sprawling beauty, even with their tacky red tassels.

"Gentlemen, take your seats," croaked a potbellied man who suddenly appeared next to us. We did as he asked and Paco grinned, smoothing out his mustache and adjusting posture—

"So what do you think, Johan?"

"I don't know. Haven't seen the ladies yet, have we?"

The music was a mishmash of pop country and heavy metal, and the women came out one-by-one for their exhibitions of flesh and soul. Again, I knew nothing of the Abyss and couldn't tell whether they were there by necessity or desire. Some danced with such vehemence that it seemed they had finally arrived, right there at the three-dollar Honky Tonk of God's Country.

"What about that one?" Paco asked, pointing towards a dark corner where a tan, short-haired girl peered at us from behind war paint. I thought maybe she was trying to hide her eyes and that if she used any more makeup she would disappear completely. But there was something alluring about her; the way she stood with arms delicately crossed and boot kicked up against the wall—a duality of being and circumstance.

"Yeah. She's nice."

I was broke and we didn't stay long. Besides, Paco was sober these days and didn't want to risk having a drink with the possibility of a random drug test. Thinking it rude to leave with a pair of legs kicking across our sights, we waited until the song ended.

I tried to separate eyes from thighs. I made the decision that very moment: Everywhere I went, I would separate eyes.

Construction Eye
Instructor Eye
Big Buck Hunter Eye
Mother Mary Eye
Teetering Toddler Eye
Baker That Made My Pie Eye

I would learn to speak the most ancient of all languages.

When Paco and I finally stood up, I felt a soft hand land on my shoulder. It was the murky-eyed medusa from the corner. She was even more stunning up close.

"We don't like to see a seat go cold 'round here," said the lady.

"Sorry. We're truckers. We have to, uh, pick something up," I responded.

"We got time, dawg," winked Paco.

Now I was staring directly into her eyes, trying to speak Eye; trying to figure out what this Montana girl wanted. Likely cash, I thought. And I didn't have any.

"There's an ATM machine behind the bar. Just hand 'em your card," she said.

Francine's face appeared inside my skull, bouncing from membrane to membrane. It even started speaking words as it ricocheted.

<blockquote>
You

               Don't

Love

               Me?
</blockquote>

"Sorry," I told the medusa. "Maybe in another lifetime."

—

BEER.

65,000 pounds bound for Tijuana. I imagined that we were smuggling booze like *Smokey and the Bandit*, straight into the trodden streets of Baja with a big chrome suitcase waiting by the beach. 'Course, Paco would have to learn Spanish by then. I sure as hell didn't know any.

We were cruising along under early snowflakes, still in Montana, headed down 15, nearly in Idaho, while I traced lines on the map and Paco hummed an old Sublime tune. I was certain that he was meditating somewhere behind those eyes, or maybe thinking about the women from the honky tonk. Meditating and mesmerized: I didn't know the difference.

Driving was indeed meditative and it's one of the reasons I loved the road. Even the truckstops were fascinating—all those pinball machines blinking, sending me into tiny seizures. Just like a girl I once saw standing in front of a chicken rotisserie for far too long.

Driving!

We were consuming road and my lids began to close as if burdened by minuscule anvils. Grabbed a bottle of lightning and gulped it down.

"You alright man?" asked Paco.

"Yeah, just a bit tired."

"Thinkin' of those ladies, aren't you? I should've left your ass back there. She wanted you, man!"

"I've got a girlfriend," I reminded him.

"Hear you on that. But it's a lonely life out here. Shit. All kinds of women start looking good after a while. Wait 'til you see some of these lot lizards—mannnnn, dawg. You're in for it!"

"Lot lizards?"

"Just wait."

My stomach gurgled. I felt the cavalry of B-vitamins working on my liver and suddenly had to vomit.

"Pull over, Paco."

"We don't have time to stop. Load is already late."

"Pull over or I'm gonna puke on the floor."

"What, you sick? Gotta drink those things with food, man."

"PULL OVER!!"

I ran into a field and meditated onto a bush.

13

THE LAUNDROMAT WAS CHILLY and I kept seeing goblins and ghouls outside its windows. They screamed down sidewalks while cars honked and screeched to tread-burning halts.

"Can't nobody drive in this damn town," shouted a black man with backpack. "Rain, shine, Halloween. It don't matter."

"I hear you," I nodded.

"Know what I mean?"

I nodded.

"Yeah, *you* know what I mean. Shit. How long you been in LA, my man?"

"Three years."

"Uh-huh. Try thirty. Thinkin' o' gettin' the hell outta here."

"Why?"

"Don't worry 'bout why. Just know that it's a good idea. Can I get a dollar? Tryin' to pick up some grub from the corner market."

I dug in my pocket and found sixty-eight cents.

"You gonna hand me pennies?"

"It's money isn't it?"

"Naw, you can keep those. I need silver. Cot damn silver!"

He walked away.

Now I was alone again with my spinning jeans and socks, zoning out. I enjoyed staring without purpose. Maybe I could stare my whole life away. Maybe my imagination would suffice. How the hell did the Buddha do it anyway? Did he not kick back with a plate of rice now and then? Chicken curry for the soul?

WE WERE BACK AT IT, Francine and I. Sex and coffee for breakfast, with waffles to wash it down. Far too bright for the beginning of November; but this was LA, and it was good to know everything was back to abnormal. I watched Francine conserve the last of the syrup by overturning the bottle onto its cap. Maybe she was trying to present a metaphor—some kind of sticky hourglass. She conserved everything. Even plastic sandwich bags were washed and hang-dried. Probably the best person I could have in my company for the impending post-apocalypse. We'd survive for weeks on sugar packets and napkins. The vultures would be on our side.

"So, how are you enjoying it so far?" she asked.

"They're okay. Could be more crisp."

"What? No. Trucking. How are you enjoying *trucking*?"

"Oh, that. That's okay, too. Yeah. Nice to finally be roaming about the country, you know."

"I'm sure it's an adventure," she smiled.

I scratched my head.

She coughed.

A slight breeze blew outside the apartment and we both turned our heads.

"Should we go for a walk?" I asked.

—

WE ENDED UP somewhere along the beach; always back to the God-forsaken beach with its washed up everythings. It brought the junk from Japan and laughs of the past. It kissed the smog before sending it back into the atmosphere. Meanwhile, the sun watched the whole thing from its perch.

Why didn't it come down and do something. Laziness? Pride?

We are indeed stars and the sun is the nearest, but who's reflecting who?

Francine brought a knapsack full of goodies, just like earlier in the year when we ended up at that park in Big Sur. The football was in the bag, too. I couldn't get away from it. Its neon colors burned their way into my conscience because I thought of it as some foam-forgotten child we never had, and that Francine would forever be asking me to chase it along the river of time.

I removed my clothes and bunched them into a pile of black. Good Lord. All that black. Like a stack of bicycle tires.

"Bet you can't throw the football all the way out here," I yelled, creating distance between the brown beauty and me.

"Yeah right! Just watch," she said.

And there it went soaring through the sky, and I was momentarily blinded but ended up catching the damn thing.

After a few rounds of this, we fell onto our blankets and dug into the bag of snacks. Francine got cozy among the sand.

Similar to Big Sur and the cliffside, I was tempted to jump into the ocean and see how far I could swim before being rescued by an oil rig and hired for their next run to ports unknown. We'd meet pirates and dine on wild caught herring.

"Let's have sex," said Francine, interrupting my reverie.

"It's the middle of the day and this is a public beach."

"I know. But we're already half naked, and besides, I have extra towels to hide under," she assured, shaking one out.

"Still . . . not the best idea, babe."

"Ugh," Francine scoffed. "All this talk about adventures and then you back down when it involves something I'm excited about. Where's *our* adventure?"

"You want to fuck right here in the open, damn well knowing we could get arrested for it?"

She nodded.

I looked around. It was fairly deserted.

I tossed the large towel over us. It was toasty inside our little cocoon. Her body pressed against mine and, truly, it turned me on. We were about to begin our great beach adventure when—

Drums.

Louder and louder they came. Some kind of high school parade tromping through our grainy bed, and we laid directly in their path.

"Shit," I said, slipping into my trunks. Francine did the same, and before we knew it we were back on our feet, marching along to the soundtrack of life.

—

DAYS PASSED.

Six a.m. and I was now slipping into jeans, which took me a total of twenty seconds due to frigid Chicago and its wind chill.

WACKY WEDNESDAY WEATHER

That's what the headlines read outside the truckstop, and I couldn't help but think about sun-drenched sex in the beach of my brain. Paco was fast asleep in the truck, and meanwhile I wandered aisles in search of a healthy morning snack. The plump girl behind the counter looked like she'd been up all night, but still held a smile and I forced one back. Her arms were tattooed. Leather bracelets. Where's the damn coffee, and was it fresh? Where's my face, and is it fresh? Found a mirror above the pot, and the answer to both questions, thankfully, was yes. My beard and hair grew wild around the ears, but my eyes were fresh. The eyes! Don't lose the eyes. If I didn't have eyes, how would I speak? If they weren't enthusiastic—

"BLACK GOLD! TEXAS TEA!!" trumpeted a man from behind. He was Paul Bunyan plus a few pounds, barging straight for the emptying pot.

"Save some for us drivers, ay kid?"

I just smiled.

—

BACK IN THE CAB, Paco shifted around in his cot, and I nearly climbed back up to mine before remembering that it was my turn to drive. Our drop-off point was Newton, Kansas, and Chicago would be the furthest east Paco and I would ever travel together, as he was assigned to the "Western 17." Essentially, Strike agreed to keep him near the Pacific, near home, so long as he worked his ass off each time out. This benefited me because it allowed me to see Francine; but I ached for the east coast since most of my family and friends lived there. This wouldn't happen until I was cut loose, and with each day I'd been getting closer; now 150 hours into training. It was the moment I had waited for—the meat of the experience—and as it neared I grew more fearful, having adapted to my new situation with Paco. I thought about the nature of dreams and desires while inspecting our truck in the pale milk morning. It seemed that once I obtained even a small slice of the cake I wanted to walk away. Or once I had adapted, I wanted to stay.

—

LATER THAT DAY the sun began to warm up the cab and I squirmed out of my sweater while steadying the wheel beneath kneecaps. Not the safest thing to do, I realized.

Land stretching through southern Illinois
Mile marker
Dairy farm
Dandelion ducks
Missouri Welcomes Me
See You Again Next Time! Buckle up!

Still focused on the subject of dreams, I thought about the colored squares of the Santa Monica map, and the dream of Santa Monica itself from behind my college desk. And Saint Monica and *her* dreams! You see, the squares had lost their color just as the city became a bedroom. Just as Saint Monica's fabled table lost its wine, when she was forbidden to bring it to the communal feasts. The bishop feared drunks. I feared what I'd do next. What did Saint Monica drink when she went home anyway?

—

Kearney, Missouri—BIRTHPLACE OF JESSE JAMES—yet I didn't see it. We were merely passing through and it bothered me. We had obligations and there was hardly ever time for exploration; but I knew there would be, just as I knew there'd be trouble when we arrived in Tijuana the previous week . . .

Not that the actual delivery went wrong.

Doesn't take much effort to unload a truck full of beer. Basically, you back the trailer up to the dock and have other people do it. Forklift drivers, pallet jack masters, warehouse workers. The trouble for the driver is the driving.

We didn't enter Tijuana, but scooted all the way up to the dusty border to some blank-faced building. After getting unloaded, two a.m., back on our way towards San Diego, we were stopped at a border patrol station under stadium-sized lights, where an officer jumped onto the climbing steps of our cab and peered into the window.

"What's the problem, officer?" asked Paco, who sat behind the wheel.

"Our dogs are actin' a bit strange out here. Seems they've smelled somethin'. Y'all got any kind of pharmaceutical drugs in here?"

Paco looked at me.

"Me? Hell no. Just some Sudafed for my seasonal allergies."

"Sudafed, you say?" asked the cop.

"Yeah, it's right here," I said, reaching into one of our drawers and pulling out a ziploc bag full of white powder—immediately illuminated by flashlight.

"Shit," I continued, "Must've gotten crushed between all the tools."

Paco winced.

"Drop the bag and step out of the truck! Both of you. Right now!"

Suddenly we were slumped on a cold bench with a canine sniffing at our balls, gnawing on his leash between licks of teeth.

Paco shook his head.

"Damn, yo. Why'd you have to pull out the bag?"

"It's Sudafed! I need it for the flowers and all that damn pollen that gets in the air."

"Flowers? It's NOVEMBER, fool!"

"Well it works for general congestion, too."

I looked over at our truck and saw the officers tearing apart the dash, undoing the radio, digging deep into the firewall; the dogs sniffing along the trailer. No barking is a good thing, I thought. Still, Paco was pacing around with his cigarette, itching to get back on the road—back in the warm truck.

Indeed it was chilly, even in the most southern of western towns, and as usual Paco wore his undershirt and shorts, but shivered this time and I felt a little guilty. Worried that maybe I had caused this situation by sheer existence. Of course, I had nothing to do with these poor cops and their slobbering shepherds. They were simply bored and felt like using their government toolkits, felt like making a scene, and we were the contestants who wandered unknowingly on stage. But there would be no prize giveaways or scantly clad sign-holders, nor a studio audience to applaud the answers:

"Sudafed is an over-the-counter medication which is used as an ingredient to manufacture *this* illegal street drug."

"What is meth?"

No wonder the officers were suspicious. I had a case of it in the sleeper berth.

"Sorry, Paco," I said.

He flopped next to me and shrugged.

"No biggie. Just hope they re-install the dash correctly. Strike will be all over us if we return with that shit hanging out everywhere."

Slow nods.

"So," he continued. "How you feelin' about flying solo? We've only got one more week together. Is there anything you're unsure about?"

"Nope. Think we've covered most of it. My only doubts are about the tire chains. I have no idea how to install them and worry I'll get stuck in nasty weather during winter."

"That's true. Shit, man. Picked a hell of a time to learn how to drive a truck."

"Is there ever a good time to start?"

"There is when it comes to the mountains! That's where you'll have the biggest problem: Donner Pass, Raton Pass, Vail Pass. They *should* shut the roads down if it gets too bad, but sometimes that's not the case. Sometimes you'll get stuck just as the flakes begin to fall. Or worse, ice."

"Okay. So will you show me how to install the chains?"

"Hell yeah, man!"

He leapt up and strutted over to the truck.

"Right now?" I yelled.

He looked back and waved me over, yanking the tangled chains from hooks on the side of the tractor; laying one set onto the ground and spreading it out across asphalt.

"What you've got to do," he said, popping an unlit cigarette into his mouth, "is throw the chains evenly over the tops of the tires. And when you've done that, you get back into the truck, put it into first gear, roll slightly forward, and then step down and hook them together with bungee cords."

"I've got to do this for every tire?"

"Not every tire; you have to follow a pattern."

He continued demonstrating the task, which I barely understood because my mind was preoccupied with a comic book I once read, which I couldn't remember the title of.

A cop's face shot around the corner of the trailer.

"Hey! What are you fellas doing? Didn't I tell you to wait on the bench?!"

"I'm giving my co-worker an education," Paco shouted. "Find any drugs yet?"

"No. But tell your wife she makes a damn good sandwich," said the officer, munching on Paco's lunch.

"Bastard pig."

—

JESSE JAMES wouldn't have allowed something like that to happen. I imagine he would have just barreled through the barricade, guns blazing and teeth to the sky. Anyhow, four days later and there we were in Missouri, closing in on Kansas. Paco emerged from his slumber and instructed me to pull over at the next rest area. In his groggy states he looked like a Mexican mobster, and I knew from his stories that he'd once teetered on the edges of becoming one.

Paco splashed into the front passenger seat and read a text message on his phone.

"No fucking way," he said.

"What?"

"My girlfriend wants to move to Compton."

"And?"

"You been to Compton? That's gang central, dawg. Can't raise a child in the slums."

"Raise a child? What?"

"I didn't tell you?" he said, buckling his seatbelt. "Gonna be a daddy."

"Wow. Congrats, man! We've gotta celebrate before our time is up."

"Absolutely. But God, man, this Compton shit is nothing to celebrate. Thankfully, I had my grandmother to keep me in check. Can't tell you how many times I was dragged out of my house by street thugs and beaten up in the front lawn. Motherfuckers tryin' to *beat me* into joining their cliques. But she would always come home and clean up my face and cook dinner. Meanwhile, my parents were too far into it. Drunk and high half the time. Man, do you hear what I'm sayin'? It's just no good. Shit circles back around. Don't give a damn if the house is twenty bucks."

REST AREA
1 MILE

I saw Paco much different than the Paco I'd seen five minutes earlier. He was going to be a father, and this warped him in a way I couldn't explain. Physically he was the same human that I'd been staring at for the past month. The tan skin and slick rockabilly haircut, mustached grin, wild construction talk, flailing limbs.

"You'll see, man!" he said, chuckling and slapping his knee. "Before you know it! One of these days. Me with a wife and baby, and you with a forty-eight inch chest. I'll catch sight of you out here and we won't even recognize each other. Maybe! Just maybe!"

winter

14

I BECAME WELL KNOWN at the Ontario Strike Transportation Maintenance Shop. The mechanics all knew my face and I knew theirs. I'd been stuck there for the past three days, waiting for the grumpy men to render my recently acquired truck a driveable machine.

Volvo VN430.

Yes, that was my birthday gift. The only problem is that the gift was leaking oil and air. I kept waiting in a long queue while the mechanics pulled my truck into the garage—"It's fixed. Get out of here"—only to double check their work and find otherwise.

This isn't my job, I thought.

They'd shake their heads, call me a liar. I'd prove them wrong. Round and round, a ridiculous carousel set to classic rock tunes of the day's overhead FM radio.

I meandered around the parking lot, kicking cans.

Paco.
Spend six weeks with a person in an 8x8-foot space, and it's bound to be someone you remember for the rest of your life.

But now was not the time to be thinking of Paco.
I'd been cut loose!

—

EAGER TO GET ROLLING with my first solo assignment, I began to prep the truck, creating a home out of its cramped interior. I placed a foam mattress topper onto my bed, brand new sheets, and strapped plastic containers onto the top bunk using bungee cords (a tool, like duct tape, which forever came in handy). Then I tucked my rolled-up USA map behind everything. It would be used for documenting my travels.

I purchased all kinds of tools, and my dad was already writing to me, asking if he could help contribute—a Christmas list of sorts. I rattled off unwrappable items such as: torque wrench, crow bar, ice scraper, vice grips. It would all be stuffed into the side compartment of my tractor eventually. But those details come later, and besides, even if they don't, they're not important. Tools are tools.

Sherry was Sherry.

Sherry was important. Important because I never forgot the way she made me feel—as though I were overseas, dabbling with the locals of . . . wherever she was from. She wandered over one afternoon while I was loading my truck with more tools (never enough preparation for the nervous). Sherry's trail of Newport smoke reached out for me like the wafting hand of a Saturday morning cartoon, locked arm-in-arm with a lover named Jane. I whipped around to greet them.

"Didn't mean to scare you," said Sherry, with an Eastern European accent.

"You didn't," I said, withholding mention of the cartoon hand.

"We been waitin' here all damn day fer this truck ta get fixed."

The accent had suddenly morphed into Alabama.

"Looks like we're in the same boat," I said. "Employees don't seem too friendly around here either."

"Hell no!" she said with a Canadian tone.

I nearly asked, but ultimately didn't want to know where she was from, as I preferred to keep the mystery. Maybe she and her blond-haired lover had just dropped from the sky onto the roof of a trailer, stealing the soul of the nearest driver; and now that driver is wandering the streets in search of a new purpose, climbing the tail end of the nearest cloud.

"Well, look on the bright side," I said. "At least we have some time to relax in sunny California."

"Shit, man, are you crazy?" she cried, spraying spit. "Who gives a damn about California? See any umbrellas 'round? We're here ta get paid!"

They soon walked away, hunched, broad-shouldered, shorts and high socks, hand-in-hand, locked, love, and blistered.

—

"YOU CAN HEAR it hissing," I told the mechanic. "Lean in."

He looked at me with a forehead that seemed to have its own face and then pressed it against one of the brake lines.

"Don't hear nothin'," he shrugged.

"But the air pressure gauges are dropping and I'm only sitting here, parked. What happens when I crest one of those steep grades with a full load?"

"Listen, kid. You're good to go. I'm the head mechanic and I call the shots around here. We've got a whole line of trucks that are much worse-off, and they're experienced drivers who need to be out on the road."

"You're joking, right? I have *no* experience. Don't you think my case is more important?"

Now he was frowning on both fronts. His earring stopped twinkling. Although, I couldn't remember if it ever did. I tried to picture him twenty years younger. Then I pictured him twenty years older. Sheesh. His face was actually starting to change shape, and I kept my focal point on his eyes, trying to speak Eye, and grew calmer as I saw that a small twinkle remained.

"Okay," he finally said with a sigh. "We'll take another look."

—

A FEW DAYS LATER, sleeping in my now-repaired truck, I was slapped awake by a vicious tone on the computer system.

PICKUP: 15:00 THURSDAY   SPANISH FORK, UT
DROP OFF: 14:00 SUNDAY   LATHROP, CA

Finally some movement.

I cracked open my brand new atlas and flipped through its laminated pages, tracing the route with a washable marker. It appeared to be a nice little jaunt across Nevada, straight through 80 past the salt flats and into the plains—places I hadn't been yet and suddenly I was amped up again, accepting the job and jamming my key into the ignition. My truck was in tip-top shape. I even made sure to run it through the wash and suck the dust from its interior. She was five years old already with nearly half a million miles on the odometer, but damn she cleaned up and whirred to life. Sure, the idle was a bit rough; but who isn't rough when they idle?

Anyway, first I had to pick up a loaded trailer from the Ontario yard, as I needed to bring merchandise with me to Spanish Fork. At four bucks per gallon of diesel, the company hardly ever sent me off without something to haul. After hooking to my trailer in the yard, I grabbed a vending machine coffee that poured like black paint, and strapped myself into the Volvo, bound for the Mojave sweep.

—

Alone and free
Alone and free inside these doors
If you're with me, then that makes four

You and me, alone, and free

My lips were forming these words into sung syllables that seemed to originate somewhere in the right lobe of my brain. But then I remembered that the left lobe was responsible for logic and thought it perfectly logical to be singing about something I was feeling; a repetitive tune to keep me focused in the moment.

Your dusty roads
Whisper west
What have you seen?
What truth is left?

I glanced over at the empty passenger seat and began to miss Paco and our antics. The Sudafed-smuggling duo of Missoula strip joints. Hot damn.

The wind picked up and rocked the trailer I was hauling, jerking the tractor and subsequently my steering wheel. They were northern winds, blowing from the direction I was headed, and suddenly I felt as though I were attempting to pierce fate; tearing its fabric enough to taste heavier breath.

What are you doing out here, man? You think you're a big shot now just because you command a hunk of metal?

At this point I was accustomed to the pesky voice and recognized it as something that had always been there, and knew there was strength to be found in the sheer recognition of it. Once identified, it became easier to manage. Sort of like Professor Jake and his meditation techniques. When it washes into the dam, breathe it back out.

Hours later, signs for Spanish Fork were popping up and I began looking out the windows for a semblance of civilization in the barren proximity. Following directions and taking the next exit, I remembered that few of the towns where I conducted the business of trucking were actually *towns*;

rather, industrial outskirts of white brick and asphalt—some named after the companies based there. The warehouse entrances were hardly ever labeled, and on this day I mistakenly turned into a shopping plaza. A place I shouldn't have been. A place where cars had room to drive in full circles, but made my truck stand out like a billboard in the Sahara.

But eventually I found my way to the warehouse and dropped my trailer somewhere on the pavement, backing it perfectly between two other trailers before scooting off to find the Lathrop-bound one. It was a gloomy afternoon. The days darkened early. I opened the side compartment of my truck and pulled out a large, high-powered flashlight, and began scanning the fronts of trailers, parked neatly in rows, numbered vertically, causing my head to tilt on occasion while trying to read them. After locating and hooking to the right one, I put the gearshift into first and began pulling away when another nasty tone pierced my eardrum:

YOU ARE NOW OUT OF DRIVING HOURS!
STAY WHERE YOU ARE OR RISK POINTS.

Shit.

Points were no good.

They were tacked onto your company record for offenses such as being late for delivery, exceeding the speed limit, or in this case, driving more than the legally allotted eleven hours. Too many of these points meant being fired, and I was not ready for that yet. Truth be told, I was exhausted, and this warning was probably a good thing. But not here.

Not on this darkening asphalt.

But it soon turned black and I cracked open a can of tuna, kicked back to Chopin, and wondered where oh where I'd find that damn cowboy hat.

—

THE SALT FLATS were purple, and for a moment I thought maybe I was still dreaming, but I looked down and felt my skin, confirmed sensation, and knew that it was just the morning hue raining down. They weren't actually purple, but they were magical—made all the more magical by the fact that there were no other vehicles on the highway (80 across the Nevada state line). Not even a bird graced the sky. It's just life, I thought. This shit happens every day. There's always some place somewhere sitting perfectly still.

Tried to warm up, shoving hands against vents.

Cold today. I could feel it coming from the window. Could see it on the horizon. The Flats were vast and I felt as though I were driving across a page in someone's notebook, panning out *their* imagined adventure, not mine. Checked the map to make sure I was headed in the right direction. Straight shot on 80. I would make a total of five turns over the next 750 miles, and they were all in the last ten.

A sign in the distance:

ELKO - 119 MI.
WINNEMUCCA - 243 MI.

My spine straightened. These were new towns and I was ready for a new slice of the American pie. Peaks were growing on the horizon, which I thought must've been the state line, and imagined a bouldery beast emerging from the cliffsides to greet me with a giant, checkered flag. Maybe he'd hoist the truck and launch it into the atmosphere.

Nah. Just more land.

But beautiful, beautiful land as I crossed the line, passing Wendover, cutting through those crumbly mountains; yawning with the sun straight ahead. Tired as I became on my routes, there was always a giddy child dancing somewhere in my stomach, reveling in all the splayed scenery. Give me a fork and knife. I'll eat it up!

113

I was hungry.

Just past Winnemucca, I stopped at the edge of Ely, parking along the street and running into a Sinclair station for a quick bite—hot dog on a stick, potato chips, apple. Apples are healthy, right? Yes. Fiber. Vitamin C. Take it.

The clerk was large and seemed to be growing a fourth chin. Wide as the counter, he saw the hot dog in my hand and licked his bottom lip—

"Those are three for a dollar, y'know."

"Yes, but I only need one," I said.

"Look like you're hungry. I bet if your mom was here she'd ask you why you wasn't eatin'."

"I'm eating. See the chips and apple? And I've got more junk in my truck."

"Truck? You're a driver?"

"Yessir."

"Must be a rookie."

"How'd you know? Were you a driver once?"

"Nope. Been workin' here since I took over for my father who fell sick in '92. I could just tell because most drivers see the THREE FOR A DOLLAR sign and don't blink twice."

"Well, I'm one of those Californian drivers."

"Suit yourself, Hollywood."

—

I DON'T KNOW HOW I got lost leaving Ely, but I assume it had to do with a subconscious desire to see something unusual. Found myself in the middle of the small town—a veritable John Wayne set—swinging the fourteen-foot-tall trailer around fourteen-foot buildings, trying not to crush bodies along the way. Skimming under dangling stop lights, brushing fire hydrants, jumping curbs. No other trucks around. These streets weren't made for this kind of weight. I felt them cracking under the tires.

Eventually I located my exit. Just before taking it, I passed a brick school building with a steeple on top. A pack of children stood outside, pumping their arms in unison, calling for a blast of the big horn. I went to tug the cord when I saw a ninety-year-old woman across the street, exiting a laundromat. Better not, I thought. Give her a damn heart attack. Imagine being stuck with that kind of guilt during the next six hundred miles.

The tots kept pumping and screaming.

Waited until I got some distance.

BBRRRROOOMMMMPPP
BROOOOOOOOOOOOOMMMMPP

15

"DIGGING FOR TRAILERS, trying to find one that isn't going to fall apart as I drive down the highway. It's one of the most frustrating parts, man."

"You kidding me? I like that."

"Yeah? What's there to like?"

"I don't know. It's a challenge. I knew this would be a challenge. It's expected."

That shaggy intellectual kid, Simon, had called me up. Or maybe I called him. I couldn't remember, wandering yet another yard full of trailers with a flashlight sometime around eight p.m., now in Lathrop at one of Strike's terminals.

Nevada. What a mystery.

More on that later.

"Let me ask you," Simon went on. "What bothers you most in life?"

"Off the top of my head? Apathy."

"Why do you think that is?" he asked.

"What are you, a psychiatrist?"

"I'm a human being asking another human being a perfectly reasonable question. Why does apathy get under your skin?"

I hopped into one of the trailers, thinking about it.

"I don't know," I said. "I suppose because I feel like it's my biggest enemy. Maybe the biggest enemy of life itself. If you're apathetic it sort of means you don't care, right? If you don't care, what's the point of life?"

"What if there is no point to begin with?"

Just then, a wall of cobweb. I emerged swallowing a sizeable portion.

"Gah! Fuck! Listen, man…I just ate a cobweb, maybe a spider, and besides, there is a point. It's just not written. So your question is *pointless* because you'll never get at it."

"So you're saying that it just *is*?"

"Yes."

"Okay then."

"Okay."

"So, have you found a trailer?" he asked after a long silence.

"This one will have to do. Anyway, tell me more about your research project. How's it coming along? Still scavenging soiled hopes?"

"Every day. God, man, if America only knew the foundation it rests upon. Lot of sad eyes for a country preaching the pursuit of happiness. Remember those notebooks in the back of my Chevy? Well I've got a truck full of them now. I use neon Post-It notes to tag the pages of people who are genuinely content, then do a quick tally by glancing at the text block. Quite the experiment."

"You're not getting paid for this, right?"

"This is all for the sake of research."

"Well, I'd love to see you published someday. It's intriguing to me."

"Signed copy, my friend. Goodnight for now."

"10-4."

—

AFTER HOOKING to my trailer, I ran into the terminal to gargle and shower. Terminals were akin to truckstops, but appeared more like offices with gray tables and chairs, corporate flyers tacked to bulletin boards, and funky sofas. Sometimes I'd catch sight of guys my age—laptops flipped open, firing away at aliens with one of those Burger King headsets. Another tribe were drivers who wandered throughout the lounge, shouting into their bluetooth ear pieces so that everyone knew exactly why they were getting fucked over on that last thirty miles, and why the Man will always be the Man and I guess that's life.

The bathroom was large, steamy, and smelled like a high school gym locker. There was usually another driver occupying one of the stalls (shower or toilet), and half of the time they sang. The other sounds I tried to ignore. And sandals. They were important to wear. In fact, I often wandered across the parking lots carrying an arsenal of bath supplies: towel slung over shoulder, toiletry bag in hand with essentials and loofah sticking out—

"Loofah? Fuck is a loofah?" one driver asked me.

"It helps exfoliate the skin. I have horrible back acne. Bacne, they call it."

"Holy cow, brother. Should be workin' at Bed Bath & Beyond or something!"

Today there was no singing to be heard, but after three days without a shower each of my pores breathed tones of joy.

Off to the vending machine afterwards.

I had no food in the truck and, tired after the long haul, wanted nothing more than a hot shower and meal. One out of two was an unacceptable fraction in this regard. Food and no shower was usually okay. It left me a little churlish, but I was a basket case without food.

The goal remained: wellness in the face of grease, and nothing behind that vending machine glass screamed health. I used one of Strike's computers to research the nearest grocery mart, only finding a Target store two miles away. Completely out of drive-time, the truck was shut down for the night. With nothing better to do, I began walking.

—

THERE WAS SOMETHING about wandering the aisles of retail stores I loved, but couldn't put my finger on why at the time.

Probably because it was my only human interaction save for truckstops and terminals. I felt like a child sneaking away from the classroom of my cab. Tagging along with all the people of the world. And they all seemed to be doing the same thing: walking around, pulling boxes from shelves, talking to each other. Toddlers in carts with bottles, looking up, looking down, looking at me.

I grabbed a basket and started loading up on goodies for the next few weeks. Anything that didn't require an oven took priority. Health came second in this case because a life on the road meant compromise, and usually I was too tired to cook after a twelve-hour workday. At least, these were my excuses at the time. Really, I think I was growing bored of my goals and looking to shake up my gut with a slathering of sodium. Might've given me something to bitch about later on, and then I'd have a new goal, which would be to return to my original goal of remaining healthy.

Anyhow, canned goods like tuna and Spam worked best for roadside breaks where I could simply peel lids and squeeze it all between two slices of bread. 'Course, it had to be sturdy, hearty bread, as the meat's juice seeped through cheaper varieties. Secondary to canned goods was microwavable packaging, and for this I preferred flavored rice, oatmeal, soups, and anything that read JUST ADD WATER AND HEAT! Some truckers had kitted out cabs with refrigerators, 12-volt hot plates, and water boilers, but not I. My meals would be served quick from cardboard. Fruits like apples, bananas, and oranges would balance out the salt; convenient and cram-packed with Vitamin C. Finally, a couple gallons of spring water to chug from, brush teeth and wash hands with when there were no available facilities nearby. And wipes, for when there was no toilet paper.

So I purchased all of this, watching the dreary cashier bag everything with slow-moving hands. She was a black woman, mid-forties, with long fingernails. Upon scanning my bag of ginger snaps, her eyes marbled with glee.

"These are my faaaavvvooorrriitte," she said with a girlish smile.

"Yeah?"

"Yeah! My mother used to serve them after dinner, but we were only allowed three each between me and my brothers."

"Well, why don't you have one right now?"

"Really?"

"Merry Early Christmas."

She tore open the bag, dug out a few, and stacked the cookies on her register.

"You just made my day," said the cashier.

"If that's all it takes, you're in good shape."

—

I SET OFF towards the terminal, and by now the sky was impenetrable; heavy like coal. My body resisted, remembering the two-mile walk. Twenty pounds of groceries would soon feel like one hundred.

These were the quiet moments.

The moments with the stars and wind.

These were the moments that, at the time, I thought were the Dreadful Bum Moments. The moments when I cursed myself for what I was doing, despite cookie cashier love. But it was only because I was tired and my emotions had gotten the best of me. It would be years until I fully grasped that all moments were great because they were part of the Life Moment.

Somewhere along the lonely highway, one of the bags decided that it had endured enough torment and cans came crashing through the plastic. There went my Dinty Moore Beef Stew, rolling into a ravine. And all I could think was, "Dammit. Is Dinty even a real name?" But more than that, I was sad. Sad because I knew it was two dollars lost that I could have spent on a hostel abroad, and because it was a meal I'd miss on one of those late nights parked behind a warehouse. And, well, just because I was sad.

Out of nowhere, I heard car tires crunching behind me and noticed the familiar flash of turn signal lamps on the asphalt. I whipped around to see a Ford Pickup.

"Lemme help you with that," hollered an old man from the window. He rushed to my aid, gathering food into his arms—even the badly dented apples that would later be thrust into a trashcan.

"Thank you, sir," I replied with a forced smile.

"What are you doing out here walking with all that, anyway?"

"I'm a trucker. And I can't drive anymore because I'm out of hours. It's a trucking thing, you know. Rules."

"I see," he said, squinting from behind thin-rimmed eyeglasses. "Lemme help you."

We gathered everything that had fallen and then he told me to join him in his pickup for a ride back to the terminal. I hopped inside. The interior smelled like pipe tobacco and a photo of two little girls hung from his rearview mirror.

"What's your name?" asked the elder.

"Johan."

"Johan. Never met anyone with a name like that."

"Honored to be the first."

"And you?"

"Andy."

"Ah. I've met a few Andys."

"Used to be a very common name. My father's, in fact."

"Well, it's a good name. Do you live around here, Andy?"

"My whole life. Just up the road. And yourself?"

"Maryland originally. Los Angeles for the past three years."

"And now you're on the road."

"Now I'm on the road."

"Life throws us curve balls from time to time, doesn't it?" he chuckled.

"Still trying to get used to that."

"Keeps it interesting, that's for sure. Depends on the curve I guess. But seems we don't have much time to discuss all that."

The turn was already coming up for the terminal and Andy gave me a little smile. "Maybe I'll see you again somewhere down the road."

"One way or another."

He parked and I gathered my stuff, thinking God O God if only I could gather these people and store them the same.

—

COUPLE NIGHTS LATER I was sent back down to Ontario for another load. This disappointed me, as I was hoping to already be on my way east toward Maryland for the holidays. There was a pending request for this hope sitting on my manager's desk, and it seemed that I had gotten pushed to the bottom of his pile. With only four days left before Christmas and 2,500 miles to go, I didn't think there'd be much chance of arriving on time. No jobs were coming my way and I ended up sitting around twiddling thumbs for another night. This was the tough part of trucking; the part that knocked the other pieces from the greater picture. The part when I'd start reaching for porn and potato chips, or stretching the lens of my Canon toward the sky in hopes that an onset of meteors would crash into frame.

My mind wandered when I could not.

I began running the film of Winnemucca through my head and remembered all the details from days earlier . . . that is, when I sat inside the cab much like tonight, staring at the last of the cherry horizon; observing drivers walking across the parking lot, trying to calculate how many years they'd been on the road when abruptly there came a knock at my door. Upon rolling down the window, I noticed a blond-haired woman of about forty, wrapped in a brown jacket, short skirt, stockings. A cigarette burned between her fingers and her eyes were half-closed.

"Uh, can I help you?" I asked.

"You alone tonight, honey?"

"I'm alone every night."

"Ain't that a shame. Too cold to be alone."

"I've got a heater in here."

"You know what I mean, baby."

She squirmed around inside her skirt, puckering lips, pulling the cigarette to them.

"Gotcha," I said. "Umm, listen, you're lovely. But I've got a woman that I'm committed to and she wouldn't like this whole idea."

"What mama don't know won't hurt her."

I thought for a moment, took one last look at the horizon, and then glanced back at her.

"You know what? You're right. Hop in."

She trotted around the outside of the truck and I unlocked the passenger door. Then she climbed in and sat down, immediately crossing her legs; revealing a lot more of them.

"What's your name, sweet thang?"

"Johan."

"John or Jo— what'd you say it was?"

"John is fine."

"Well it's nice to meet you, John. They call me Sass McGrass."

"Sass?"

"And don't let the broken blouse fool you, I do got class."

She unzipped her jacket, revealing heaps of cleavage.

"Are they real?" I asked.

"What?"

"Your boobs."

"Does it matter?"

"I want to know what I'm paying for."

"'Course they're real! Born and bred Nevada nookie; that's what you're gettin' here."

"I see. Look, I'm gonna be honest: I've only got twenty bucks and I'm just as lonely as you at the moment. How about you sit here in the warm truck with me and I'll pay you the twenty for good old fashioned conversation."

"CONVERSATION!? Listen, honey, I ain't got time for conversation. Twenty bucks'll get your dick sucked. Now d'y want it or not?"

"You'd rather suck my dick than chill out and talk?"

"For twenty bucks."

"Listen. Time is money, right? Does it matter to you how it's earned?"

She stared out the window for a bit, watching the other trucks drive past, cocks zipped and waiting, buckled behind seatbelts.

"Alright, you got yourself ten minutes. Whadddyouwanna talk about?"

"Tell me about your childhood."

She threw back her head and laughed. "Gotta be shittin' me."

I winked. "How was your day?"

She went on to explain how she'd woken up inside of some dingy motel room that morning next to a guy she'd never seen before, and how the bathroom light didn't work, so she had to unhinge the mirror and do her makeup in the living room. And then her heel broke and she twisted her ankle and some kindhearted trucker lifted her from the pavement and hammered the heel back on with a nail—"And I ain't never seen a hammer used for somethin' like that before. He was pure MacGyver."

I hardly spoke a word the entire time and could tell that she was loosening up in a different way than before. Unfastening more than her blouse—a slackening of pucker and posture. It seemed that, for the time being, she had jumped out of her skin and was dancing in the light of herself.

"So that's what I told 'im. I said to get the hell out of my house if he didn't want to pay rent or fuck me. Ass, cash, or grass."

I think I had been nodding the entire time.

"Well, our twenty minutes is up," she said after a long sigh. "Maybe catch you next time around. Thanks again for listenin'. This was really nice, you know?"

She leaned across the shifter and planted a fat lip print on my cheek. Then off she went. God knows where. Last thing I saw was her hiking up her skirt as she trotted towards the next bulk of metal and bone.

—

THERE CAME A KNOCK at my door around eight p.m. I had somehow fallen asleep while sitting upright at the wheel and everything was hazy. Was it even a real knock?

KNOCK.

Yes, it was.

Couldn't be another lot lizard, could it? Not here at Strike.

KNOCK.

I peered out the window to find a pair of familiar brown eyes. Francine stood below, smirking.

"Babe! I came to see you! And I brought some treats."

She held up a basket with a bow on it, larger than her whole upper torso. I hopped down from the truck and gave her a big hug, picking her off the ground and spinning her through the air. Ten kisses to follow. Or one long kiss which felt like ten.

"Didn't expect you to come all the way out here from LA."

"Are you kidding? We haven't seen each other in, like, forever."

"Hop inside! Get warm!"

She climbed into the cab. And damn she looked good after all the time away. I followed her into the sleeper berth, dropped the shades, popped a CD into the stereo—mellow blues tune. Francine handed me her basket. "Early Christmas gift," she said.

"Thanks."

I couldn't imagine what was inside the woven token of love, and when I dug through the tissue and bows I uncovered a genuine Stetson cowboy hat, perfectly creased.

"Whooooaaaaaa," I gushed. "Think it'll fit?"

"I *know* it will," she said with a wink.

"You didn't measure my head while I was sleeping, did you?"

"Maybe."

"Be honest, babe. Are you a creeper?"

She laughed and I dropped the hat onto my cranium.

"How'd you know I wanted a cowboy hat?"

"Girlfriend's intuition."

I jumped up and admired my new look in the truck's side mirror. My hair had grown quite a bit, having gone uncut since I began the journey, and it fanned nicely out the back of the brim. Yeehaw. I wanted to light a cigarette and punch through the windshield just for the hell of it. Just to give my energy somewhere to go. Instead, I dodged back to the bed and thanked Francine until midnight.

16

SHE WAS UPSET the next morning and left me with one of those kisses that barely touch.

Flustered when I finally told her that I wasn't planning on staying for Christmas; that I wouldn't quit the job. That the sky didn't collapse while we were sleeping and bury us under perfection.

Kiss
Kiss kiss kiss
All your kisses are doomed, brown woman!
You think they infect me?
You think they plant seeds beyond my subconscious in some gold-plated vase?

Well, they do.
I love every slobbering last one.

But eventually I left her and headed east.

I was bound for Hagerstown, Maryland and still somewhere in California. Zooming through Fresno, zooming straight for the Sierra National Forest, or Mammoth Lakes, as you wish. When I saw the city name I thought of a woolly mammoth, and prepared for a beast of a climb across the spine of the Great West. I wondered why Strike had sent me on such a precarious route considering I was still a rookie.

Up I ascended.

Somewhere along the way I stopped at a rest area because I noticed the road thickening with white and an upcoming sign that read:

TIRE CHAINS STRONGLY RECOMMENDED

I parked, shut down the truck, and went to use the toilet, shuddering my way onto its frozen seat. The faucets dripped like a liquid quartet—the perfect accompaniment to carved lyrics:

PERCY WUZ HERE 10/6/98

CALL THIS NUMBER AT MIDNIGHT: [SCRATCHES AND SCUFFS]

WHAT'S THAT SMELL?

YER ALL A BUNCH OF PUSSIES!

Wind howled outside, and the muffled Weather Radio echoed throughout the bathroom, indicating high chance of precipitation and an estimated five to ten inches of snowfall. Gusts of forty miles per hour expected. Whiteout conditions. Twenty degrees Fahrenheit. This message will repeat.

I dropped my head upon hearing this because I knew that it meant I'd have to wait even longer to cross the state, nonetheless country, in time for the Christmas feast that surely waited on the other side.

"'Could be worse, right?"

The voice came from the neighboring stall.

"Yeah," I replied. "Guess so."

"Where you headed?"

"Maryland."

"Maryland!? Hell of a run for the holidays. What outfit you with?"

"Strike."

"Yeah, they have a tendency to push the new guys, don't they?"

"Actually, it was my choice. Trying to see my family."

"Ah. Wife and kids?"

"Nope. Just family."

The voice ceased, followed by a couple of grunts. I flushed the toilet and went to wash my hands, only to find that the soap dispensers were dry. As I pulled emergency hand sanitizer from my coat pocket, a stall door flung open behind me and a thin man emerged—plaid shirt, skin hanging from cheekbones, anorexic by trucker standards. He had a withering mustache that lined his top lip, receding into his nostrils.

"Name's Ben," he said, extending his hand.

I squeezed sanitizer onto it.

"Johan."

—

BACK OUTSIDE, Ben and I walked to our trucks, again noticing the TIRE CHAIN warning. We didn't speak much about it because there seemed to be a quiet code among truckers regarding safety: If you're going to be unsafe, be *safe* about it and don't blabber on. Just do it or don't.

"Listen, partner," said Ben. "It's gettin' dark and the snow ain't gonna stop anytime soon. I have a feeling that's not gonna *stop you* from tryin' to get home. Seein' as you're a rookie and I've got a decade under my belt, how's about I follow you up the mountain to make sure you're alright?"

"You sure?"

"Just offered, didn't I? Ask if I'm sure again and I might not be!"

He slapped me on the back and coughed up a laugh.

"Should we throw chains?" I asked.

He took another look at the sky, spit in the snow, did a little shuffle.

"Nah. We'll be alright. They'll block off the road if it gets too bad. It's only a *warning* right now, see?"

I scaled the cab of my truck and knocked the snow from my boots before settling in. The windshield whistled and the few vehicles on the road seemed to be crawling along. Maybe not such a good idea, I thought. But Ben was already releasing his brakes and rolling forward.

"Channel twelve!" he yelled out his window.

I turned on my unused CB radio.

"Alrighty," he said. "Can ya hear me?"

"Loud and clear."

"What ya waitin' for? Let's get a-rollin'!"

"10-4", I confirmed.

I put the shifter in gear and got behind Ben, salt kicking up from his tires. The sky was growing dense as we drove, and the mountain widened like a gaping mouth with ten-mile tongue. I couldn't tell if we were driving upward or downward. When everything goes black, you lose your sense of direction. And with nightfall came an unfortunate perspective where only the road and Ben's disappearing taillights led me.

I grabbed the CB mic.

"Uh, Ben?"

Static.

"Ben, you copy?"

Static.

"Yeah, I he-ar you, bud," his voice chopped in. "Still ba-ck there?"

"I'm here, but I can't see you anymore. Could you slow down a bit?"

Syllables.

"Didn't catch that, Ben. Where are you?"

Suddenly I desired the Ben-voice of the scarred stall. The still-shitting-Ben.

Dammit!

The grade steepened and I knew that he was long gone, somewhere in the falling flakes, leaving me alone with the mountain on the worst part. The part where the tires completely lost traction and I could only watch the speedometer drop from forty miles per hour to fifteen; the tug of Swedish furniture dragging me down. The only thing I could do was pull over, but didn't know where the edge of the mountain was. Didn't even know if there was a shoulder, or if I'd mistakenly park the 60,000 pounds onto a powdery plane. I turned on the high beams. Snowflakes. "Fuck!" Don't panic. Just do it. Do it with trust. Do it like you *know*.

I inched my way off the road and parked with half of the truck jutting into the highway. Then I strapped on my gloves and hat, took a breath, and went outside to open the tool compartment, from which I retrieved cones and flares; setting them alongside the truck to warn oncoming traffic. Except there didn't seem to be any. Five minutes and not a single car or creature.

Coyote, squirrel, vagabond penguin!
Where have all the beating hearts gone?
Where is the face of the carved cliff?
The Ventura sun sphere?
Surely, somewhere beyond all this black
it radiates faith and good times.

My hands grew numb and I could hardly feel my fingers inside my pocket. Eventually I found them and trudged through the snow, which was now calf-deep, and sat back down inside the chugging cab; thawing my body to sounds of a lame wiper blade. I didn't know what to do next, but I knew that I wasn't going to spend the night sleeping in a truck that was stuck on what could have very well been the ledge of a 200-foot drop. I imagined dozing off only to be awoken by a crashing sound, followed by more crashing sounds, the crunching of bones.

A peculiar noise snapped me back to the road.

Glowing lights in the distance—one pair ahead of me and one behind—slowly approaching. Extraterrestrial angels. Or snow plows. I preferred the former because I had never seen an angel before, but plenty of snow plows laced my memory. As a child, the sound of their shovels scraping asphalt was synonymous with jubilance and play. Indeed, neither plow nor angel would be a bad sight.

I jumped down from the truck and began waving my arms, but the plows roared past, pushing snow against the truck, further walling it in, along with me, waist-deep. "Hey!" I yelled, standing on the steps of the cab and waving my glowing phone at them. Surely they saw. The flares. They'd return. But no, they blared into the distance and I sat back down. The only explanation I had was that the trucks were operated by drones, neither angel nor human.

Climbed back into the sleeper and dug through the cupboards for food. My supply was dwindling, but I grabbed a couple pieces of bread, ripped open a can of Spam, and began piecing together a cold cut. Food would bring ideas! Get the synapses firing again. As I munched, I realized that the truck's fuel level was low and began to worry that it wouldn't last throughout the night. I'd have to keep warm somehow. But the flares would soon die, and that would be no bueno in my position. Had to get off this damn mountain.

Full stomach, I went back outside and pulled the snow chains from the rack on the side of the truck. I had forgotten how to install them, but they were going on one way or another. I tossed them over one of the tires and followed Paco's hazy instructions. My fingers were dying again and I had to work fast. To my relief, I managed to successfully wrap two drive-tires and began working on the trailer when a blinding light washed over me. Shielding my eyes, I made out the distinct shape of a plow, and saw the figure of a man next to it, breath billowing into the atmosphere. He held some kind of shovel or axe and lumbered forward with a hunched back, gray beard down to his breastplate.

"The hell you doin' up here?!" he hollered.

"Chaining up at the moment," I said, watching the mysterious tool wave around in his hand.

"Chaining up?! Didn't you see the signs?"

"Yes, but they were just warnings when we... When I passed them."

"I see," he said, finally lowering his arms. "Guess the City didn't account for elevation. They never learn. 'Cause they don't spend any *time* up here in winter! They're all down in Havasu sippin' Mai Tais!"

He aimed a flashlight at the white wall surrounding my truck.

"You're a lucky man. This was our last run of the night. Finish puttin' those chains on and I'll carve a path for you."

"Thanks so much. I really didn't expect this."

"Don't mention it," said the man, walking away. "Just remember: This ain't LA. This is Alpine Country! Ha-*ha*!"

I never did see his face.

Only the beard, the axe, and laugh.

—

EVERY VEIN in my skull throbbed when I awoke the next morning. Where was I? Couldn't remember. The taste of Spam was still on the roof of my mouth; stenches of sweat and stale air. I threw open the curtains and saw a narrow street in front of me lined with shabby houses, rotting fences, campers. In the other direction was a brick diner with clean glass windows and smoke pluming from its chimney.

Now I remembered why I stopped here.

I sloshed my way across the parking lot, grumbling and growling, seeing the chains strapped to the tires, knowing I'd have to yank them off before getting back on my way. Surely some kingly meal awaited behind those diner walls, in the hands of the cream-colored waitresses of Mammoth. That, or I'd wake up in the back of the cab, realizing it was all just an oasis of the mind—even the bearded axe-man and his icy eyes. But then I smelled the fried oxygen and knew it was time to warm the soul.

I took a seat at one of the round tables in the back of the room—a window seat that faced away from the truck, with a view of the mountain ridge, prompting me to recall my Big Sur experience with Francine. Remorse washed over me and then I didn't know where to sit; so I moved near a young couple chatting over coffee and crumb-specked porcelain. They were about thirty and clearly in love, and kept spinning smiles in my direction.

A waitress appeared before me. She was the Wonder Woman I'd creaked knees to consult.

"Nice to see a pretty face," I told her.

"Wow. Thank you," she giggled. "Do you still need a minute to look over the menu?"

"I'll take anything hot and filling."

"Ha! We have quite a few dishes like that."

"What is the most hot and, uhh, *fillingest* thing you've got?"

"Oh," she threw back her head, "I'd have to say the Mammoth Omelet, made with five eggs and about ten different ingredients. Comes with a side of hash browns and your choice of pie."

"I'll take it."

Off she went, blushing past ethereal windows and mounted television sets. Meanwhile, the couple in front of me was still hanging out, holding hands, squeezing against each other. I didn't intend to stare at them but soon realized I was.

"Hey there," said the woman. "You look like a traveler. Where you coming from?"

"Ontario," I replied.

"Canada?"

"No, the one on the other side of this mountain."

"Where ya headed?" the man butted in.

"Maryland."

"Maryland! Whew. Quite a trip. Are you driving?"

"Have to. I'm a trucker."

"Really? That's so cool."

A yonger man sitting in a nearby booth turned halfway around, as if looking for a mosquito. He had a beard and trendy plumb pants with brown suede shoes. Student, maybe. The love-struck couple caught his glance and invited him to join the conversation. I soon learned that he was a recent film graduate, working in the nearby national park to capture footage, which would be used to whet the appetite of tourists. He reminded me of Simon with the same ambitious energy; and I could tell that somewhere beneath all the pretentiousness he was starved for truth.

"I think maybe a few more years of this and I'll head out to LA, see what I can make happen," he said.

By now, I was ripping into my omelet head-first and hardly heard a word the guy said. He mainly spoke to the couple, and I caught fragments of sentences, intermixed with the yapping TV and clacking heels.

"I overheard you were a trucker," the scholar eventually said to me.

"That's right."

"Well, where's your truck?"

"Volvo right outside," I said, inhaling hash browns. "Parked along the curb there."

He craned his neck, saw the dirty beast, and then nodded at me. "Don't they feed you guys in that profession?"

—

THE TRIP was smooth sailing from there. The only problem was that I kept pushing myself to run ten-hour days and it naturally took a toll on the mind. Sometime after the seventh hour you start to retreat inward—the cobwebbed corners. A trip within a trip. I thought of Professor Jake from the academy and his meditation, wondering if he had found Nirvana this way; from years of endless horizon. I remembered Paco's words, too: "It gets in your blood." Yes, the Neo-Buddhist drives a truck and willingly submits to worldly pleasures like the bacon-flavored ice cream I saw at Denny's on Christmas Eve just outside Stratford, Texas. But

I wouldn't try it. I would sit there and wallow about how I wouldn't be home for Christmas and attempt to remain healthy with whole grain toast and pea soup. It was the first time I'd miss being home for Christmas, and as I sat staring out at the truckstop lot watching the other glowing rigs, I felt a sense of unity, finally understanding the sacrifices that these men and women made. Their children tucked in bed halfway across the country. Wives and husbands spooning cold pillows, lulled by Leno's late night banter. Hell, I just wanted a beer and hug.

17

THE HUGS CAME FIRST, then the beer.

I was happy to be home. Home is where the good people were. The people with the beer and lasagna. And it was heaping as expected, served with love straight from the oven. By the fourth lager I was overflowing with stories from the road, and my mother and stepdad, Arthur, listened with the eyes of children. My younger sister, Kelsey, was due at the table any minute—we were still awaiting her arrival from Virginia—along with my four-year-old niece, Bella.

The house was just as warm as I remembered, and it made me forget about my truck, which I had parked in Southern Maryland near my father's house, next to what used to be a Kmart. It wasn't the safest area to leave a $100,000 vehicle, but I left the curtains closed across its windshield as a security facade, hoping to fool potential thieves into thinking someone was sleeping inside, clutching a steel pipe.

My mother was on edge. Wondering whether I'd been eating well and all the other things mothers worry about. For the first time ever my belly showed beneath my shirt, and I reassured her with a slap on the stomach. Art was nose-deep in the politics of the week, grunting the occasional acknowledgment from behind cigarette-stained teeth, and the smells of cheese and tomato swirled despite pundit projections.

"So how much longer do you plan on doing this?" asked my mother.

"Don't know. Until I grow tired of it I guess."

"I think you'll be doing it for *quite a while*," Arthur said with a smirk that befuddled me.

"We'll see," I said.

My mother nodded, distant. "But where will you live? Where are you planning on *living*?"

"I'm living in the truck for now. Maybe afterwards I'll settle back in LA."

"Don't you want to come home, back to the east coast?"

I began to feel the sting of responsibility, a sticky guilt. I noticed that people were getting older, streets were expanding, commonalities becoming differences. And there I was, missing out on it because I wanted to drive a truck. Is this the price we pay for doing what we want? Is it all too selfish? No. Couldn't be. It was the quest for happiness—the thing often confused for selfish behavior. At the time I didn't understand any of it, but it hurt to see loved ones missing me so badly; to see everything changing.

"I mean . . . I'm sure I'll return home at some point. But I don't know if I'll ever settle around here," I said, doing my best to reassure.

"Just wish everyone lived closer," answered Mom with a sigh, getting up to pull lasagna from the stove.

Soon after, the front door flung open and Kelsey pushed her way through with a bursting suitcase and bright-eyed Bella. "Woooohooo! Finally made it!" said Mom, stretching her arms and trotting towards the two of them.

"Traffic was crazy," quipped Kelsey. "Got stuck behind one of those damn *Strike* trucks!"

We all laughed and sat down to eat.

—

AS WITH ALL holiday breaks, the days passed quickly. Pennsylvania was beautiful with freshly fallen snow, and the sky seemed to be speaking more than ever. It darkened, grumbled, powdered. It shuddered at the thoughts that shook me. Thoughts of the sky's own demise, and one day it would happen when the sun decided it was time to die. We all shared this same terminal secret, and the trouble was that it both bonded and separated us. Death itself a faithful friend who tagged along, wanting to be accepted, never leaving our side, pestering like the young forgotten child.

Snap out of it, Johan. You're on vacation. Plenty of time to think about death while careening down the highway.

> Yes, the days passed quickly
> And before I knew it I was back in Maryland
> Back with the good ol' boys
> Burning with my own thoughts of childhood
> And the forgotten town of my youth
> The gifts came, too
> Crowbar, boots
> and the one I bought myself
> *Johnny Cash's Greatest Hits*

Kelsey and I spoke little. We'd have our moments in the years to come, but this was all before we bonded over booze in the taverns of our time. For now we were brother and sister; mother with child, man with dust.

Snap out of it.

—

FRANCINE AND I had been talking during the entire vacation. She wanted me back on the west coast, understandably, and from where I stood it seemed unlikely. These were the quiet moments when everything seemed to be simultaneously at peace and war. I had achieved the dream of hot Honda Civic days. I was no longer surrounded by bathrobe assholes and yearnings for colored squares; but it seemed that new desires began to replace the old. Now that I had my cowboy hat and Johnny Cash and Christmas—gifts unwrapped and revealed—I could only look again to that damn bow-tied horizon.

—

THESE THOUGHTS stayed with me all the way back to Maryland, where I met up with two good friends the next evening, Tariq and Veronica, a happy young couple. The ground was burnished with frost; the air hinted at snow. I stood outside my father's house and took a few deep breaths to clean my lungs. Something baritone approached.

My old pal boomed into the driveway with his sporty Subaru and waved his arms around, motioning for me to jump in. Tariq was not one for formality. He greeted me from the front seat alongside Veronica, the brown-eyed brunette. Within seconds we were off flying down the highway, and despite having been immersed in street racing culture during my teenage years, I became terrified, unexpectedly, at the speed and size of his car compared to my behemoth. It was like being in a damn go-kart, and I grew nauseous sliding around in the back seat while Tariq twisted down the turnpike.

"Damn this thing is fast!" I yelled over exhaust notes.

"Fucking-A," Tariq yelled back. "Four hundred brake-horsepower. Stage two turbo kit. Even upgraded the suspension and tires. Had to."

He swerved around to demonstrate its nimble handling. Veronica looked back at me and rolled her eyes.

"Shit man, how's life?" asked Tariq. "No, wait. Wait 'til we get some alcohol in our system. Let's just listen to music. What are you into nowadays? I've got some new trance mixes. Underground hip hop? Black metal? Post punk? Post rock? Electro-folk?" CDs were flying in my direction like ninja stars and I caught a couple of them, trying to make out Tariq's scribbled Sharpie. "Truck driver! Johan the trucker! Holy shit! Dude. You gotta tell me more about this. Veronica, babe, where should we eat?"

"I don't know. Maybe the Horny Toad?"

"Horny Toad. Now we're talkin'. Johan, do you believe in horny toads?"

"What?"

"Strange name for a restaurant, right? But Veronica and I were wondering how horny toads really were, or could be, and then we found this . . ."

He handed me his cell phone and wouldn't you know it: two toads fucking their brains out.

—

AN HOUR LATER, head still pounding bass and vibrato, we all sat around with tongues drooping onto menus. As with the car, it was an odd feeling to be surrounded by so much speed. The patrons at the bar were chattering over cocktails and their mouths seemed mechanical, wrists flicking up and down, eyes darting, legs crossing and then uncrossed, feet flopping, joints bouncing. I couldn't keep track of it. Tariq snapped fingers in my face, trying to get my attention—

"Hey man, we're over here! You're dazed tonight. Too much time on the road, huh?"

"Maybe."

"Shit. Let's get some drinks in you. What's your poison?"

"Afraid I can't join you guys on drinks. Need to be back on the road in the morning. Company does random drug tests."

"You're kidding, right?"

I shook my head.

"One little drink won't make a difference. It'll be out of your system by morning. Trust me. My uncle's a doctor. He educated me about this when I was very young."

Veronica rolled her eyes again, then looked at me— "You'll be fine, Johan."

"Alright then. Jameson on the rocks. But just one."

"Good deal," said Tariq, calling for the waiter who returned almost immediately with our order—a continuation of the high-speed frenzy. The moment my lips touched the glass rim, I thought my entire head would fall into the liquid, as I hadn't had a drop of booze in months.

And it tasted good
Tasted like freedom
Like the thing I'd been searching for on the road
My tongue, the tarmac

141

The sun, Jameson
The son, me

Tariq opened a tab and kept ordering drinks, and for some reason I kept drinking them, knowing it was a big risk. Part of me desired a certain chaos of the mind. I wanted to lose myself in the amber glow like a prehistoric mosquito, stuck for centuries—millennia! Rescue me! Take me to your museum of eternal bliss!

"Dude, are you drunk already?" asked Tariq.

"No. I'm good."

"You look like you're deep into something."

"Just thinking about stuff."

"Shit man, thinking is no good. We've gotta order a bottle. These highballs have too many cubes."

"No. I really can't."

"Really? That's a shame. So anyway, tell me more about this trucking thing. Why'd you decide to do it?"

"Pretty simple actually. Wanted to travel but needed money, and trucking provides the opportunity for both."

"Meet any hot chicks or just old men with boners?"

"*Tarrrriiiqqq!*" sighed Veronica.

"Just so happens that there are female truckers, too."

"Hot?"

"Occasionally."

"Damn. How long you gonna do this for?"

"Don't know yet. Need to save some more money, then we'll see."

"If you want," he said, "you can quit today."

"Hm?"

"My boss is looking for someone to shoot videos of a protege aircraft we're testing out in the desert. Needs to promote it to maintain his contract."

"I don't know, man. I've jumped through a lot of hoops to get where I'm at."

"Yeah, but you're done with trucking, I can tell. You wanna move on. And this is the next step. Lots of dough in it, too."

He had a point. I needed money, and a government contractor was sure to pay heaps of it. And the invisible crowd of people seated in the back of my brain told me to take it.

We've been through this. Don't be an idiot.

What about the road?

Forget the road. What more is there to see? It's a road.

It's a road that has spoken to me.

Do you want to be a fool speaking to inanimate objects or do you want to make money and have a good life?

"I'll have to think about it," I told Tariq.

"Okay, but understand that it's a one-time offer. Right? Not everyone gets an offer like this. Shit. Fuck it. Let's have another drink! Waitress!!"

Another glass and I was surging into oblivion—forgetting the voices, forgetting the reasons, forgetting the motivations and goals. Travel where? Travel here. I'd arrived at the promised land of tablecloths and hoop earrings. Veronica, you haven't spoken a word. What do you know? What lies behind those hungry eyes and lustre smile? Stay for awhile. I wanna know. I wanna know.

Pick me up, bartender
Pick me up, Tariq
I wanna know
I wanna go

—

SOMETIME around three a.m. I awoke in my childhood bed, staring up at the ceiling—the glowing star stickers that plastered its surface. They seemed to be shape-shifting, reaching for me; amorphous and amorous all at once.

I felt as though I were going to be sick and dodged to the bathroom, only to belch into the mirror. As I stood there at the sink listening to my father's rhythmic snoring, I considered Tariq's offer and all the possibility of a good job. His words played on my mind:

NEXT STEP

LOTS OF DOUGH

ONE-TIME OFFER

I saw Veronica watching Tariq with her warm brown eyes, and the warm cold glasses in our hands, swinging through the voices and evening moxie. I saw everything sparkle and thought the new job might shimmer the same. Protege aircraft dangling in the hangar. Get me a cup from the break room, Carl. Make it steam and full of caffeine. I've got to fire up this camera and capture these sparkles! Sure, sure, it sounded like a fine gig, and I thought for a long time under the fluorescence. Then there was sweet Francine and the highway, which still had yet to unfold completely. Hell, I hadn't even seen the Great Northwest yet! The tremendous land of Canada. And all the on-foot explorations of fantastic cities along the way. More than that, I thought of the World that awaited at the end of the adventure once the grand scale of my vision was complete.

It struck me: Francine didn't know about this ultimate world travel goal, and I started to see little holes in my plan. I saw myself returning to LA only to tell her that I was leaving again for nine months and six continents. I saw her retreating. I saw myself feeling like shit—falling back into the pit, which had no name but seemed to exist regardless of where I went. Although, wouldn't she react the same if I stayed in Maryland? It seemed none of the options were good enough and I tried to listen to my Vodka-soaked gut. "What do you say, gut?"

Take the damn job, fool!

"No, not you. Gut."

Oh.

Gut to Johan: "Keep on truckin'."

18

BELLA BOUNCED around in the back of the cab while my father played with that damn on-board computer, which wouldn't stop barking orders. I had hoped he was using his technical skills to reprogram its sounds. Give me wind chimes or bicycle bells. Toes brushing against carpet.

"This reminds me of old MS-DOS systems," he commented.

"That's what I thought. It's got the traditional vomit-green backlighting."

Stomach gurgling, I couldn't think of any other adjectives. At least my balance had been restored and I was sure that, as Tariq said, the alcohol would exit my system within the next twenty-four hours.

"How do you like it back there, Bella? Think you could sleep in here?" my father asked.

Bella nodded and kept bouncing on my bed, climbing up to the top bunk and bouncing on it. "Careful now! Don't fall!"

"Wanna go for a drive?" I suggested. "You can come with me as I leave town."

"Yeeaeaahhhhhhhhhhhh!"

I quickly planned my trip—straight shot from Maryland up I-95 where I would pick up a new load in Philly. Then I turned the ignition, released the brakes, and off we went down the street, pulling an empty trailer that bounced like Bella. It was unusually warm and I rolled down the windows and ran my hand through the cool air. Everything seemed clear—much clearer than the night before—and I couldn't tell if it was my lingering buzz or the fact that I was surrounded by loved ones while doing something I loved. On a major level, yes, I knew that I loved this journey, and remembered the times when I loved it most. They were the times with good people. This notion would prod me during the next few months, but for now I was happy just to breathe the air.

"Look out the window, Bella," said Dad. "Look how high up we are."

There it all was. Shopping centers, housing developments, fast food chains, billboards, and the crispy sleeping trees, quietly waiting for their moment. The sunlight was best. I think we all appreciated that. Still, Tariq's proposition continued to haunt me. And meanwhile, Francine reached her hand across the country and tapped me on the shoulder. And Paco! Where was Paco? Somewhere on this big plane, sipping energy drinks and singing Sublime.

I parked at the edge of town and Kelsey soon arrived to pick up my father and Bella.

"When do you think you'll be back around?" she asked.

"Soon enough."

"We'll miss you."

"Yeah, we'll miss you!" chimed Bella.

"Miss you, too."

"Be safe out there," said Dad with a quick hug.

I climbed back into the cab and watched the three of them disappear. Then I pointed the nose of the behemoth north, sun bouncing behind.

—

"WHY can't *you* pee into it?"

"Well, I just got back from Christmas break, and it just so happens that I was drinking last night. I'm a new trucker and can't lose this job. Please help me."

"Alright, but you should know better," said the man, fumbling for his jug of water to facilitate the process."

"I'll pay you."

"HA! Don't have to pay me, man. Just gimme a second to conjure somethin' up."

Somewhere around Bordentown, New Jersey, I had been phoned by my manager for a random drug screening, which left me scrambling the parking lot of the nearest truckstop for a kind soul. My new friend, Trucker Jim, just so happened to be standing around with a half-full bladder and nothing to do. I questioned the randomness of this screening, occurring just after the holidays when drivers were sure to be celebrating in some capacity.

Trucker Jim disappeared behind the curtains of his sleeper berth, returning five minutes later with a honey-colored Aquafina bottle.

"Might wanna go wash your hands," he said with a laugh.

"Duly noted. Thanks."

I threw the bottle in my truck and dodged down the highway, parking the trailer along the curb of the nearest medical clinic. Upon arriving in the gray office, I was nervous and damp, hoping my sweat didn't reek of substance. Jim was duct-taped to my thigh, concealed by my baggiest pair of jeans.

"You know the procedure?" asked the sassy black woman behind the counter.

"Walk into the bathroom, pee into this cup, return it to you?"

"And *don't* flush the toilet!"

"Got it."

Once the door was closed, I ripped the bottle from my leg and carefully poured its contents into the cup. The rest went into the toilet and I felt just as accomplished as if I had done the deed myself. The empty bottle went back onto my leg and voila, I flushed the toilet and . . .

"I flushed the toilet."

"What'd I tell you!?!"

"Sorry. I'm just coming off holiday break. Still getting back into the swing of things."

"Well, you might have to swing-a-thing again, 'cause we NEED this sample."

"I've got an important delivery to make and it must be on time. Can't you accept this? Please?" I begged with pouting lips—the lips that never worked with Bear, but maybe here. The woman shook her head, tapped her nails.

"Alright," she said, "Lucky I'm a trustworthy person and you have a trustworthy face. Don't lose that face. And next time, don't *flush* the damn toilet!"

—

I TOSSED THE BOTTLE into a nearby trash can and shuffled through the parking lot, dodging dollar signs and protege planes all the way back to the truck. It was natural to second guess in this circumstance: maybe it's all a big mistake. Maybe Tariq was right. Maybe Francine was right. Mom and Arthur. They were all right.

Or were they?

What was right?

Smart phone? Is the smart phone right?
And the mailman? He right?
Chinese clerk?
Is the birthright?
And the coffee bean?
Textbook?
Facebook screen?
Is the hoagie right?
And the lawyer mouth behind it?
News anchor? She right?
Snake right? Brake light?
Girl on scooter right?
Was last night right?
Is the monk in cave in robe right?
Is the principal right?
Grain right?
Is the temple right?

Are the sane right?
Mother?
Father?
Brother?
Lover?
Preacher?
Teacher?
Sunday afternoon brown paper bag sleeper?

Is the crow right?

Look at it fly

Sky
Sky

Are *you* right?

Then it rained

It rained
It rained

—

THE NEXT FEW WEEKS were like that. Me questioning what was right while I hooked, dropped, and drove loads across a land I had yet to know. Sometime during the middle of the month Arctic winds swooped down and January became brutal, and as a result I pushed south, turning down the Boston and Maine jobs, despite an eagerness to see the northernmost parts of the country. Besides, Francine waited at the other end. We continued to speak on a daily basis— bluetooth headset securely fastened around left earlobe while I steered through the I-States: Indiana, Illinois, Iowa, and the state of 'I' itself. Me, the ego, the mind, and the third eye, which spoke to me when she did not.

Francine's New Year's resolution was to create a change of scenery by moving to Hollywood, and she had already found a place tucked beyond the Tar Pits in a surprisingly quiet neighborhood. She was uprooting her life and subsequently spiraled into a process of evaluation, sifting through the pieces of our relationship, as if it were something to either pack or toss. Whatever the case, her impatience was palpable. She kept reminding me of the distance between us and how long it had been since we last kissed and touched, etc.

I grew tired of the situation but didn't have the guts to sever ties and go separate ways. Pesky voice still present, I continued to question the whole shebang: Dream, O dream, where have you led me? Where will you lead me next? And does it matter if I say no or yes?

For the moment, the dream had led me back to Kansas. I was parked at Xact Technologies, docked and waiting for crewmen to load my trailer with twenty pallets of car batteries. I watched each one drop with a crash and knew it wasn't going to be an easy haul across the Rockies to Pacoima, California. Not in this weather. The ground was already covered with a couple inches of snow and it was falling fast. I had hoped to escape the Arctic by the time I reached the Heartland, but it only followed and reminded me that I still hadn't been to Boston.

I sought refuge inside the warm warehouse break room— walls comprised mostly of metal lockers, splattered washbasin, and a mirror turned grease-collage. I snagged a two-pack of Little Debbie snack cakes from the vending machine and drained a nearby coffee pot. The cakes tasted like nothing, but it was a good nothing that, when combined with coffee, became something.

Two female employees entered the room and ripped off pairs of latex gloves—SMACK! SMACK!—and sat down with smiles that told me they were about to eat. The smiles were the smiles of people who didn't smile very often— distant, forced, resurrecting old wrinkles with weakened winks. Or was it weekend winks? It was Friday, after all.

"Did you hear about Yolanda?" one of them asked the other.

"No. What? Why?"

"Oh nothing."

"No. What?"

"She's having another baby."

"Pregnant? Again?"

"I know. Ridiculous isn't it? She's like a walking pair of ovaries."

"Perks of being the CEO's wife. She's only a secretary after all. What does it matter when you sit behind a desk filing papers all day?"

"Yeah, but at *her age*?"

"She's only thirty-seven."

"No."

"Yes."

"No."

"I'm sure of it. She's thirty-seven. That's what twins'll do to you, I guess. Could've sworn forty-seven myself."

"Lord almighty. Good luck to her. I've had enough with my son. Lazy pot smoker. Won't do anything! I told him to get a job like this young man. What's your name?"

"Johan," I said, mouth jammed with bread, trying not to get caught up.

"You're a driver, right?"

"Yes ma'am."

"See, there ya go. How can I get my son to work like you?"

"Not sure. What's he interested in?" I asked.

"Pot."

"Does he sell it?"

"What?"

"Does he sell the pot or just smoke it?" I clarified.

"What kind of question is that? I don't know what the hell he does with it!"

"I'm just saying, there are jobs in the medical marijuana field. Out west especially. Maybe you could look into it."

"Ha! And *encourage* this kind of behavior? Why in God's name would I ever do that?"

"Because he needs a job and that's what he's interested in."

They stared, slack-jawed.

The intercom crackled: "Driver Johan, your load is ready! Driver Johan to the dock!"

"Anyway," I concluded. "There are worse things."

—

I PUT THE SHIFTER into first and rocked away from Xact, down the street to the nearest truckstop, as I had to weigh the load before setting off towards Colorado where I planned to spend the night with chicken soup. The trailer lumbered onto the concrete scale and, judging by its bulging tires, I could already tell that it was overweight. Good God, they're going to burst! Lo and behold, I exceeded limits by one thousand pounds of plastic and acid on each axle. If it were only fifty pounds—one hundred even—I might risk it. After all, I'd burn that much weight in fuel alone over the next few hundred miles. But driving off like this was "askin' for it," as my mother would say.

Back at Xact, I showed my scale printout to the dockworkers and they shuffled around, rearranging pallets, as if their tactics were going to magically dissolve the two-thousand pounds.

I walked into the break room. The two ladies had returned to work, or work had returned to them. Or they disappeared into the walls and were watching me stab my can of tuna with a Swiss army knife—"He must be stoned! He must be stoned!" Alas, there were no can openers in sight and all the running around had my blood sugar low. I shook, careful not to slice a ligament.

I had enough time to cram two forkfuls down my throat when the intercom blasted the room: DRIVER JOHAN,

DRIVER JOHAN, TO THE DOCK, DRIVER JOHAN!!
LOAD IS READY, DRIVER JOHAN!!

Driver Johan is indisposed, dammit!
Call back when he's full of fish.
Leave a message at the
BEEP
BEEP BEEP

Now the workers were coming to *me* on their forklifts, parking outside the break room entrance. A large man poured out of the machine ass-first, waving papers in my face, telling me that everything was A-okay; then rushing to the vending machine for Sprite. I dodged out of the room, back to the truckstop, back onto the scale, and wouldn't you know it: 1800 pounds over. A mere two hundred shed from the rearrangement. "An hour of my life I'll never get back," I groaned. Now I was upset, and the snow kept falling, darkening with twilight, and I wasn't making money during the process because if the wheels weren't turnin', I wasn't earnin'.

———

XACT strung me along all evening.

I drove back and forth with scale printouts, and they rearranged, removed a pallet, then removed two pallets, then put one back on, then shifted some more. On their fifth attempt it was night, and I stood with crossed-arms and eyes, fuming at the pudgy manager who was sick of my face, and the two women sick, too; finally driving off in their pickups. My body ached, sticky with sweat, salt-powdered jacket, boots, and jeans, which reeked of fart and seat cushion.

"Just lose a pallet!" I yelled into my trailer. "Another truck can haul it."

A man in ball cap jumped down. "What's your problem, buddy?"

"I've been standing around here all day and you guys know damn well this load is overweight, and nothing you've done has fixed that. Meanwhile, I'm not getting paid a dime."

"You coppin' an attitude with us?"

"Wouldn't you?" I asked.

"Listen, we've got orders from our boss to ship as much of this order as we can. Our jobs are on the line."

"With all due respect, this weather isn't letting up. Once I return to that truckstop, I'm staying put. If the load is overweight, I'll call *my boss* and set things straight with him. I'll have my boss call your boss, and they'll get their bosses involved, and so on and so forth. We don't want a boss war over a single pallet, do we?"

The worker laughed, spit in the snow. "Whatever you say, bud."

He removed the pallet.

ME: 1
WORKERS: 1
BOSSES: 1
PROFITS: -.001

—

THE SHOWER WAS as I hoped it would be: hot.

The humans as I expected them to be: grumpy.

All the drivers forlorn, shuffling around the truckstop with their shower bags and bluetooth headsets. Some of them, I thought, never removed those headsets and never ceased to have a directory of people to talk to; feeding them conversation and anecdotes. Words like warmth, blanketing eardrums for the dream haul. The Driver's Lounge television cast shadows on the faces of at least ten men and women who sat tired and plump; steaks like weights heavy on the lungs.

Feeling as though I deserved something more than a can of Spam, I made my way to the diner that was located within the truckstop and finally saw the quandary drivers were faced with: they really weren't required to move much. Between sleeping and sitting in the truck, and the multitude of services provided within truckstops—from shower to full buffet—they were akin to caged seals. It was apparent that it took effort to break the chains of routine with so few options and encouragement in any other direction. The more I eased into the job, the more I saw myself conforming to this patterned lifestyle. I began to fear that this danger existed with all lifestyles, and that trucking was just one of the many paths on the heartbeat symphony scale. I also began to see that the trick, regardless of chosen path, was to maintain enthusiasm, and that the cage awaited those who didn't.

Anyhow, it wasn't a time for thoughts like these. In that moment I was focused on the path of the menu, which led me through a labyrinth of appetizers, entrées, and treats piled high with whipped cream. Half of the menu's pages were painted with whipped cream, and for a moment I thought I'd have to ask the waitress to hold the cream on my meatloaf and veggies.

"Know what you want?" she queried.

"Meatloaf looks pretty good. Is it good?" I asked without looking up at her.

"Probably the best I've had outside my mother's house. Are you from around here?"

"I've been to this diner in other truckstops; so in a way, yes."

"You messin' with me?"

I looked up and smiled. The waitress, Carla, was short and pale with round, black-rimmed glasses and a white blouse undone one or two buttons. Her hand rested on her hip. She was waiting for my response.

"Yeahhhh I'm just playing around. Been through Kansas once or twice, but never Salina. What's the town like, by the way?"

"It's nice. When the streets aren't frozen over!"

"Damn. Wish I could see it."

"Where ya comin' from anyway?" asked Carla.

"Northeast."

"Bet y'all got some snow up that way."

"Warm actually. Scientists say climate change. Others say it's Mother Nature throwing us a curve ball. Speaking of, I need a nice warm meal. I think I'll take that meatloaf and veggie soup."

Carla grabbed my menu and spun away. While waiting, I pulled my laptop from my backpack and set it up on the table, preparing to write. I glanced around the room and tried to draw inspiration from its checkered walls and frosty windows, but nothing came. The spent waitresses bantered back and forth behind the counter, and I thought of the women from the break room and wondered if they, too, were talking about the street corner stoners and babies to be. Or maybe husbands to be, or husbands who didn't want to be. Or babies they wanted to see and husbands they did not. And the backpack next to me. Last night's downer sex, and the ecstasy sex to free.

Or maybe just the weather.

I switched to the internet, signed into my bank account, and evaluated my savings-to-date: $4,843.20 minus meatloaf. Shit. I felt like a slowly deflating basketball. Five months deep and I had yet to hit five grand, and none of this pretty white stuff outside boosted esteem. The plan was twenty grand, for which I'd calculated one year on the road. At this rate, it would take at least twenty months to hit that mark. I thought that I had accounted for student loan payments, credit cards, health insurance, mobile phone, etc, but it seemed that I missed something. Maybe I hadn't factored in the initial months of training, waiting around, and the flat pay during mentorship. Maybe things would pick up in the coming weeks. Maybe when the weather did.

"Head's up, hon."

The plate landed with a dull clink, and in front of me sat a meal worthy of ten thousand taste buds. "That's what you wanted, right?" asked Carla, hand back on hip.

"That's it alright. Meatloaf and soup."

"Strange combination, you know," she commented.

"Why's it strange?"

"Usually meatloaf is served with potatoes or green beans or somethin'."

"Consider me a rebel."

"Gettin' smart with me again?"

"I apologize," I said. "I turn sarcastic when I'm tired. Sit down, let's talk."

She glanced around at the other tables, then nodded to her co-worker and sat down. "What would you like to discuss?"

"Something other than meatloaf and snow. And babies and work, for that matter."

Carla scanned my eyes to see if I was joking again. Meanwhile, I cut my meal into little squares and dipped a piece of toast into the soup. "What?" I asked. "I'm not kidding. I'm looking for real conversation, know what I mean?"

"This ain't a date!" barked Carla. "And I'm sure as hell not here to entertain you while you eat."

"Let me ask you," I said. "Who's the most interesting person you've met while working here?"

She looked up at the ceiling as if waiting for a memory to drop through. Her eyeliner was smudged, treading across her lids like charcoal. I wasn't sure of her age. Thirty-two perhaps, but she looked older, as if the years had stolen the years from her.

"I'd have to say Old Miss Brinkley," Carla finally said.

"And why was she the most interesting?"

"Well, she ate here every afternoon and always wore the same floral dress. I mean every day it was the same white and blue dress, but always clean and perfect. And the handbag matched, of course. When you saw her, it was like looking at a picture from an old magazine or newspaper clipping, except in color, y'know? She hardly spoke a word to anyone. Sometimes she just pointed at the menu to let you know what she wanted. Anyway, I thought maybe she was just super religious and went to church every day, so one afternoon I clocked out early and followed her after she left here."

"You followed her?"

"I did. I got in my little Ford pickup and she got in her big boat—Cadillac or somethin'—and I drove behind her all the way through town, keeping an eye on that floppy vintage hat. Wasn't sure where she was going at first. Seemed like she kept making turns through one neighborhood and into the next. She was just goin' through neighborhoods! Thought she'd notice me after awhile. Anyway, at one point she finally parked outside a shabby house, walked up to the door, met with somebody—but never walked inside—and then left again. I was gettin' pretty tired of followin' her at this point and thought about quittin', but I was just so damn curious! And so I continued and eventually we came upon a cemetery and she finally parked, got out, walked away. Once she was outta sight, I followed on foot to see where she went. It was weird walkin' through all those graves, and I never liked cemeteries, but it was still daylight and I thought okay, why not. Miss Brinkley's here after all. How scary can it be? Wow…lookin' back…it really felt like I was on an adventure . . ."

"You were."

"I guess. So, to finish the story, I couldn't find Miss Brinkley anywhere and thought I had searched the entire graveyard, but remembered there was this hill section—some of the graves were up on a hill, you know—and thought I'd give it a shot. And wouldn't you know, there she was, Old Miss Brinkley, sittin' next to a tombstone, smokin' a joint, watchin' the sky."

"Getting high? Alone?"

"All by herself! With the grave, of course."

"That is interesting."

"It *was*! But that's not the end of it. The next day here at the diner, I told some of my coworkers about my adventure, and they were super curious to see Miss Brinkley walk through the door. They just wanted to *see her* after hearing the story, y'know? And we waited all afternoon, tending to customers and what not, but she never came. The next day we waited, same thing. Now, mind you, this is a woman who'd been showin' up every single day for three years. Well, on the third day of us waitin' around, our manager, Paul, comes over, looking all tired and beaten up, and he sets a newspaper onto the counter:

HATTIE BRINKLEY, LOCAL FOUND DEAD
SUSPECTED SUICIDE AT HUSBAND'S GRAVE

…and there was a picture of her from about forty years ago. Black and white. Floppy hat. She looked the same."

19

THE ICE WAS THICK.

It took me ten minutes just to break the windshield free.

Everything encased in ice—even the side mirrors, which began to look like an avant garde sculpture. Then the wiper blades needed worked loose, and the spray nozzles, as I was sure to get splashed with grit heading west. The headlights were also glazed over, and before long I just walked around whacking the truck with a lengthy scraper I'd purchased; beating the hell out of it; feeling as though I were beating the job itself from the truck, hoping to shape it into a spaceship that would transport me to another land.

But soon I broke free and hit the open road, tapping into the Buddhist mindfulness techniques I learned back in LA when life had first grown sick and I sought to restore its health. On this Saturday, I was only trying to keep the tractor and trailer in line while rolling over patches of white and black ice. The four-wheelers (cars) zoomed on past, sometimes spinning 180s and 360s, causing me to veer to the right or left as delicately as possible. It seemed that we were all doing some kind of figure skating routine to the next Walmart.

Francine called many times and I told her that yes yes, I'm coming, I miss you, can't wait to see you, can't wait to hang out and do great things, so on and so forth. I missed my girl, but mostly I just missed remembering the purpose of things. Feeling the fire of certainty in my gut; red buzzer indicating **RIGHT TRACK!**

—

OAKLEY, KS
GRAND JUNCTION, CO
RICHFIELD, UT

None of the signs read RIGHT TRACK, but they passed day and night, and the states merged and blurred and became one. This wasn't so different than my time in LA, I thought. Everything blurring once it became the norm. Even with my cowboy hat and Johnny Cash, the spikes of experience were rarer, and in my mind I saw it as the panned-out waveform of our fundamental song. Occasionally I'd come across someone like Carla who tossed spice into the soup, but the recipe grew watery.

Tried to listen to new music. I wore a baseball cap. John Deere cap. Craftsman cap. None of the caps made a difference, nor did Mick Jagger or Metallica. Great tunes, but the song—the song! The song was flat. The music must mesh with the *song*.

—

WHEN I FINALLY reached Pacoima I parked along a curb outside of a small building, seeing no docks and not knowing where else to stop. I limped out of the truck and walked over to what appeared to be the shipping office, but all of the lights were off and the door was locked. I looked around for one of those BE BACK IN __ signs, but there was nothing to be found. I lolled the lot, basking in blue sky, eighty degrees, and suddenly began to laugh because I was struck by the extremes of America.

—

TWO HOURS LATER, as I was preparing to leave Pacoima and head back to the Strike terminal, a VW van sputtered up to me and buoyed to a stop. A green-eyed woman leaned out the passenger window, hair dropping to the street. "Hey you!" she called.

"Hm?"

"You look hungry! Want a nice meal?"

She presented a styrofoam container with both hands, as if it were an offering to the gods of…wherever. "It's not warm, but it's nutritious."

I opened it and saw a splash of peas, macaroni, and something wrapped in tin foil, which I assumed was meat. "That's kind of you," I said, handing it back. "But there might be someone else who can use this."

"We've got a whole *van-load* of this stuff," said the driver, squinting through circular sunglasses. "Just take it, man!"

"But I'm not really homeless or anything . . ." I continued.

They waved and drove off.

Then they backed up again.

"Forgot to provide utensils," said the woman, tossing a package my way. "See ya!"

It dawned on me: they think I'm homeless.

But I didn't feel homeless. Just looked like it.

—

I SAT DOWN on the curb and began picking at the food, and sure enough there was fresh chicken breast under that foil and I started to work on it with the knife, taking little bites to make sure it wasn't poisoned. If it were poisoned, at least I'd only be poisoned a little bit. Halfway through my meal another vehicle pulled up, and this time three Armenian men came running towards me, waving arms and yelling "Sir, sir! So sorry, sir!" Turns out they were the owners of the automotive parts company receiving my shipment.

"Where's truck? We'll meet you at truck."

"My truck is out back, but where's the dock?"

"We don't have a dock. We'll meet you, we'll meet you. Just go to truck."

So I went to truck and stood at truck, and sure enough the guys met me with a forklift and pallet jacks right there along the street.

"Do you have a cone?" I asked them.

"Why?"

"Safety? To warn other cars, people."

For the next hour I waited, without pay, playing traffic coordinator while the workers unloaded pallets of Kansan-constructed batteries one by one, hauling them over to a small garage. No clue how they fit everything inside. All I wanted was a cup o' joe. How can I manifest a coffee? No one had coffee and the cars zipped along, skimming past my body while I directed them with the cone like a disoriented dunce.

—

LATER THAT NIGHT Francine met me at the Ontario terminal and whisked me off to Hollywood, where I'd see her new apartment for the first time. "You're gonna love it," she kept saying, weaving down the 10. "Right next to a convenience store, too. You know, in case we ever need to make an emergency run and don't want to drive. It's also got hardwood floors, babe! They're a pain to keep clean, but they look brand new."

"Sounds great."

"It really is. And do you know what else?"

"What?"

"Two bedrooms."

"Oh yeah?"

"Yep. Don't know what to do with the other one yet. Was thinking of getting a roommate."

"Would help cover the cost of rent," I suggested.

"Exactly. Yeah."

"Yeah."

"So how's trucking? Make any cool trips lately?"

"Just got back from Kansas, and before that I visited my folks as you know."

"Wish I could've met them. When are we gonna take trips together to see your family, babe?"

"Soon."

"How soon?" she pressed.

"Soon."

"You don't seem very talkative."

"Just finished a fourteen-hour work day. Only natural that I'm tired."

"I know. But it's frustrating when we only have a couple days together."

"Let me squeeze in a nap and then we'll go out tonight."

The car hummed and weaved, and all the signs read LOS ANGELES.

The ten p.m. palms were mysterious.

Forever speaking to me.

—

IT WAS ALL cardboard boxes and coffee the next morning. Pots and pans poking out, being unloaded, placed into cupboards, burnt toast, and Francine and I hanging out as usual. It was at this point that I felt as though I were becoming schizophrenic to some degree—if only temporarily. Being in LA was like returning to a past life; the trucking life paused. A comatose dream that I slipped in and out of, mending both lives at once, attempting to stitch them into a quilt of the moment.

The apartment was as described, and the hardwood floors were in fact nice and polished, echoing our footsteps with sharp notes. Though comfortable in the new surroundings, I desired movement, and hopped a bus to the beach once Francine sped off to work. It seemed that ever since leaving LA I appreciated the beach more and wondered why I hadn't visited while living next to it. Routine, as I would come to learn throughout the remainder of my twenties, was a flypaper of sorts, and that only *movement* would strip me from its surface. This would be an ongoing battle, I knew. Easing into the waters of LA only to ease into the cab of a truck, and once the easing had commenced I was damn near done.

But how would I break the cycle? How would I make peace with it all?

As I bounced off the bus onto Ocean Ave., I thought that maybe one day I'd hit a wall and it would all be clearer. Then again, I didn't want to hit any walls. The walls are what led me to the walls of the truck, and those walls pushed me back to the open ocean.

Get with it, Johan. There's the sun, see?

There's the sand. Go feel it with your toes.

Remove a layer or two. You're baking in all that black.

I crossed PCH and strolled down to the shoreline where I sat shirtless for about an hour, hoping to even out the "driver's arm" tan I had acquired in the sunnier states.

The beach was dead. Only a few blankets and bodies sprinkled about, and the seagulls swooping down, landing, looking around—looking for answers maybe. Back to the beach! Hot damn hot beach! Always back to the beach. Five years earlier it had been the land of promise. Two years ago, the land of grind and try. Now, just land. Everything merged. It no longer mattered where I was, and that was the scariest thing of all.

—

LOS FELIZ.

My preferred neighborhood if I decided to move back to LA. On this indigo night, it's where our dinner restaurant was located. The place had a patio with thick white bulbs strung over round metal tables, and Francine seemed to be powering them with her smile. I wanted a beer. Between the bulbs and teeth, it was too much to take. Fuck the beer. I didn't even want to be there. Her smile looked genuine, but I suspected that it was loaded with stratagem; motives hidden in molars.

"You look pretty tonight," I said, followed by "Fat Tire" to the waiter.

"Thanks, babe. You do, too."

I knew that she meant nothing by it, her smile. But I couldn't stop feeling as though I was standing in front of a firing squad.

The beer appeared before me, and after a quick toast, I was three gulps deep.

"Easy, babe," said Francine. "Don't want to lose your job, do you?"

"Not gonna lose my job."

"Would you want to?" she asked.

"What?"

"Would you *want* to lose your job? Are you trying to?"

"No. I'm trying to enjoy this beer."

"Oh. Because it seems like you're tired of it already. The job, I mean."

"No, no. Stressed at times, but not tired."

"But you like my new place, right?"

"It's great. Perfect. You found a real gem. Didn't think there were decent apartments left in Hollywood without having to spend a few paychecks."

"Me neither. Anyway, I wanted to ask you something. I know you're still on this adventure of yours, but in case you'd want to return, I do have a spare bedroom, and would really like to live with you, even though I have reservations about doing so prior to marriage."

I was now halfway through the beer and loose at the limbs. I flailed my arms around a few times, but forgot what was said in the moment. Not that I was drunk or anything. I just forgot. Something about "maybe" or "I don't know."

I don't know.

I don't know.

You're pretty.

I don't know.

Waiter.

—

THEN I STOOD at the edge of a cliff. Still with the strange urge.

It had been two weeks since the teeth and beach, and Utah was looking lovely on Valentine's Day—rocky red. Soon I'd call Francine on my headset and talk for an hour as I headed east into Colorado.

But *now* was not the time for talking. Now was the time for staring headlong into the abyss of the canyons. They were magnificent, and I was the only person standing there at the scenic view area—truck parked behind me, still idling, muted by the northern breeze. It was a hazy day. The exposed sediment was evenly lit; chalky crimson with shrubs sprouted above. I thought about screaming. A good scream would do me good. Clean out the esophagus. Release the hounds.

I stood for a while longer and unleashed the thoughts of the day, and month, and my entire life, and tried to focus on the present moment. Get swept up with the dust. Yes. That would be a hell of a trip, sucked through the air filter of the truck. Then I'd really become one with the beast. That is, until I got belched out through its pipes. Then I'd have my scream!

—

LATER, back on 70, I was huffing and puffing up the Rockies, hauling sheet metal or something. Whatever it was, it was heavy, and I was lazy, missing gears, slowing down to a crawling pace and cursing myself.

Fucking bastard! Pay attention!

Ah, there you are. Where've you been, old friend?

Vacation.

And where does one's inner critic vacation?

In the unconscious. So get back to being conscious so I can rest in the Rockies.

I shifted into third and finally gained momentum. Momentum! Momentum was synonymous with movement, and the truck would soon become a rolling reminder of the concept.

Despite movement and momentum, I kept stopping at scenic areas and sitting for long periods of time. Maybe sitting was also movement, I thought. Must we move to move? Did I not move while I sat in the truck? Was sleep not movement? Does it not regenerate cells and repair muscles?

What's right? What's right?

—

ALL THIS TIME the truck was becoming filthier and filthier. I noticed this somewhere in New Mexico, when it had been weeks since she'd had a good wash. It didn't help that the Volvo was painted Polar Bear White and that I'd spent the past couple of weeks in the bone-scorched Southwest pushing through dust clouds. Eventually I decided to paint a message onto the grime, right there alongside the truck, wiping letters with a wet rag:

IT'S NOT
THAT BAD

I added a fat smiley face to the design.

It's the way I felt at the time. That, despite all the uncertainties of my youth, trucking, and the grand journey itself, everything was A-okay. I had my health and I was a breathing being like the rest of them. The bathrobe asshole, ol' Army, and the bedazzled Persian of the Palisades. I had my Spam and right hand for shifting gears. I had music. By God, *music!* How could I forget my foundation of bass and treble? The jolt of magic electric guitars, snares, synths, and occasional psychedelic overtones. Most importantly, I still had enthusiasm. Although it had recently waned, I kept the glowing ball under lock and keen observation; monitoring with the nodes of what I knew to be true.

Still, the questions came:

"What the hell you got written on the side of your truck?" asked a shipping clerk.

"It's a philosophy of sorts," I told 'em.

OR

"It keeps me sane."

OR one driver who simply walked over to the truck, looked down at the message, then back up at me with firm-pouted lips.

"No. No it's not, is it?" he said, turning and walking away.

I drove for weeks like that and kept running a rag over the letters to make sure they were visible. The message became more legible with the accumulating dirt. I thought it might change the world in some way.

—

I LOVED THE SOUTHWEST and it soon became my favorite part of the country. Didn't want to leave. Just close enough to LA to be far enough away; just hot enough in Tucson to savor Flagstaff. Regardless of temperature, the desert roads were all beaten the same, with snaking black lines and barely filled potholes; and me trying to avoid them while I rollercoastered across spreads of cacti, pin-pricked crows, and crow-pecked kills. The land was pure and untouched— the forgotten territory that America bought for expansion and aestheticism, save for the aforementioned and Albuquerque. Santa Fe. Las Cruces. Names that seemed to belong to active tribes existing in tunnels below shopping centers and croaking oil rigs.

In these lower left states I became unhinged from time. Once, after banging my head on the cab's cupboards due to a delivery rush, I ripped off my wristwatch and launched it out the window, straight into the sand. "Fuck this thing! What's the use? Time doesn't exist, it doesn't *exist!*"

For as much comfort the cosmic landscape offered, it also grabbed me by the collar with its quietude. Cliff after cliff, I saw everything as it was. Sometimes I parked in the middle of nowhere to do nothing but sit on the hood of the truck and eat a bag of chips.

> On an old road in Arizona
> Thinkin' how I'm on my own now
> Trying to remember my hometown
> But it's hard when there's nothing around

I sang and sang, and somewhere in the distance my watch kept ticking. It had a ten-year battery and weatherproof casing. It would tick for a long time.

—

MY NEXT PICKUP was in Gallup, New Mexico, but I awoke in Kingman, Arizona. It was early and I still had hours before I needed to be on the road, but couldn't sleep for some reason.

I stepped outside the truck for fresh air and a stretch, and watched the sky burn with subdued pastels and FINGERLICKIN' FRIED CHICKEN! $1.99! next to buzzing diesel rates. My bones snapped into place and I lingered for a while, ass against trailer, hypnotized by the roaring morning traffic—trucks silhouetted amid fiery blue backdrop.

I splashed water onto a thickly pasted toothbrush and scrubbed my teeth before heading over to the convenience store for coffee that would ruin them. Hot damn hot coffee. Twelve-ounce'll do. Add some hot water on the side for my instant oatmeal and almonds. Raisins for fiber. No, I've got almonds. Watch the fiber, dammit. Keep the bowels loose but not too loose. Too early for this kind of thinking. Walk. Find something to do.

Wandering through the convenience store, slurping my breakfast, I came across a curtained-off room with black foldout chairs facing a podium. A few people were sitting around, holding pamphlets and scratching their faces. They were mostly men—mostly truckers—and the gentleman standing behind the podium wore a white, buttoned-up shirt. Clean-shaven, combed hair.

"Come. Sit. Join us." he told me, arms stretched wide.

"Hm? Me?"

"Yes, *you*. You're welcome just as anybody else."

"Okay. But what is this?"

"Well," he started, rubbing his hands together, "It's a sort of community counseling session sponsored by the truckstop. We like to think of it as a spiritual retreat. A place to unwind before you begin your day. Do you have a place like that in your life right now?"

"My bed."

The man laughed, and behind the laugh I could hear zapping arcade machines in the neighboring room.

"My name's Roger. Why don't you take a seat?" he said.

I sat down and continued spooning heaps of oatmeal into my mouth. Outside, the sky had extinguished to a cloudless blue and trucks were pulling away from their spaces, sauntering onto the highway. Men and women began to fill our small room, and an old man soon joined Roger. The old man wasn't nearly as polished. He wore a plaid shirt and jeans with large bronze belt buckle that fastened them to his thin waist. He whispered into Roger's ear while simultaneously scanning the room.

"Okay, friends," said Roger. "We're going to begin now. Does everyone have their Bibles on hand?"

I looked around, and sure enough, everyone had mint black copies.

"I see someone over there on the side who doesn't have one," noticed the old man.

"Me?" I muttered.

"What's your name, son?" asked the old man, waltzing over.

"Johan."

"Johan, I want you to have something very special," he said, handing me a flimsy black and white paperback. On the front cover: a Peterbilt truck with tacky chrome grill.

"Trucker's edition, and it even has the verses in bold," he pointed out.

"Thank you."

"My sincere pleasure," the man replied with a nod, moving backwards and taking Roger's place at the podium. "Now, before we start our daily prayer, I wanna do a little activity."

The old man distributed single sheets of paper the size of golf scorecards. A checklist.

"Don't read just yet!" he cautioned. "Wait 'til they're all passed out."

I was curious and jumped the gun:

ARE YOU A SINNER???
A CHECKLIST FOR THE DOUBTFUL

1) HAVE YOU CONSIDERED THE EXISTENCE OF OTHER GODS?

2) HAVE YOU SHAPED GOD AS A FIGMENT OF YOUR IMAGINATION?

3) HAVE YOU USED THE LORD'S NAME IN VAIN?

4) HAVE YOU KEPT THE SABBATH DAY HOLY?

5) HAVE YOU EVER DISRESPECTED YOUR PARENTS?

6) HAVE YOU MURDERED?

7) HAVE YOU BEEN WITH ONE WHO ISN'T YOUR SPOUSE?

8) HAVE YOU STOLEN ANYTHING? (EVEN A CANDY BAR?)

9) HAVE YOU LIED TO ANYONE? (RECENTLY OR IN YOUR PAST?)

10) HAVE YOU BEEN COVETOUS OR JEALOUS OF OTHERS?

>> IF SO, THEN **YOU ARE A SINNER**. REPENT AND BE SAVED!! <<

"So, are you?" came a voice from above.

I looked up and there was the old man hovering over me with chapped lips. It appeared as though his entire face were about to melt.

"I mean, apparently. Aren't you?"

"Son, we're all sinners. That's not the point of this exercise. The point is right here at the bottom," he said, pressing a bent finger onto the REPENT AND BE SAVED text. "Which leads me to my next question: Will you?"

"Will I . . .?"

"*Will* you?"

"Do . . . do what?"

"For Christ's sake, son, will you allow yourself to be *saved*!?!"

The room gasped.

"I apologize for that," said the man. "You see, I'm no shining example. I know where my faults lie. But I've also followed the Word and given myself chance at redemption. And that's what I'm bidding for you this morning, young man. To accept Jesus Christ as your Lord and Savior."

Roger seemed inaccessible. He was somewhere beyond the ridge of the old man's shoulder.

"I'm going to be straight with you," I said. "You're creeping me out a bit."

"Creepin' you out?"

"Yeah. None of this feels peaceful or comfortable."

"No. Indeed not. Sin is never a cozy thing."

"I'm speaking more about this situation. Although I realize I'm a sinner, I've always sought God on a more personal level. This feels forced."

"I see. You're one of those spiritual, non-religious types. Well let me tell you somethin', Jack. That might feel nice and cozy, but it's like sittin' in a Mercedes-Benz without any fuel for the destination. As drivers, you should all understand that analogy."

The room nodded.

"So what'll it be?" he asked me again.

"Are you going to baptize me right here or what?"

"Sure as heck will. I'll get a bowlful o' tap water from the soda fountain and bless it."

His eyes were hungry, feverish, clawing for something. Desire, it seemed, had consumed him like a rubbernecking window shopper, and I didn't know to what end.

I looked down at the Trucker's Bible in my hand.

"How about I just read some of this and find my own way?"

I stood up with my oatmeal, waved to the faces, and left.

Pausing outside in the hallway, I heard the man continue: "I remember what it's like to be young! He'll be back!"

—

FOR WEEKS, the Southwest.

I made sure to remain there so long as it served me, turning down loads to other places despite the prospect of more money. I was not done absorbing. Running from place to place with money on the mind was insanity, I knew, and it defeated the whole purpose of the trucking adventure. The adventure was not the adventure without the adventure, just as life was not life without the living. I had to remember that things were happening as they were happening, or risk them happening after they'd happened.

Today! TODAY!

Today the turquoise Navajo Travel Plaza had me transfixed with its fiberglass yellow horse attraction and hand-woven blankets. Hand-made jewelry. And the hands of the Navajo people themselves, dry and work-ready. Once, I stumbled past an old Coca-Cola machine into one of those wood-propped shops and found a face in the shadows, traced with ancient lines untold in any history book I'd ever read. The lines spoke of stories with mystical nights and tragic endings. Endings that I would come to see along the highways of northern New Mexico while straddling either side of the Great Divide. Endings of tin huts and bottom shelf bottles strewn across grassless lawns. The children, rampant, naked, looking for a new story on The Rez.

> This isn't the America I know
> This can't be America
> How have we forgotten all this?
> Have we grown beyond our beginnings?
> Like rife vines
> right over top
> right down the line
> assembled from the ass-end?

I downshifted and drove upward into a maze of roads that led me to a series of squared farms. I was supposed to pick up potatoes, reportedly used for Pringle-making, but didn't know from which square. I kept going in circles and the on-board computer was freaking out.

On one of the dirt roads, thinking I had finally arrived, I parked and got out. I was walking towards a barn with my clipboard and pen when suddenly I heard the sound of footsteps and panting. Something moving in the distance. Only when I lowered my sunglasses did I see the large coyote huffing at me. Coyote? No. Dog. Looks like a coyote. Doesn't matter. Run. No. Stay. Fear makes it worse.

Too late to decide, I stood my ground and prepared my pen as a potential weapon. Thankfully the brown and white creature slowed its pace, and by the time it reached me, it was wagging its tail and begging for pets, which I promptly kneeled to give. I couldn't make out the breed, but the dog looked like a stray—collarless and unkempt. And as I continued to search for signs of human life, the dog trotted alongside, following me everywhere.

"Where'd you come from anyway?" I asked, speaking with the childish tone reserved for when we're alone with animals. "Is your owner around?"

Back at the truck I located a jug of water and poured a plastic cup, which the dog dove into nose-first. The wind whipped up nasty clouds of dust and sprayed it into our faces like hurricane sand, leaving the sun to clean up our frowns.

"You looking for someone?" I heard through the grit.

I turned around and saw a Native American man of about forty-five with deep black hair, chubby face, straw hat. Similar to the dog and myself, the man remained standing and waited for me to approach him.

"As a matter of fact," I said, smoothing out the documents on my clipboard, "I need to find G&D Industries. It's supposedly in the area. Think you can help?"

The man took a look at my directions, scrunching his features and nearly losing his eyes in the process. I considered handing him my sunglasses, but his hat seemed to suffice. His hands weren't unlike the hands of the clerk I saw back at the travel plaza—rubbery, wrought, and shaped so solidly that I wondered whether they were ever smooth. Perhaps he had been delivered from the womb calloused and confused. In any case, I wanted to know more about the Native American people, and observed with fascination as the man drew a shaky diagram of local streets, complete with starred stop signs and angular arrows; pointing into the wind to ensure I got it all. After I confirmed with plenty of nodding we shook hands and I walked to my truck, again followed by the affectionate coyote-dog.

"Whose dog is this, by the way?" I asked.

"Yours if you want him," said the ancient man.

"You mean he has no owner?"

"He hangs out and I feed him. Other than that, he's a wandering creature."

I looked down at the comical tongue, the fire and zeal. This dog had the spirit of the West and I needed it, now and always. I opened the truck door and helped my new friend inside.

"What breed is he?"

"Hell if I know."

spring

20

They sent me Pharr.

Pharr, Texas. All the way to the Mexican border where armed guards stood erect before the Rio Grande, waving cars and trucks over the wide International Bridge. Meanwhile, I stood in a crowded dirt lot next to a trailer of Tecate and Tecate himself, my coyote-dog that I named after the imported lager. It seemed that whenever I went to Mexico, or near Mexico, I was handling beer but never drinking it. Beer loads were the most depressing of all. Especially in March when Texas temperatures were crisp but strangely rendered my cab an oven.

Tecate lapped up a cup of water while I toyed around with an unopened beer plucked from mud. Once again I found myself at a deserted warehouse, and once again I was working for free. Thus, the can was cracked with a PSSSSSSKKT CLUNK and GLUG-GLUG-GULP. Even Tecate had a few sips. The dog was beautiful and I couldn't stop admiring him, inventing stories in my mind about *his story*. Where he came from, what he'd seen in the Great Land of Natives, and what it felt like to not have an ego.

Oh, one day the Bodhisattvas would tell me over a steaming cup of water!

I turned my attention back to the shipping office, banging on windows and asking the sun where everyone was. Tecate was pissing all over the place and I knew that he would soon need a bath. I'd never bathed a dog before, and in fact, never owned a canine until now. The whole thing seemed daunting. But I enjoyed his companionship and pushed pragmatism aside in lieu of unconditional love. Still, stink is stink, and Tecate was a fly trap.

—

HOURS LATER, finally relieved of my beer conscience, I was back on my way up north to marry myself to a new load somewhere in Laredo. Leaving Pharr, I drove through another small border town with stray cats and children running across the streets; causing me to buck my way through, burying brake pedal into carpet every twenty seconds. Shops held together with glue and rusty nails, and tattered signs advertising REFRESHING COCA-COLA sold from out-of-order vending machines. It was all very vintage—an abandoned America—with a freedom of its own. A living, breathing country of its own, slave to its appointed government of nobody. It was bordered by walls of boys and girls and their beliefs. It was guarded by the drone of flies and steel hubcaps. These barbed-wire lands existed separate from the fertilized lawns of my youth, and again I thought about the Native Americans and wondered if anyone considered the contrasts of our vast territory.

Anyhow I stopped at one of those shops to grab another jug of spring water, having underestimated Tecate's thirst. Inside were clerks with Spanish tongues and babies slung across chests; men pandering with girlfriends over broken condoms of last night's sex; and when I closed my eyes I heard the cash register ring the price of society, and all but the newborns were buying. There's the water. In the back. The fridge next to the broken one with punctured glass and rotten eggs. Got it. Go. Gone. Out the door and around the side to the lot, past the man selling fruit: "Orange! Orange! Sir! Five dollars!"

Stop.

They were stacked all around him, glowing, rotund. The salesman's face reflected their brilliance.

"Here," he held out his dusty hand with a dripping piece. "Fresh."

I took it and tried it, and indeed it was fresh, and the sun seemed to beckon that I buy a sack, which the man was already preparing. But I made him wait, savoring the splice of scenery. His smile. The taste. The warmth. The voices. Tecate's snout poking through the truck window. Professor

Jake would be proud. Bet he's meditating right now to the cacophony of a thousand coffee makers.

"Yessir. Uno bag, por favor."

I was happy to hand over the five bucks and even gave a couple more as a tip, swinging the sack over my shoulder and swaggering back to the truck. My friend, the Mexican orange-salesman. My loyal Tecate. Yes, this was in fact the great dream sequence, and I acknowledged it as it happened; as I'd often forgotten.

—

IN LAREDO I parked at the local Strike terminal and immediately noticed that it had special rooms for special drivers to sleep in—those with "a million miles under their belt" and such. Essentially, these rooms were boxes with beds and no different than the truck, save for the added benefit of heating without hearing the engine idle. But that wasn't much incentive for me. I'd grown to appreciate the rough diesel chug over the months, which always rocked me to sleep and occasionally awake. It became expected and I could no longer doze without it. Let the boxes blanket the Million Milers; I was diving fist-first into a bag of fruit.

The night was cold and so were the oranges. I picked one out and dug my nails into it, prying away the tough skin while Tecate watched with pouting eyes. I still wasn't sure whether or not he'd been vaccinated, and concerns mounted each time he neared my face. That's the last thing I wanted: to be found running wild and rabid along the border at two a.m. As I continued to pick apart the orange, I noticed that it had soft areas, causing my fingers to fall into its mushy interior instead of peeling it. Upon turning on the light, it became clear that the orange was browned rotten. I rummaged through the bag and…sonofabitch…I'd been duped! All spoiled. I threw the fruit to the floor and Tecate tackled it with his teeth. Seeing how much he enjoyed them, I took the sack outside and began launching the oranges into a nearby field, prompting a game of catch in which all the balls would be thrown and none returned. Tecate jogged back with a dead snake. We watched the stars and fell asleep.

———

I DIDN'T KNOW what I was in for the next morning.

Only knew that I needed a shower.

It had been a few days and I felt a gritty layer of salt on my face, neck, and arms. Furthermore, I had a weighty bag of laundry that smelled like a mechanics' locker room. And so I left Tecate by the truck with a can of tuna and moseyed inside the terminal. As I walked, I felt my spine sagging below the clavicle and quickly straightened out, conscious of the ever-evolving trucker's hunch. Folding! Already! Ah, it had been no different in the office, gangling over keyboards like some medieval drudge.

The water hit my scalp first and I turned it off immediately—not because it was cold, but because I wanted to savor the feeling of being cleansed. There was something transformative about a shower after days gone without one. Felt as though I was emerging from a shell of sorts; that I would draw conclusion about the direction of my life by the time I reached my toes. That it would all become clearer by the last comb and brush.

As was habit for me to do, I inspected my body while scrubbing, and on this day something caught my attention: a black spot on the head of my dick. Some strange dirt, I thought, and began to scrub it as I had everywhere else.

It wasn't going away.

I didn't have any birthmarks in that region—I was sure of it. Had to be after twenty-six years. A stubborn scab perhaps. I began picking at it, and eventually pulled the spot away from my privates, holding it up to the light for inspection.

The spot was now moving.

It had legs. They were kicking about.

Shit! What the fuck is it?

Closer, I looked, and finally determined that it was a tick, hastily burying its way into the skin of my finger. I quickly found a piece of tissue paper and nabbed the bug, flushing it down a toilet.

"Must have been that damn field last night," I said to myself. "Bet Tecate's crawling with them. Shit!!"

—

I WAS WORRIED.

I'd heard about lyme disease and all the other viruses derived from tick bites, and as soon as I got back to my truck I tip-toed around Tecate and phoned my doctor back in LA. He wasn't available. I left a message, then went into the convenience store and bought a large bucket, to which I added warm water and some of my shower gel. Better than nothing. I also bought a hefty sponge, which was apparently meant for washing cars, but today it would be used to un-stink and de-tick my furry friend.

Outside again, I untied Tecate. He finished his tuna and flung the empty can somewhere like the bony remains of morning prey. I set the bucket down and sloshed the sponge around, showing it to Tecate, allowing him to smell it and gather some sense of what was coming. His eyes bulged, he backpedaled. Desert dog or not, surely he's been exposed to water at some point, right? Right.

Right?

I removed my boots, rolled up my pants, and began washing my legs with the sponge to further our understanding. Closer and closer he came to me, until I scooped out some water with a cup and splashed the side of his body. He jumped back, startled. Splashed him again. He shook out his fur, spun around a few times, then returned for a full-on bathing.

—

Moments.

—

LAREDO GIRL.

O she was a woman!

But Laredo Girl is what she would forever be known as, and today was the day that I'd first lay eyes upon the face that would come to haunt me for the rest of my life. It was at the border patrol station, a customary checkpoint similar to the one Paco and I got hassled at on that chilly autumn night. Tecate was curled up on the passenger seat, which he barely fit on; a sizeable portion of his body drooping off the edge. I had set the heat on full blast with all vents aimed at him and windows half down. He seemed relaxed, and meanwhile I remained rigid—mind racing with epitaphs:

> HERE LIES JOHAN NIVENS
> LOVER OF LIFE, TRAGEDY OF BITES
> HE DID NOT LOOK LIKE A TRUCKER
> BUT WAS ONE
> FOR A SHORT WHILE
> WE'VE ALMOST RUN OUT OF SPACE
> ON THIS VERY TALL HEADSTONE
> ENJOY YOUR DAYS
> REPELLENT SAVES

O she was a woman!

And when I finally inched up to her under the shaded station, I immediately fell into her eyes. They were big, lovely, and it seemed her whole body was buttoned into a uniformed world of its own. Dark black hair tucked under a hat, which furthered my curiosity and nearly drew me from the truck. Alas, I had to stay high up in the cab, observing from above, answering her questions as they came: "Where are you going?" "What are you hauling?" "Are you alone in the cab?"

The last one hurt the most because I wanted to say no.
Wanted to say no because I wished be with her.

186

And when I said no, she said "Okay." And she said it in such a way that mirrored my own regret, as if she too felt the sadness of staying and going and the gaps of desperation that lie between. What if, what if, what if?

Her face followed me as I drove away.
It summoned urges and random visions.
Laredo Girl was more than just a woman. She was spirit.

—

"SO WHAT KIND of tick was it?"

"I-I don't know, doc. It was a tick."

"Okay. I need a little more information to make a proper diagnosis over the phone. What region of the country are you in?"

"The South. Texas."

"Okay. And on what part of your body is the bite located?"

"My penis."

There was a short pause.

"Your penis?" the doctor repeated, as if not hearing correctly the first time.

"That's right, on my penis."

Another pause.

"Is that bizarre or what!?!" I asked, chuckling.

"I'm a doctor, Johan. I've heard *and seen* stranger things."

"So what do I do?"

"Hmmmm," my doc continued. "Luckily, you're in a low-risk area for lyme disease. Definitely keep an eye on the bite mark as it heals, but I wouldn't worry too much. You sound pretty shaken up. Is that all that's bothering you?"

"Medically speaking?"

"Generally speaking. Your general well-being is related to health, you know."

"General as in my . . . *mental health*?" I asked.

"Mental, spiritual, emotional. I can't advise you in all of these areas, of course; but I like to remind my patients of them once in awhile."

"Yeah, I see. That's nice of you. Come to think of it, I guess you could say I've been a bit stressed lately. For example, there was this girl I saw about fifteen minutes ago—well—woman. She was a woman. And I immediately wanted to be with her, know what I mean? Err—not just *sexually*, but really *be with her* and get to know her spirit. To run away. I immediately wanted to drop everything and run away with her. And you know me, doc—it's uncharacteristic for me to think this way. I've got a girlfriend that I'm committed to. But these urges are conflicting and they come from a strong place within. I can't ignore them, they aren't going away, and at the same time I feel a disgusting guilt despite the purity of these thoughts. It's like I feel guilty for who I *am*. And hell yeah it stresses me out, because it's a questioning of the truth of everything that has preceded this moment. They're such pure thoughts, doc. Pure and evil and confusing as hell."

Silence.

"Doc? Still there?"

I looked down at my phone. NO SERVICE.

Damn you, Texas. Damn you and your dick ticks.

21

AAAAGHHHH-CHHHHEWWWWWWW!!!!
SPLAT.
UGH.

Allergy season was in full bloom and pollen coated everything in Ohio. Yellow. Like mustard powder. On the windshield, mirrors, blowing into the cab, my eyes. I wondered where all the shit eventually went. Did the rain just wash it away? Blew my nose. Ah, there's a trace of explanation.

Tecate didn't seem to mind. He was rolling around in the stuff, and I ran after him, brushing him off, pulling out the bucket for bath after bath. I had underestimated the rascal's intelligence. I was pretty sure he did this just to get more baths. Meanwhile, the cottonwood trees were creating their own spermstorm of white fluff that breezed through the air while I rattled down old Amish roads.

Weeks. Constantly itchy. Constantly tired. Everything blurring together.

This was the part of my journey that I dubbed "cruise control." The part where nothing really seemed to be happening. Driving, sneezing, cramming my face with protein bars. I had taken things for granted, and taken to complaining because there was always more to take and I didn't have it yet. The trees, with their budding branches and hints of green, did not register with the dulled senses. Mother Nature merely passed along with the mile markers and ol' Father Time himself. I had snubbed both parents, focused on the never-ending horizon, and dammit I knew I'd arrive sooner or later with polished shoes and lavender-scented Tecate. The gates would open and I'd be placed upon a throne with unfading, youthful face; all my Laredo Girl dreams actualized and documented, and ready to be replayed at a moment's notice—a DVD plucked from the shelves of my better self.

Sounded good to me.

So I kept going.

—

LATER THAT NIGHT, driving east towards Youngstown, Ohio, I became hopeful that I'd see my mother again, as she only lived a couple hours away in western PA. Pleasant thoughts entered my head: warm hugs, sitting on the porch with beers, and introducing her to Tecate. But that was what *could be* and now was *now!* It took a hard slap on the face to remind myself of this—of the *night that was now*. The night, heavy with black, and me, pale peach, cutting through with sharp beams. A mix CD was playing on the stereo—the same mélange of music I'd been listening to for weeks. I ejected the disc and whipped it out the window like my watch (still ticking).

All was quiet for a few minutes, save for the hum of the road, whistling windshield, and Tecate's sighs. I thought nothing, and it was my biggest accomplishment of the day I thought.

The phone rang.

I fastened my earpiece and answered.

"Hello?"

"Johan, y'bastard! Where the hell are ya?"

"Uh, who is this?"

"Ya bastard! You don't recognize my angelic voice?"

". . . Simon?"

"Damn straight. And guess where I am."

"No clue," I said, rubbing bloodshot eyes.

"Less than two miles in front of a Texas tornado!"

"Seriously? Why the hell are you on the phone with me?"

"Don't know," said Simon. "You're the first person I thought to call. We're on this adventure together, right? Besides, it's an itty-bitty thing. F1 probably."

"Damn. What's with the bizarre weather lately? Heard the entire South is getting ravaged."

"Nature can be wild. It's not like we've documented all 4.5 billion years of earthly climate. We humans might be an extreme pattern of life itself. But I know one thing's for sure: Damn it feels good to FEEL something!"

"'Course it does."

"I mean, that's why we're out here, right? To *feel* *something*. That's why I came out here. How you feeling about the whole ordeal? Gah—hold on—the thing's chasin' me down. Wow! Just wow!"

"Simon, why don't you call me back? I don't want to be accountable for you getting sucked into oblivion."

"No, no, no. It's fine. Just hopped up on adrenaline. All good. So anyway, what's new with you? You feeling anything?"

"I'm feeling, yeah."

"Yeah?"

"Yeah."

"What are you feeling?" asked Simon.

"Well," I said, looking over at Tecate, who was suddenly sitting with perked ears. "I guess it's a mixture of emotions. Partly excited to continue the journey; partly eager to move on to new experiences."

"Yeah? Like what?"

"Don't know. Feeling kinda stuck, I guess. Like I've painted myself into a corner. LA no longer appeals to me, the road is wearing me out, and being in my hometown is like putting on old clothing. What are your feelings, outside of Texas tornados?"

There was a pause.

"Simon?"

Silence.

"Simon!?"
"Yeah, I'm here."

"Shit," I exhaled. "You're freakin' me out here. I've got nothing but headlights in front of me, and you're projecting bad images. Why don't you call me back?"

"No, no, it's all good. Just had to gather my thoughts. On one hand, I empathize with you, and on the other, well, I'm just goin' with the flow as they say. I've had a few ideas, though, for what I'd do if I were suddenly forced out of this trucking thing. Some of my loads take me to interesting places. Recently delivered a very large wrench to a shack in a Nebraskan oil field, for example. They offered me a job on the spot with twice the salary of what Strike pays. It's in the middle of nowhere—the nearest town has a population of 150. It became an instant dream for me and I froze up because I suddenly had this unexpected, uncontrollable urge to take the offer and construct a house out there. Powered by solar panels or something—the irony, I know—but damn, why not? It's cheap, beautiful land, and I figure I can make runs to Omaha for romance."

He bellowed a laugh hinting nervousness and joy.

"Doesn't it sound like a dream?" he asked. "Why the hell are the simplest dreams the best dreams? Do you feel that way?"

"Yeah, I do. Passing through the mountains."

"So why don't you go live in the mountains?" asked Simon.

"Because I'm afraid that when I get to the mountains I'll see another one."

"We always want what we don't have, that's true. But won't that ideology prevent you from ever settling down?"

"Settling's overrated."

"Everyone settles at some point, Johan."

"Tell that to some of these old timers behind the wheel."

"Haven't they settled in their own way?" quizzed Simon. "What did you do back in LA anyway?"

"I was a filmmaker and reality TV story, uh, inventor."

"You produced stories for real people living in fictionalized worlds."

"Mostly."

"So do you think that now you're inventing a fictional narrative for your true self in the real world?"

"It's possible. The lines that separate fiction and reality are thinner than we think. Tell me, Simon: What's your latest entry in that project of yours?"

"Ah, my Humanity Journal! Well, it's—

JOHAN NIVENS. TWENTYSOMETHING TRUCKER. LIKES MOUNTAINS. DOESN'T WANT TO RETURN TO LA. DOESN'T KNOW WHERE TO GO. RELATIONSHIP ROCKY. PASSIONATE ABOUT TRAVEL.

IF GRANTED ONE WISH:

"Goodnight, Simon."

—

SIMON'S WORDS shoveled down my throat and sucked the gall from my gut. When I awoke the next morning they were all I could think about. Words spinning through the stale morning air at Youngstown Big Mamma Truckstop. Hmmmmm. Wondered where Big Mamma was. Maybe, like Mother Nature, she could offer interpretation in all her twirling glory. But no. Big Mamma was only a logo with too much makeup.

I stepped outside the truck and wondered what my wish was.

Yawn
Stretch

Sniff
Diesel

A couple stretches more and I noticed a man approaching in my peripheral.

O young town, what do you have for me?

The man, scruffy and plodding, was accompanied by a boy with Down syndrome.

"Hey brother, how ya doin'?" he asked, throwing an arm around the boy.

"I'm alright," I said. "Hungry."

"Hungry? Well that's perfect. Me and my son here've got just the thing for you." He swung a bag around his torso. Inside were packaged snacks, ranging from pretzels to Slim Jims and Twinkies.

"Whatcha need, man?" he urged.

"Oh, wow," I said. "You know, it looks like tasty stuff, but I'm on a health kick."

"*Health kick*!?" he cried, incredulous. "Ain't got an ounce o' fat on ya."

"Well, it's not so much a question of weight as it is—" I stopped, transfixed on the boy's face. He hardly knew where he was, and I could tell because he kept shifting his magnified eyes behind spectacles. A pure spirit with virtuous intentions, botched by this man's game, in which all the food was expired and his pitch lame:

"C'mon, man," he continued, glancing over at the boy. "It's fer school. He's gotta sell the most stuff or else he loses the competition."

"Alright," I said, reaching into my pocket for cash. "I'll take a bag of pretzels."

The boy stood there in a daze and the man poked him with so much force that he nearly fell over. "You heard him, son. Get the damn pretzels!"

"No rush," I told the man.

But he seemed insistent that this be a quick transaction, and ripped the bag from the boy's slow-moving hand, digging for the elusive treats. Upon closer examination, I could make out traces of track marks along the man's forearm. It was all too obvious, and I felt helpless for his son's magnified eyes, as though my own eyes had shrunk under their pleading.

"There it is!" said the man, finally, tossing the pretzels my way.

"Thank you very much," I replied.

The man looked at the boy—"What do you say?"

The boy said nothing.

"C'mon now, we went over this. What do you say?"

The boy said nothing.

Clenched jaws.

Then the boy pulled a Slim Jim from his back pocket and handed it to me. "This is for you."

The man nearly snatched it away, but restrained himself—"N—Aww, innt that nice. But you should've said thank you. Say thank you."

"Thank you."

"Thank you."

"Thank you."

"Thank you."

———

My mother was waving from the parking lot when I arrived at Vagabond Truckstop the next day. I had a load of 'dry products' shipping to a Walmart store in upstate New York. More junk to be slapped with price tags and sold to the masses. Maybe it was good junk, maybe not. While I had once been curious, I now stopped questioning the contents of trailers. They had become nothing more than rectangles, blocks; a game of Tetris with no fitting end.

My mother was waving from the parking lot.

It was late afternoon.

I wasn't supposed to be clocking out—there were still another two hundred miles to be driven—but I stopped questioning that, too. My trailer, like all trailers, would eventually arrive along with the customers and their wallets, purses, carts, children, smiles, frowns, bubblegum chomping, finger pointing, fabric thumbing, soul redeeming, glance arounding, bargain hunting, head nodding, head shaking, and low-blood-sugar-time-to-go-home-will-you-please-carry-the-bags-for-me routines.

My mother was waving from the parking lot.

It was late afternoon and the sun was still high enough to cast tall shadows across stark concrete. I maneuvered my Tetris block into one of the parking spaces and greeted her with a hug. "Arthur's waiting in the car," she said hurriedly. "He's pretty hungry. Hop in and we'll take you to one of our favorite restaurants."

"Okay," I said. "But there's someone you have to meet first."

I opened the cab door, gave a loud whistle, and Tecate came jumping down.

"You bought a dog!?"

"Not quite. Found him. In New Mexico. He's my new travel buddy."

Tecate, as with most strangers, was very cautious— mannerisms muted and distracted—focused on everything but the new face glaring before him.

"How old is he?" asked my mother.

"No clue. He's got a lot of energy, so I'd guess somewhere between two and seven."

"I see. Have you had him vaccinated?"

"Not yet. Seems healthy enough, though."

My mom's eyes grew big—"You gotta have him vaccinated, Johan! It's a dangerous thing to go driving around with a stray dog. You remember the story I told you about getting attacked when I was a little girl, don't you?"

"Yeah."

"Well?"

"It'll be alright, mom. Trust me. Let's get some food."

I whistled again for Tecate and he came trotting alongside me, and alongside him, a beastly black shadow. Then he hopped into the car and devoured half of my face with his tongue. Oh, he was alright.

—

AFTER WE'D HAD OUR FILL OF FISH, Arthur, my mother, and I wound up at the local drinking spot, leaving Tecate tied up nearby. Bucket o' cold water and chicken scraps, but still he was pissed. That love-creature had once wandered the canyons from dusk 'til dawn, but now he needed to be tied up, lest he go wandering the traffic lanes of Route 40. Anyhow, Arthur kept him busy with copious petting and stenches of fresh cigarette.

It was a rustic locale with twenty and thirtysomethings hunched over the bar, sweating alcohol and wiping foreheads with five-dollar bills, begging for more. Old Lincoln would be proud, I thought. Ol' George Washington himself, who had once led his troupe through bush and branch, waving onward, waving flags, waving towards what would finally become . . . the bar.

The *bar*! With its own troupe of polished glass and skin, called to me more than ever, and for a moment I stood stunned at the sight of society, plainly gathered in youthful grandeur. They were generational kinsmen and kinswomen, which my mother pointed out from across kitchens; glittering crystal.

"She's pretty," motioned mom.

"Yes, she is."

"So is she. I like her dress."

"It's nice," I agreed.

They all glowed the same, and they all seemed single.

"How are things with you and Francine?" Mom went on.

"Not bad, but not exactly good either," I responded, lowering my head to the floor, conscious, picking it back up. "We're okay."

Mom, conscious of my lowered head, lowered hers. "That's good."

The barman, conscious of us, shouted from across the way—"Yinz look like you need somethin' cold in your hand."

"Two beers, please," I said, planting Lincoln on the counter. The drinks were whisked to us with the force of a thousand hangovers, sloshing in frosty mugs. Washington for tip.

"I just want you to be happy," said my mother.

"I'm happy, Mom. Francine is great, but we may have reached a fork in the road. As a driver I'm used to forks, but I've always got the map right next to me, you know?"

"Yes, I know *exactly* what you mean," she agreed. "I've had my experiences, and you know what they are unfortunately."

"Art's a good man, Mom."

"He is, and I love him, God bless his heart; but it's been fork after fork until now. You know . . . I like to think that's just how life is. We're all whizzin' around the map. Everyone wants to be happy. It's sloppy business, but in the end, if you stick with it, you'll find your travel partner."

"Cheers to that," I smiled, raising my mug.

"I'm glad we had this time together, Johan."

"Me too, Mom."

Swig.

Swig.

"Now what am I supposed to do about all these gorgeous women?"

—

IT ALWAYS disturbed me whenever I'd spend a day or night away from the truck. The outside world served as a reminder of the life that I'd put on pause. The one that waited with crossed arms for my return. Similar to the pesky Angelino sun, it tantalized me with its godly rays. It was the circling mobile that I'd brushed with fingertips only to watch it raise another notch. Good grief. What if all of life was this way? What if Mom was right? Whizzing, skidding, slipping up and down hills. What if...what if life...were no different than trucking? Who, then, was the beeping, buzzing machine? Who pushed us along? What was our fuel? Our destination? Were there more destinations after the destinations? Do we arrive only to drive?

I let my head fall against the steering wheel.

Tecate barked out the window.

Here we go again.

Clutch.
First.
Gas.

22

MOM: Stick with it.

Simon: What's your wish?

Me: Where's the toilet?

"We ain't got no toilet!!"

"But where do *you* go to the bathroom?"

"At home, 'fore I come to work. What's your beef, brother? Go find a Mickey-D's or somethin'."

"I told you, I'm out of driving hours. I'm stuck. Do you mean to tell me that you contain yourself from nine to five?"

"Listen bud, I ain't got time for this. We're closed. Good luck to ya."

I was stuck.
Mom said to stick with it.
My wish was toilet.

I knew that much at least.
And I knew that this shipping clerk was an asshole.

Because what *he knew* was that there wasn't a trace of civilization for miles.

Fields of dry green
Raw, bald soil
Dying daylight of another
Dead end day

—

MIDDLE OF THE NIGHT, I awoke to my screaming bowels. Gurgling, gut-wrenching screams. Screams that stirred Tecate and made me hop into action, fumbling for shoes in the dark.

"Dammit, Tecate! Fuck that clerk! FUCK that clerk!"

Tecate tilted his head, indicating that he had no clue what I meant. He didn't understand the process of self-loathing that encased certain people in thorny shells: curmudgeons carved by spite and spat. He didn't grasp the Abyss, or that these folks had fallen into the Abyss of themselves and in the process shelved their good graces. He didn't understand the empty refrigerators they return home to; the cupboards of malt liquor and juiceless potato. He couldn't fathom the hard-springed couch, the hard-boiled brain, the sameness of nothingness that one may thrust themselves into when all is lost beyond receding hairline. For he—HE!—the mighty Tecate himself, with all his wild fur and soul, with endless energy and enthusiasm, with no attention to past or future, with no bones to pick save for scraps, was merely beast.

"Dammit."

I jumped out of the sleepy Volvo and rushed across gravel and dirt, into the hollow night, remembering my Honda nightmare. Not again, I thought. I'm only a man who wants to sleep, dammit! I didn't sign up for this shit.

I dropped to my knees and let out a yawp that shook with the brush. Yes, I knew it to be true. The rollercoaster of life would continue in its patterns of ups, downs, straights, and loops, regardless of place, profession, or disposition. No one can escape Shit, and when I saw a successful person just as when I saw a crotchety clerk, I knew that Shit occurred to both, and that ultimately how one dealt with Shit made the difference.

My knees, stabbed with stone.

Had to get up and go, but where?

A rhythmic tone beckoned me. It came from beyond the nearest hill. I peered over its curve and saw a construction truck crawling around in the next field. Two high-powered lights shone upon the site: one illuminating the truck, scooping mounds of earth, and the second radiating like a halo over an ocean blue Porta-Pottie.

—

ONE PARTICULAR AFTERNOON I was driving up an old country road in the backwoods of North Carolina, hauling barrels of paint thinner. It was heavy. Whenever I hit the brakes I could feel the stuff sloshing back and forth, buoying the truck like a ship at sea. Moreover, it was the first dangerous HAZMAT load that I'd hauled, donning FLAMMABLE signs on all four sides of my trailer. I wouldn't have worried so much if it weren't for the tiny towns I'd been routed through. At this point, I thought maybe the company was torturing me for sheer pleasure. Maybe they'd mounted a tiny surveillance camera above my windshield and laughed at each bead of sweat. I grew paranoid at these thoughts, so I stopped thinking them.

Anyhow, while stopped at one of the traffic signals, I saw a nasty hill waiting in front of me. It was going to be hell. It didn't even have a slope; just shot straight up into the sky. Even worse was that there existed a line of trucks behind me, and none of them would be able to pass on the narrow two-lane highway. They would all have to wait and stare at my dirty ass.

On green I started off, rocking through first gear, clunking into second. For a while I stayed in second gear because I didn't think third would provide enough power for the hill. Choosing this method meant that I topped out at a whopping twenty miles per hour.

"Hey, Strike!" I heard on the CB radio. "You jerkin' off up there or what?"

Kept my hand on the shifter.

"C'mon, wankerboy! You got seven more gears!"

My gut tingled with anger, and somehow I desired the fire. I wanted to hear every word that was about to be said.

Damn straight you do. 'Cause you're a wankerboy and you know it!

"Wankerboy!"

Kept my eye on the hill and shifted to third—slipped—missed—and dropped down to ten miles per hour, barely jamming 'er back into first.

"Just like a rookie. Strike is the worst, I tell ya. Goddamn bottom-feeders put a bunch of dickless pussies behind their wheels."

You hear that? Dickless! What'd I tell you! Should've quit when I said.

The truck struggled.

"Need a bump?"

WHAM!
Got smacked from behind.
Chortles shook the small CB speaker.

I could feel my blood boiling and thought that I should've been the one donning those FLAMMABLE signs. Sure, I could have turned off the radio, but I wanted to hear it all. Hate seemed to have a hold on me—an unhealthy addiction that served no purpose save for my own destruction. Maybe it was the thing I sought when I drank heavily. Even the haters themselves, I thought, were engaging in the practice of self-destruction by hating others. Hating others and hating yourself are two sides of the same coin. A hater's goal is to hate themselves into the ground. I would say that each hateful word is equivalent to a shot of whiskey, and the hater behind me was on a bad binge.

"Pussies, I tell ya! Pussies! Strike, why don't you get yourself a nice cushy desk job in an office, or jerking off onto Playgirl centerfolds. You weren't cut out for a man's world. Bet you're whacking off right now to the sound of my voice. Just drippin' with jizz aren't ya?"

I was shaking. Wanted nothing more than to grab the mic. Wanted nothing more than to slam the brakes, jump out, and smash this guy's face with my stainless steel vice grips. More than anything, I wanted to *see* his face. I wanted to see the face of hate. I wanted to really *see it* and soak it in. Let's stoke the fires together! Let us burn! That's what you want, isn't it?!

"Wankerboy!"

Eventually I made it over that big hill.

—

THEN THERE WAS this bee.

It was like an eight ball with wings, and somehow it made its way into my truck while cruising down the highway in Alabama, buzzing throughout the cab. Good God. I ducked and dodged, and Tecate barked bloody murder. The dumb thing couldn't find its way out, despite open windows.

ZZZZZZZZZZWWWAAAAAAAAAAAAAAA

Like a moped.

I swerved all over the place, nearly eating Toyotas in the process. The bee smacked against the windshield, trying to comprehend the glass.

ZZZZZZZZZZZWWAAAAA

I took the very next exit and parked alongside the road, immediately jumping out.

I watched and waited.

Then I heard a yelp.

Shit. Tecate hadn't followed me out as I expected. I moseyed back up to the cab, peered inside, and found him whimpering and licking a wound stuck with a long stinger. The bee, on the floor, kicking its fat legs. I put it out of its misery.

Now Tecate was angry.

I didn't know how to handle the situation. Whenever I got close to inspect his wound, he snapped at me, clamping large chompers. I'd have to sedate him, I thought.

And so I rolled into a small town and parked at a dingy truckstop, scanning the aisles, hoping they had some kind of medicine for this sort of thing. Past the rotating hot dogs. Maybe I'd just feed him into a greasy coma. One idea, at least. Then the lady behind the counter told me to buy Benadryl—"Knocks my cat out cold." Worth a shot. I grabbed a big box and, sure enough, one of those hot dogs, sticking a couple tablets inside the meat. As much pain as Tecate was in, he was hungry and ate it all up. Well ahead of schedule, I popped one of the pills for my allergies and we both clonked out. But not before I yanked that damn stinger.

—

HOURS LATER, I awoke in a slather of sweat and immediately ripped off my shirt and boots. It was five p.m. The sun burned hard over lush treetops. Tecate was still asleep, breathing rhythmically, occasionally twitching his ears.

Then a black man landed on my hood.

Where he came from, I didn't know, but he appeared suddenly with a spray bottle and rag, and began cleaning my windshield.

I stuck my head out the window.

"Hey there."

"Have a nice sleep?" he asked, wiping furiously.

"Yeah. It's peaceful here in the south. What are you doing, by the way?"

"Cleanin' your windshield, man!"

"Aw, you don't have to do that," I said.

"I know I don't have to, but hey—listen, man—I got the heart of a saint and the blood of a slave."

I took a closer look at the man and indeed there was something of the old south in him. He was scrawny and long-limbed with muscles that seemed to have adapted to his stretching movements. His clothes were akin to slightly clean rags; his goatee, coarse and untrimmed. But my observation extended further than appearance. The man had resigned to his work. He seemed to accept it as destiny.

"Whatcha starin' at?" he asked. "Ain't never seen your windshield so clean, have you?"

"Nope. And since this is my first time in the south, I'm glad you're improving my view. Whereabouts you from?"

"Oh. 'Roun here."

"Yeah?"

"Yeah. I get by, know what I'm sayin'. Got to. For the kyds. The *mouths*. Mouths to feed, my man! You got kyds?"

"Can't say I do."

"Alone out here, huh? That's a sad thing to be in life."

"What?" I asked.

"Alone."

"Yeah, but it can also be nice at times."

"Oh yea?" he shouted, nearly flattened across the hood, reaching the far corners of the glass. "How so? Come outside so I can hear you better, my man."

I climbed down.

"Well, for one, I've got a lot of time to think about who I am and who I want to be. Not so easy to hear your own voice in a crowded city. Lot of opinions."

"Go on," he said, now finished with the task, walking over to me, wiping fingers. "What's number two?"

"Number two?"

"Yeah."

"Number two . . ."

I looked around, trying to think of something profound. The bushes? Sun? Fuel pumps? Clouds? Dumpster? Bird? Bird! No.

Then I looked at the guy again.

"Number two would be having the chance to meet people like you."

"Awwwww shit. You 'bout to make a black man blush!"

I laughed. "But it's true. Humans are amazing, especially when they're kind. Speaking of, what do I owe you?"

"Whatever you want, man. Imma freelancer with no rate."

I handed him a few bucks and he disappeared into the trees.

—

IT WAS MY FIRST TIME in the South.

It was also one of the worst weather seasons the south had ever seen.

Within a two week period, a gang of tornados had ripped through Oklahoma, St. Louis, Louisville, and parts of the Great Plains. And now, on a dark Tuscaloosa afternoon, my CB radio rattled off the hooks with warning reports:

"EXTREME WIND AND VIOLENT GUSTS TO BE EXPECTED. THIS MESSAGE WILL REPEAT."

Violent gusts? Even Tecate seemed to comprehend this message, hiding behind the sleeper curtains.

Traffic crawled along. Confused lane changes, uncertain maneuvers. It was all very symbolic—a collective display of fear translated through muscles and metal. Shit, I thought. Gotta get out of here.

HONKKKK HONNNNNNNNKK

"Move it, dickwad!"

"I can't go anywhere, asswipe!"

"You calling me an asswipe, bitch?"

"Maybe if you'd take your hand off that horn, you'd of heard me!"

I was momentarily distracted by these two nearby Stooges. Although I was happy to have the entertainment, it seemed that they only roused everyone, causing further ripple in the traffic. Meanwhile the sky darkened to an ash-grey color, gargling its own energy and spitting out big bolts. Suddenly I was reminded of Simon and hoped that he didn't get sucked into that Texas twirl. As I sat there, I imagined it happening. I never wanted to think these kinds of thoughts; they spawned uncontrollably. I saw his truck bending, folding.

I've got to call Simon!

But I didn't.

The moment was pressing and we had all come to a standstill; a feeling of beginnings and endings in the atmosphere. Tecate shivered behind the curtains. My windshield wipers were on, but there was no rain. The sound of rubber against raw glass irked me. I quickly flipped them off and switched on the CB. It was like walking into a cocktail party where voices stood out one at a time:

"Any y'all know how bad this thing s'posed to be?"

"Heard it was a big one. But Christ, I'm stuck!"

"No shit, Einstein. We're all stuck!"

"Got a wife and kids at home. Can't even call 'em. Anyone got reception?"

"Towers are down."

"Where's the nearest exit?"

HOOOOONNNNNKKKK
HOONNNNNNNNNNNK

"Who keeps beatin' on their horn? Ain't gonna make no difference!"

"It's those two dumbasses in the four-wheelers."

"I'm about to give 'em a piece of my mind."

Finally, I broke through the commotion:

"Everyone chill out. It'll be alright."

"*Chill out?*" a raspy voice responded. "Who elected you the authority?"

"I just think that it's better to not add fuel to the fire," I cautioned.

"Ha! Tell that to that to the grumbling God above."

"Well that's what I'm asking all of us to do," I said. "If you have any faith, you'll trust that we'll be alright."

"Trust? How old are you, driver?"

"Twenty-six."

"Well there ya go. Wait 'til you get to be my age. You'll see."

"What will I see?" I asked.

"You'll *see*."

"Enlighten me. We've got time. I don't understand what age has to do with trust and faith."

"Just does. All I'm sayin'."

The radio was quiet now.

Everything was.

Then: a train in the distance. Or what I *thought* was a train. Only after a couple of seconds had passed did I recall that we were nowhere near train tracks. What I was hearing, rather, was the arrival of a spiral over one mile wide. A cyclone of disastrous proportions, stripping away asphalt and collecting its less-than-concrete contents.

"Holy mighty she's a BIG'N!"—on the CB.

The mass grew quickly, efficiently, as if it had a mind of its own; aware that it was hovering over homes and electricity. An evil that defied all of my trust-logic, and suddenly I was questioning everything while simultaneously looking for a way to take cover. "TECATE!" I screamed, throwing open the curtains to a pair of gnarly incisors. "Calm down, boy. You're safe."

"NO ONE'S SAFE, GET THE HELL OUTTA HERE!!"—on the CB.

The F4 zigzagged, threatening to venture down our path (Interstate 20 NB). I saw its rage in full bloom, closing in, flinging what looked like trees and rooftops through the air. Traffic was moving now—not much—but it was moving. Bumpers smashing into bumpers, pushing the cluster of metal around like dead dominos. The sight of this hysteria was infectious. It roused me and, not knowing what to do, I flung open the door and jumped out with Tecate following close behind, nearly tripping me.

SSSSCCHHHHRRROOOOOOOOOOOO

There it was.
Death.

"HEY!" yelled a commuter, standing halfway between their car door and the highway. "Where do you think YOU'RE going?"

"There's a DITCH," I screamed, pointing to the roadside. "I'm gonna LIE DOWN in it!"

The man shook his head—"You're NUTS!"—and ducked back inside his Jeep.

Maybe.

Sure enough I found the ditch, but by the time I got there I'd lost Tecate somewhere in the traffic. No. Dammit. Get back up and search.

"NUTS!"

Nuts!

"SHUT UP!!"

I slid across hoods and skimmed past bumpers, searching the crevices between cars, under cars, beyond cars. Searching for any signs of a dog that looked coyote.

"TECATEEEE!!!!" I screamed, gulping grit.

And then, when all hope seemed lost in the miasma, I just stood there among it. I shrunk before the sight of mad Mother Nature wondering why. I had trusted. And where. Tecate went. And that was all I thought. The ashy gremlin kept on, stripping its path, whipping Ikea furniture, disappearing to further destruction. And I watched and wondered and wished.

23

"WHAT A GREAT AGE to be doing something like that," said the old man, pouring another vanilla-flavored creamer into his styrofoam cup. "It's inspiring, really. I'm gonna go home and tell my son about you. He's about the same age, just graduated college, doesn't know what the 'ell he wants to do with his life. Just sits around all day staring at the computer screen."

"You know," I said, "I stared at computer screens for a long time myself."

"Well that's what I mean! You found something else. I'd say you broke through to something more *substantial*."

"Yeah?"

"Absolutely. You're out seein' the country! A lot of people wait 'til they retire to do something like that. But let me tell you a big secret: retirement's overrated."

"I've had that assumption for a long time. I'll take your word for it, sir."

"Please do. Hey, lemme buy you a coffee," the man offered.

"You don't have to do that."

"Well that's what you came in here for, isn't it? You're leaning over the pot after all."

"Yeah, but I've got money."

"I know you've got money, but it's something I want to do. Geez. You kids gotta learn another secret: When someone wants to do something nice for you, let 'em! Even if you don't think you've *earned it* or whatever. We're all in this together. You just helped me out by providing a good example for my son. Now, what'll it be?"

—

THE MAN WAS NICE and I never got his name. But I preferred not to know people's names when roaming about, nor their age, nor where they came from, or where they lived or worked. I strived to keep the mystery, and besides, it allowed me to focus on their human qualities. Character, gesture, and smile.

Sat down with my cup and scanned the truckstop.

It was not unlike the other realms of the trucking world, with its bright overhead lights, sectioned off arcade, and t-shirt racks (and snacks). But tonight it had lost whatever charm could be extracted from pale-plastered walls. Which meant nothing. There was never any charm in those walls to begin with. They were just walls. Insulation, studs, plaster. I was fucked.

Tuscaloosa had been a tragedy—sixty-four dead—and I couldn't shake the memory, awestruck at the timing and circumstance. Despite the old man's words and my hot cup, I was fucked because I felt fucked. The outer adventure no longer aligned with the inner, and of course I had been feeling this way for weeks. But Tuscaloosa had taken it to a new level, and had taken my dear Tecate to God knows where. Underneath a car, into the bed of a pickup or nearby field. Maybe the dog had the same idea as me, but different direction, different ditch. Maybe it was time to part ways. In my mind I pictured him running.

Onward past the cyclone, past Jackson and Mississippi
Onward through Texas Plains
Onward through pain
Onward down highways, Historic 66
Onward jumping cacti
Onward getting pricked
Onward hot and heavy
Onward needle wound
Onward smile your smile, love creature
N'Mexico, see y'soon

—

IT WAS ABOUT this time when I felt the need to head back to LA. I don't know whether it was the tornado, losing Tecate, or what, but I felt a strong tug from the Pacific, and from all the love I'd left behind. Moreover, I was scheduled to meet with my father who was flying in from the east coast for business; staying somewhere near LAX.

My current load was to be picked up in Mississippi and hauled all the way to Yuma, Arizona. It was hot. My first real taste of summer and only two days into May. When I say that it was hot, I mean that I was sweating like a pig, pissing bottles of water from face. I looked like a glazed doughnut. My shirt and underwear clung to my body.

I wasn't sure what the contents of my load were, but when I walked into the shipping office, chilled by an AC unit that would satisfy the most perturbed of penguins, I was immediately directed into a managerial office adorned with gold-plated plaques: #1 IN CUSTOMER SERVICE. The family photo resting on the desk showed a balding, sun-beat man who'd enjoyed one too many Big Macs. Or had a thyroid problem (one shouldn't assume). And the desk itself, a polished mirror and shrine to his pride, undoubtedly used to comb stray strands in brighter daylight.

He's probably a wankerboy just like you!

He's probably a wankerboy.

He's probably a dirtbag father. Look at that fake smile. Like a slap-on sticker.

He's probably a dirtbag father.

Ah, quit all that. This is how it starts. Lose a dog or tooth and you're chin-deep in the Abyss. Indeed, we humans are fragile beyond facade; beyond pomp and intellectualism, diamond studs and buffed veneer. Have some compassion or you'll harden. Compassion keeps you soft. Pliable. Young.

Assumptions are a surefire sign of slipping. They lead to prejudice and other crotchety penchants.

The door behind me pushed open and in walked the man from the photo, who sat down behind the desk and faced me. He sharpened a pencil slowly, as if it were a subliminal threat-message—a potential death-weapon that would be employed should I defy his authority. But he sharpened with a smile that projected as genuine, and it seemed that my mind was still working against me.

"So," said the man, shuffling the BOL documents. "I see that you'll be hauling one of our HVLs (High Value Load). And quite a distance at that!"

"All the way to Yuma."

"Mmm, yes. I want you to understand that, for a young driver like yourself, this is quite a responsibility. You've got over ninety thousand dollars worth of scotch whiskey at hand."

"R-Really?"

"Yes. You weren't aware?"

"No."

"Geez. Thought Strike would've briefed you about this by now. Okay then. Are you still willing to haul it?"

"What are the requirements?"

"First: You can't stop for the initial 250 miles—not even to urinate. Secondly: After the first 250, you must inform us whenever you stop and the *reason* you've stopped until you reach the final destination. Oh! And another thing. You must park in well-lit spaces whenever you shut down at the end of the day. Think you can handle all that?"

"Don't see why not."

—

HAULING NINETY GRAND worth of whiskey really wasn't a problem, nor was the no-stopping-for-250-miles requirement. I had gotten used to relieving bladder into empty bottle when time was of the essence and bodily functions came second in the trade of delivery and deadline.

It would be cake with all the sweat. I could drink gallons so long as I kept the windows down and my face in sun.

No, that wasn't the problem.

The problem came somewhere in Arkansas, just outside a town called Hot Springs, which is when I got lost reading my map and took a wrong turn down a twisty backwoods road. Three hours into my trip and already lost! Like the paint thinner, I could feel the alcohol sloshing around with each turn and tap on the brakes. The road had no shoulder and no parking lots to circle around in. Only residential neighborhoods and tiny strip marts. Shit. Now I really had something to sweat about. Get me outta here. Even more terrifying was the fact that I kept drifting into the oncoming lane when I approached a turn; only because I had to in order to *make* the turn. On and on, the road snaked and twisted into swamp-black riverside woods.

Then I saw it.

Around one of the bends was a small creek bridge with a MAXIMUM CLEARANCE 12' sign. I hit the brakes and a chorus of horns reigned down on me. Fuck 'em. There was no way I could clear that bridge and every driver behind me knew this. For a moment, I did nothing.

Breathe
Breathing
Breathe

And the lonnnnnnnnnggggggg exhale, which Paco would remind me is the oneness of myself and truck and workman's life cusped into the bulge of Now.

Or calm down, as Professor Jake might say.
Is what I pictured him saying.
Calm down.
It's nothing.
Cake.

HONNNNNNKKK HOOOONNNNNNNNNNKKKKKK

At this juncture, I had begun to separate humans into two basic categories: those who honked and those who didn't. But most honked, and it was my observation that we were always honking at one another.

Anyhow, I stepped down from the truck and walked around to the back of the trailer, surveying the roadside landscape, trying to make sense of it, trying to find a way out; waving a "one-minute finger" to traffic. Hmm. Saw a dirt path that had been carved thirty feet back into the woods, bordered on one side by a steep embankment leading to the river. With nowhere else to go, it was my best option.

I trotted over to the car parked directly behind my trailer. It was a small Ford Escort with large man crammed inside.

"Excuse me, sir. I'm going to have to back my truck into that dirt space over there and I need you to move."

"Need me to *move*?" said the man.

"Yes."

"Where to?"

"Anywhere but here."

"Ugh. You truckers need to learn not to come down roads like this. What were you thinkin', anyway?"

Yeah. What were you thinkin'?

"I was thinking that it led somewhere it didn't. It was a mistake."

"Yeah, well, try to make fewer of them for us commuters."

He moved, and so did the minivan behind him, and classic Corvette.

I sat back down inside the truck, still unsure of how to manage the maneuver. It was tight and the path was rocky. And then there was the small cliff of doom. No time to think anyway. I placed my clammy palm on the control switches, ready to release the brakes and dive into it, when suddenly my hand froze up.

You can't do this.

"I can't do this."

Raindrops peppered the window and the bridge stood defiant with its crisscrossed sabers. An animal trotted past just beyond the structure, and for a moment I thought it looked part coyote.

HOOOOONNNNNNKKKKKKKKKKKK

Sick of the noise, I mustered the muscle to release the brakes, put the shifter in reverse, and spin the big steering wheel while backing towards the dirt. But the angle was funny and the truck became jackknifed in the middle of the road—the cab and trailer positioned at an ugly ninety degrees. Raindrops. I kept pushing, spinning and twisting, watching the mirrors. Sweating, wiping, sweating, sighing, damn near crying while cursing the horns. Finally, the trailer tires touched down on the pitted path and I could feel my entire world shifting weight.

BEEEEEEEEEEEEEP

What now?

BEEEEEEEEEEEEEEP

The onboard computer glowed a message:

WHY HVE U STOPPED? THIS IS A HVL!
NO STOPPING FOR FIRST 250 MI!!!

I kicked the thing off its hinges and kept backing. But now I was further distraught because I remembered the 90k worth of whiskey lumbering behind me.

CA-CHUNK, CA-CHUNK

The trailer must've hit a pothole because now it was leaning scarily towards the embankment and I didn't know which way to turn the wheel. Fuckers! I engaged my brakes again and sighed. Wondered why all the shit lately. Was it to be a sign of some sort? Maybe *I* was the fucker who was meant to get the fuck out of trucking. I tried to recall when all the shit began. Surely there was a more glorious period of this whole shebang. Maybe I'd lost sight after Simon started talking about wishes, or possibly before that, when Francine sat me down under the starry Los Feliz lights.

A knock at my door.

I turned to find a kind-faced man standing on the steps of my truck, signaling for me to roll down the window.

I did.

"Hey," he said, adjusting his baseball cap, "looks like you got yourself in a bind."

"Unfortunately."

"Don't worry, it's not the first time this has happened. Did a stint as a driver myself, so I know how it feels to be stuck. Can I help get you out?"

"That would be awesome. You don't mind?"

"Not at all. That's why I ran over here. Besides, I'm stuck in that line of traffic until we get you unstuck!"

"Sorry about that."

"Don't worry!"

And so the man stepped down and directed me, and I didn't worry, and soon after the whiskey was on its way, along with the drinkers and classic Corvette, minivan, Escort, and all of humanity, of which a small corner had been restored that afternoon.

—

When I finally arrived in Yuma, after dropping off the booze with a swipe of sweaty relief, I found the nearest truckstop and parked; then prepared my shower bag, put on the ol' flip-flops, and hunched my way across the asphalt. Eyes fixed on ground. Moving along. Step, step, step. Counting the seconds and thinking nothing except warm water and meal. Reduced to the basics: flip-flops and hot dogs. Eight months in and Professor Jake was right: humans are pros at adaptation. Sure we complain at first; maybe even protest and pick fights. But survival is survival. Loads need delivered. Stomachs satisfied. Adapt and survive or carve a new path.

"Hey man! Dude! You!"

A voice, getting closer. I looked up.

"Yeah man, you!"

It was a Mexican guy, late thirties, with long tied-up hair, tank top, and cargo shorts. He was an obvious nomad, donning a large backpack and unwashed face. And in general he was an obvious nomad. You just knew who they were after awhile. There was something in the face—a desperate joy.

"Me?"

"*You!* You're a truck driver, right?"

"That's right."

"Sweet! 'Cause I—I didn't wanna assume or anything, but I thought I saw you step out of one of those rigs."

A gigantic soda cup in his hand. The guy twitched around as if he'd been sucking from it all day.

"Yep. That's me over there. Polar Bear Volvo."

"Sweet, sweet, sweet. I'm Fabio, by the way. Nice to meet you."

"Johan."

"*Johan!* Right on, man. Where'd you get that name?"

"My parents."

"Oh."

"So what can I do for you, Fabio?"

"Oh. Oh! Well check it out, man. I'm stranded. Girlfriend drove me all the way out here, broke up with me, and now I gotta get back to LA to make ends meet. You don't happen to be going that way, do you?"

I *was* going that way, but something about Fabio's twitching told me that he'd ingested more than sugar. Still, after the encounter with my Arkansas angel, I felt that I had something to pay forward.

"Yeah . . . I'm headed up there tomorrow. To San Bernardino, though."

"Ah! Perfect! Hey listen, I don't have cash or nothin', but I'd be extremely grateful if you could give me a lift."

"Sure thing. Just be ready at six a.m. when I leave. Knock on one of the cab doors if the curtains are still closed. Sorry to run off now, but I really need to—

"Wait. Be ready at six?" asked Fabio.

"Yeah."

"Listen, man. I been hangin' around this truckstop for two days now. They've kicked me out twice already. Said I can't sleep here. If I fall asleep, they kick me out. But I gotta drink hella soda just to stay awake. I'm passing out on tables even with the caffeine. So I was thinking that maybe…I don't know…maybe I could sleep in the cab with you. You got two beds, right?"

I wasn't comfortable with the idea.

"As a matter of fact, the top bunk is loaded with containers of my belongings."

"Aww. Really, man?"

"Sorry. See you at six."

—

Breathing
Digesting
Dreaming

—

SIX O'CLOCK came and there was no Fabio to be found. Must be inside the truckstop, I thought, and set off to look for him. Past the buzzing sign and chugging chrome mugs; past the piss puddle and padlocked gates, leftover remains, stray chicken bone, and crushed cigarettes. Past regret. I yawned. Too early for yawning. These hours were meant for sleeping or waking, but certainly not walking across parking lots in search of nomads. Alas, it was the adventure, and the adventure was not the adventure without the adventure.

I nearly tripped over him.

His legs were twisted across the pavement, jutting out from a nearby entranceway—an unused entrance to the convenience store—right next to a thoroughly used dumpster. He looked peaceful, wrapped in some old jacket, clutching his big cup like a stuffed animal. His face had lost both its joy and desperation, and now showed the universal portrait of slumber.

"Fabio," I nudged. "It's six o'clock. Do you still need a ride?"

He jumped forward, limbs flailing, spilling soda. "'Course! Shit! Did I actually fall asleep?"

"Apparently."

"Would you believe that. Stay up all night only to fall asleep the moment I'm kicked to the curb." He took a deep breath and whacked me on the back. "That's life anyway. Let's hit the road."

Now, I wasn't in the mood for talking, but Fabio was a wind-up toy. Constantly cranked. This usually wasn't a problem. In fact, I actively sought the enthusiasts of life. I'd dig ditches and excavate for them if there were ever a shortage. The exception here was that Fabio disrupted my routine, and I only had time to grab a pre-packaged apple pie loaded with sugar and lesser-known elements of the periodic table.

"Wanna check my bag?" asked Fabio.

I looked at him, puzzled.

"Why would I want to do that?"

"You know . . . just to make sure I don't have any knives or bad shit in there."

He opened it and showed me the insides, shifting around old shirts and books, toothpaste and comb.

"See? Clean as a baby!" he yipped.

"Good deal."

"So where's the truck?"

"It's the white Volvo, remember?"

"No."

"I told you yesterday."

"Shit. I'm out-of-it."

We got inside the truck. Fabio set his stuff down. I finished the last bite of my pie. Then he grabbed my hand.

"What are you doing?" I asked.

"I think we should pray before we take off."

"Okay."

"The road is a dangerous place, you know? I've had a lot of *shit* happen to me out here. Gettin' ditched by my girlfriend is nothing compared to…well…I think we should pray anyway."

"Okay."

"Dear Lord, our Savior and ultimate source of love," he began. "Today we are driving from Yuma to San Bernardino, Joe Hann and I, and we ask that you protect us with your large hand of guidance and good graces. Keep Joe sane and steady at the wheel. Help me get back home to my sweet Maria. Help the air conditioner work. Protect us from sin. Forever and ever. Amen."

"Amen."

"Jazzy, brotha! Let's ROLL!!"

—

"SO THAT WAS…that was…about the time I was serving pizza from delivery trucks in San Antonio—we sold so many pizzas, bro—but I lived in Maine before that. Working down by the sea at a fisherman's port. Anyhow, this San Antonio business was no joke. We made loot. I was pulling twenties out of my pocket like one of those fucking…what do you call 'em…clowns at the carnival who have the long line of colored fabric—ha! You know what I mean, man. It was dough—haha! Night after night, too. We'd go to parties and deliver these huge fucking pepperoni pizzas to big corporate wigs with white chicks in bikinis—you know, pool parties and shit—and anyway—*mon-ey*. I even became part owner after awhile. Ooh—look at that sunrise, man! Salton Sea isn't far either. Coming up in a bit on the left side. So yeah, pizzas. They were good. You like pizza? Who doesn't like pizza? But you see, San Antonio was only a fraction. I've lived in almost every state—shit you not. Up and down the coast... OH! This song is sick, crank it. And I'm talkin', like, up and down *each* coast and everywhere between. I even lived in Alaska and did a stint as an adventure tour guide, but I've never loved anything as much as spinnin' pizza. Reason I liked pizza so much is because I was passionate about it. You got to have *passion*. Like you! You've got passion and I can see it in your...your fuckin' light...it's coming off o' you. Hey man, I'm gonna read you some funnies real quick while we drive. You like the funnies? Comics? This one sounds like a riddle: 'What is the longest word in the dictionary?' Don't even try to guess. It's not worth your time. Give up? 'Smiles, because there's a *mile* between each "s".' Ha! I get a kick. Really. Can't tell you how many times I've read these things to keep a *smile* on my face. By the way, I need some smokes. You probably think I'm on drugs don't you? But like I said, I'm clean as a baby. Check my bags, check my blood. Can you stop at the next—ahhhh! Salton Sea! Look! Gas station, three o'clock."

24

I MET WITH MY FATHER that evening at his towering hotel. From behind tall glass windows, I glanced down at the dizzying traffic. There it all was. Los Angeles. Swaying palms and smog skyline flanked by billboards.

"I'm done in the bathroom, if you want to take a shower," interrupted Dad, emerging from the humidity.

"Sure, thanks."

"And how about a nice clean shave?" he said, tossing a towel at me.

I smirked and walked into the steam, wiping down the mirror. Truly, my beard was out of control. It had begun to curl into cursive letters at the edges. I reached into the thick of it and pulled out a gray strand that seemed to mock me—'Hair is long, life is short.'

Fired up the trimmer.

—

"AH!"

My dad nearly fell back in his chair.

"What have you done with my son?" he asked, followed by a chuckle.

I had cleaned up enough to feel presentable to his work buddy awaiting us in the lobby. We were to meet and have dinner at a nearby restaurant.

"Ha!"

—

"YOUR FATHER tells me you're a trucker."

"Yes," I told the blue-eyed man with fork half stuck in his mouth.

"He wanted to see the country," added my father. "Couldn't settle for a simple vacation. Had to drive a truck."

"It's an adventure, not a vacation," I corrected.

The man nodded and mopped a glob of sauce, satisfied with the two short explanations. "Well that's cool. But where are you living at the moment?"

"In his truck," said Dad. "He's *homeless*."

"Well you don't *look* homeless," said the hungry man.

"'Cause I made him shave!" jested Dad.

"It's true," I confirmed, wiping a bead of sweat from the top of my forehead. "And you? I know you work with my father, but what do you do?"

"Well," chomp, chomp, "I'm a Systems Engineer."

"So you test things—equipment and such?"

"Yep. Make sure everything's running to par, make adjustments if necessary. Not as interesting as what *you're* doing of course."

"No?" I asked, confused.

"It's uhh…you know. Work."

"Hm."

"Not to say that what you're doing isn't work."

"'Course."

"You know what I mean, though."

"Food's good here"—heard from a nearby table.

"Delicious, yes."—heard.

"Anyway, bet you see a lot of neat things out on the highway," continued the man, scraping meat-sword against teeth.

"Lot of signs and numbers," I admitted. "But also some amazing sunsets, landscapes, people. You meet a lot of characters. It's work, but also fun if you want it to be."

"Pays good?"

"Okay to start. Gotta stay in a long time if you want to make a decent salary."

"And what about Hollywood?" the man questioned.

"What about it?"

"Well, don't you see any potential here? This is what you went to school for, right?"

"For Hollywood?"

"Yeah. Movies and stuff."

"Sure. But I believe that there's more to life, with respect to . . ."

I could sense that the man knew where I was going, and I stopped before I got there.

" . . . It's material for new stories. Screenplays."

"Ahh, I see. Great plan!"

My dad smiled and seemed content with the checkmark that validated this strangely tense exchange. Society itself just a little more at ease that night. Everything as it should be. The waiter came with dessert, tips given, electric bills skyrocketing, songs blasting, beds rocking, orgasms, spaghetti, and somewhere up north, an Eskimo wondering how it might have all been different.

—

THE NEXT DAY I wound up wandering Abbot Kinney Blvd with Francine and Dad, pushing our way through crowds of sunburned hipsters in what appeared to be a reenactment of the '67 Be-In. Everyone in dashikis, fedoras, Lennon specs. And all the faces: young and happy. It seemed that I had found temporary home in kindred company, save for the scene and facade. The hang-up was that I felt as though I were dabbling somewhere between the truth that I sought on the road and the stylized image of truth. As with all relationships, philosophy and fashion were a beautiful marriage when fused as strong independent entities; but it had been my experience that most people were all fashion and no action. It's what happened with the whole damn hippie movement—watered down and sold as Coca Cola and Halloween costumes. World peace, but first, drink up.

Yep, there we were. The strange trio soaking in all of the faces; dodging tattooed limbs, dancing gorillas, snippets of conversation . . .

"Right on! MGMT is rad, but I'm into this new group . . ."

"Soooooooo crazy."
"I don't really llliiikkkeee it."
"Her politics are dishonest. Then again . . ."
"They serve tofu dogs."

Strange trio.

Kept thinking that life shouldn't be this way. Shouldn't be so strange. I should be back on suburban basketball court with Dad, or married to Francine, with job (*job*-job) and debtless summer porch, Ford and friends, Gold's Gym on sore muscle leg day, rub Bengay and eat pizza.

O but it was strange! It would always be strange, pondering the unforeseen. I think my father knew this, and I was just happy to be walking and breathing alongside him in the moment. Francine was mostly quiet and it was nothing new. She'd been this way lately. Some sort of test that I was supposed to interpret. Still, I couldn't look away from her brown skin, kissable as ever in the silky sweat of her Sunday dress.

It was a nice stroll and we eventually made our way to the notorious boardwalk, where a man in top hat and suit waved a stack of flyers at us—"Step righttttt up, friends!"

I reached out and grabbed one of the glossy papers:

ZANY ZACK'S FREAK SHOW EXTRAVAGANZA
MAGIC AND FOLLY AWAIT!
$7 ENTRY

"What do you two think?" I asked.
"What else we got to do?" posed dad.
"Never been to a freak show before," said Francine.
The consensus was unanimous, and so we entered the dim red-and-yellow checkered room, strung with lights and mounted theatre masks. At the center of the place stood a shirtless middle-aged man with gauged ears, nose ring,

mohawk, nipple-piercings, and all countenance of counter culture. A Venice thoroughbred led by LSD.

"What is *that*?" mused dad.

"That's…a man of passion." I uttered.

"Passion for pain!" he quipped.

Francine had drifted off near the funhouse mirrors, squeezing her body into strange shapes, then jumping back; startled at the sight of a mangled clown mannequin. "This place is creepy." But I pulled her in for a kiss and reassured her that we weren't going to die. Meanwhile, the man with the mohawk began pulling items from a red bag, one of which was a rusty bear trap. "Come one, come all!" he hollered, garnering a crowd of spectators. "See what the human body is capable of!"

Again, I thought of Professor Jake—*We adapt, see?*

The bear trap was casually tossed aside in place of an industrial staple gun, which the daredevil presented to onlookers like a shining jewel, grinning toothlessly.

"This next trick's for all you cash-carriers out there. If you got a five-dollar bill, I will let you take this gun and staple it to my hairy chest. A ten, and you can tack my stomach. Twenty? Take Mr. Jackson and plant him right here," he pointed, "onto my forehead."

Uncomfortable shuffling.

"If you got a higher amount…well…we can negotiate other lowwwwcations."

Nobody wanted to play.

"C'mooonnnnnn. I can take it! This is my *job*. Some o' y'all spend your day in the office. Look around! Cubicle!!"

Sick of all the waiting, my father dug through his pockets and yanked out a twenty. "I got your cubicle right here!" he motioned, waving the bill around like an American flag before handing it to Francine.

"No," she said, aghast.

"Go for it," he said.

She turned and looked at me—I shrugged—and Mohawk seemed thirsty for blood, egging her on with outstretched arms. "Put 'er right here, smack dab in the middle!"

She looked at me.

I shrugged.

She looked at him.

He pressed finger to forehead.

She grabbed the gun.

Cameras raised.

She put twenty to skin, metal to twenty, and with a grimace and whimper, squeezed the trigger.

Snap.

"Awww—oooohhhh—aahhhhh—owwwwwww—are you okay?"

Mohawk's eyes went heavy, entranced in sadistic gratification. We all lost him for a moment as he took a few steps back, laconic, riding his nerve endings to dulled edges.

Francine gently laid the gun on the ground. "I'm really, really sorry."

Then, a burst of madness as the man jumped onto the center table, flexed biceps, and proclaimed to be the Great Pierced Prince of Venice.

Suddenly I didn't feel so strange.

Oh but I was.

We all were.

—

AFTER THE WEEKEND, after the sad kiss send-off at Ontario, when I waved goodbye to Francine from behind an unclean windshield, I sat in my truck hesitant to move. I had arrived at another crossroads of coming and going (or going and coming). In fact, I wasn't sure which was which anymore. My father was on-plane: going. Francine was in-car: going. But what was I doing?

Exploring.

That's right.

Your great adventure, remember?

That's right.

Right as you want it to be.

You're starting to make sense. I'm not accustomed to this.

Fuck off then!

That feels right, too.

Right as you want it to be.

—

WITH JUNE just around the corner and a mere seven grand in the bank, I knew that it was imperative to seek new experiences in order to keep my adventure alive. And so while traveling in the vicinity of Strike Headquarters the next day, I made sure to barge into the HR office and demand a run to Canada. The way I did it wasn't exactly brash, but it required tapping into the charm reserves. I already had the necessary paperwork filled out; it was just a matter of convincing the company to bypass the six-week approval period.

I was itching. I needed the stamp today.

Was hoping for a cute intern when I walked into the office, but instead met with the eyes of a man six inches taller. Bald, chiseled dome. He looked like a trucker who'd finally squirmed out of the driver's seat and into a swivel chair. Still, the charm method was my only plan and would have to work.

"Hello," I said. "Why, that's a nice blue shirt you have on. They should make them standard for us drivers."

"Thanks," he said, smoothing it out. "What can I do for you?"

"Well, I've got some paperwork to submit regarding a request to haul Canadian loads. And for a nice blue shirt like yours."

"Please, no more compliments about my shirt."

"It is nice, though."

"Thanks," he nodded, smoothing it out again. "So you want to go to Canada?"

"Yep. Mostly for the syrup."

"The what?" asked the man, tilting his head.

"You know . . . they make maple syrup up there. But it's, like, really pure."

"Okay."

"For pancakes."

Uh-oh, I thought. Losing him.

"Anyway," I bolstered, "It's a place that I've always wanted to visit and was hoping you guys could approve the request today and get me on my way."

"Do I look like a travel agent to you?"

"No. I mean. You could be. With that nice—uhh—demeanor you have. Professional, you know. You have a professional aura."

"Aura?"

"Were you once a driver, by the way?"

"Do I look like a driver to you?" he asked.

"Just curious," I assured.

"Because I'm tall and bald?"

"No."

"Because I'm not actually a travel agent?"

"What?"

"Because you need a travel agent and not a bald, ex-trucker?"

"So you *were* a driver?"

"Maybe."

"Well did you ever make it up to Canada?"

"Maybe."

"Was it a beautiful country?"

"Yes it was."

"Can you help get me there?"

"Yes. But only because you like my blue shirt. My wife hates this shirt."

25

I WAS AFRAID of myself.

I knew this because I had carried a tape recorder during that year and never had anything to say; yet when I sat on the edge of my cot at the end of each shift, it all came gushing out as I drifted into courageous bliss. Day after day I'd lift the machine to my lips and knew the words—*really knew them*—but it all translated into empty anger. A beast slipping between teeth, piece by piece, vomiting, watching traffic, hollowed out, sun beating the hell out of my face, left with nothing to taste save for the remains of last night's paste. And those are the moments when I put the recorder to rest and sought refuge in breakfast.

JUNE 5TH ENTRY #1

"Top o' the fucking morning! Gaaarrrrgggghhhhh. Need coffee. Coffee-coffee time. This is my coffee-coffee rhyme. What am I saying here? What am I saying, what am I doing? My gums…some kind of film on them…think it's toothpaste, but not quite sure. I've never experienced this before. So many things start to change…teeth grimy, yellowed…bones aching…cracking…farting like a frog…horrible diet…don't know what happened to my health plan."

—

JUNE 5TH ENTRY #2

"Back on the road. Ninety westbound just outside of Buffalo. My stomach is…filled with grease. I'll probably have to shit in the next two hours, but hopefully reach the border by then. Because I'm going to Canada, baby! CANADA! Hell yeah. Finally something...new. Other than the same road. It's all the same. How did it become the *same*? Worried that this is life. Is this life? What do you think, Stan? Who's Stan? I don't know. Stan's the man, man. Stan's the man you talk to when you don't have anyone else. You're goin' insane! I thought you bought this recorder to, like, outline movie screenplays and stuff."

—

AFTER SHOWING my paperwork to officials at the border, I was back on my way towards Toronto, not knowing what to expect from The Big Smoke and its ominous CN Tower, already showing on the horizon. My final destination was a town called New Liskeard, smack-dab between Ontario and Quebec, where I'd deliver 67,500 pounds of laundry detergent.

I was bouncing to familiar beats on the stereo, happy to see that Strike had granted me a fair tour of Canada. Another seven hours and I'd be on the shores of glittery Lake Temiskaming, where I planned to park for the night and book a motel room. Maybe I'd rent a boat and spend the evening on that lake, watching the blue moon, rowing nowhere naked, sleeping, waking. Maybe mosquitoes would leave me alone. Maybe I'd have a cooler of beer and a Canadian coyote, and a violin would play from somewhere in the treetops, and I wouldn't question where the sounds came from 'cause my brain's numb and that's all there is to it.

In that moment, however, I was slithering through traffic, trying to find my exit north while simultaneously craning my neck to get a glimpse of the tower and buildings beneath it. Like Manhattan, there was a heavy feeling of industry and sweat that hung in the air. I was both attracted and repelled by it.

I'm just cruisin' through, man.
I'm lookin' for a new view, man.

That's what I told the Los Angeles man.
That's what I told Toronto Stan.

—

ALL SIGNS POINTED NORTH, and the firs, cedars, and pines came to greet me at the roadside, dancing in the breeze. Unscarred earth, just as the Natives would have it, teeming with vegetation and arcadian ponds. I switched on the radio, scanning for a local sound—something that would further entrench me in Canadian culture. Pop music, pop music, French game show . . . yes, I think that will do, despite not speaking a word of the language. Something about *le gagnant* being *super* and *special!* Sure, I follow you now. We are all super and special winners when façade melts away.

In any case, it was not the time for philosophy, even on the most *fondamental* level. It was time for conserving energy so that I could enjoy my one night stay in the upper reaches of North America.

I pulled over at a rest area to take a breather, and upon stepping out of the truck, realized that I'd chosen a lucky stopping point—straight across from a pawnshop. It was about three p.m. Children played in a nearby park while cars whipped past and mothers bit nails and tugged on lounging husbands. Closer I drew to the shop, crossing a few lanes of traffic to arrive at its entryway. The place looked as though it were held together by bubblegum. Under an awning sat two curious creatures—faces that would inspire the most apathetic sculptor. I guessed they were in their eighties.

"Young man," the older gentleman called out. "You look different. Where ya comin' from?"

"I look *different?*"

"Yeah," said the other. "You got a different look."

"What do I look like?" I said, taking a step back.

"I don't know. Like somethin'. What's your ancestry?"

"Slovak, German, Italian—"

"That's it! The Italian. I could tell. That's where I'm from originally."

"Cool. When's the last time you visited?"

"Not in eons. Maybe when I was sixteen, seventeen. We immigrated here, my family and I. But it's a beautiful country. I can still remember it."

"Do you remember anything specific?" I asked.

"The women. They're gorgeous. Gorgeous! I've been struck by their beauty many times. It's like walking into a wall when you see 'em. They're so damned pretty."

I thought of Army.

Here I was two thousand miles away, and it was no different than when Army and I sat at his Palisades table surrounded by 8 x 10's and Ella Fitzgerald. Army had talked to me about surfboards. This man was all about the ladies. They were beings of everlasting passion. The ones who refused to fade; the proud, the hungry, lonely-happy warriors.

"Well anyway, I won't keep ya," sighed the man. "Go. Explore. See what we've got in there. It's all junk, but it's our junk."

It was musty inside the shop. The walls were lined with shelves that held dolls and memories, kept them in place; a chamber of stuffed love and glass where only light escaped. Price tags flapped in fanned air, humid and haunting, drawn from square windows and vents. A museum of the mysterious, and they were the only museums I sought; just like the museum streets and people, museum Tecate in museum New Mexico.

I rounded a corner and sat down in a vintage recliner, breathing the fresh attic smell. The wall in front of me was covered with rusty license plates both American and Canadian, and I thought of my father, as he was a collector of these types of things. With Father's Day approaching, it would make for the perfect gift. Carefully, I reached up and pulled a blue 1980 Ontario plate from the collaged spectacle, dusted it off, and tracked down one of the museum men outside.

"Found something, I see," said the Italian.

"My dad collects automobile parts."

"This is a good one," he nodded. "Pulled from my Ford back in '87. Surprised it took this long for someone to snatch it up."

"Maybe it was waiting for me," I jested.

"I believe it!"

"Think my dad will like it?"

"He'll love it. Parents love all things from children, no matter how old they get to be. That's gratitude at its finest, being a parent. Got to have gratitude."

"Is that your secret to staying so enthusiastic?" I asked.

The man waddled behind the register, placing my plate into a paper bag and scratching his chin.

"Never thought about that," he said.

"What?"

"That I . . . Whether I was an enthusiastic person."

"I'd say you are."

"In that case, probably, yes. Gratitude. Every day. If you can't be grateful, what's the point of life?"

"I don't know. Some people would say love."

"Love is the point?"

"Yeah."

"Sure it is," the man went on. "But what's love without gratitude?"

"Hm. Wow. You're like the wise man of the mountain, except I didn't have to climb a thousand steps to see you."

"Aren't you grateful for that?" the man smiled.

—

The old man said gratitude!
Gratitude, says the old man!
Maybe that's what we've been missing
in Americaland!

Perhaps we've become obsessed with *things*, and what irony, I thought, to hear such advice from a man who sold them. My heart welled and wondered about Francine and whether I was grateful for her. I wanted to throw myself out of the truck for questioning the past three years, and I thought of those who questioned twenty, and entire lives, and knew that gratitude might possibly be the most important truth yet. Really, I wasn't sure. I knew that I loved Francine. I knew that she was beautiful. But it's almost as if I were collecting her in the pawn shop of my life. Collecting love but dead to it. What is love without the aliveness? What is it without . .

Without . . .

Up ahead, I spotted a roadside hitchhiker holding a sign that read NORTH. She wore some kind of tattered western jacket, brown, tassels, earrings to catch dreams, eyes, hair, tied, dimpled, freckled, sign: NORTH.

I stopped.

She climbed inside the cab and threw down a bag, immediately extending her hand—"Name's Juliette, from Vancouver."

Her palm was cold despite the warm day, and I thought this made her special somehow.

"Johan."

"Nice ta meet ya, Johan," she fluttered. "Where ya headed?"

"New Liskeard. About three hours—"

"I know where it's at," she interrupted. "There's a music festival up that way. It's where I'm headed."

"Music festival? What kind?"

"The kind with music."

Somehow I kept meeting smart-asses on the road; although I didn't mind in this case because Juliette was a sarcastic smart-ass with charm and sass, and incredible youthful mystique. Her face puckered with each remark and suggested that she liked me right off the bat, rather than wait to display her best wit as we pushed north. NORTH! Because of Juliette, North quickly became the new West, and part of me wished that she would never find that festival; that it would dismantle and move out of town before we arrived.

"You don't even know me," Juliette remarked.

"Huh?"

"I know what you're thinking over there," she said, squinting.

"What are you talking about?"

"I mean…it's okay. I've been stared at by guys before."

"Am I staring at you?"

"Little."

"Well, you're a new person that I've never seen. You're interesting to me. And pretty at that."

"Thanks, but I don't date guys with girlfriends," she said, peeling a photo of Francine from the dash. "Or wives. Or whoever this is."

"Wait, wait. Let's start over," I urged, waving my arms through the awkwardness. "I'm Johan. Yes, I think you're pretty. Yes, I have a girlfriend. But I also give compliments when they're due. Yes, I will take you to your music festival."

Juliette blushed, dissolving freckles, and went quiet. We sat there in the hum-drum dusk and things continued on as usual—drone and rattle, itch and shift. Perhaps Juliette was to be a final test.

"So what kind of music festival?"

"You already asked me that question," she reminded.

"Just trying to make conversation."

"I know. Thanks, really. Thanks for picking me up. But I'm tired. I'm going to sleep now."

We were an old married couple celebrating our ten-minute anniversary. I watched as Juliette pulled a blanket from her backpack, bunched it up against the window and rested her head. I noticed that she had an eyebrow ring the shape of a barbell. What an amazing woman. Out here tramping, laughing in the face of risk, not giving a shit, jumping into trucks and passing out under the gaze of strange men. I wondered where she came from—Vancouver, sure—but where she really came from. What her childhood home looked like, what was whispered into her ear on the playground that one day, what the birds and the bees really turned out to be.

"Can you turn off the AC?" she said. "I'm cold."

—

I WAS an hour outside of New Liskeard when my phone rang, stirring Juliette, her eyebrow ring flashing in the moonlight—"Where are we? Who is that? Your wife?"

"She's not my wife," I whispered, answering the call.

"Hey babe," came Francine's voice.

Juliette continued to lie against the window, eyes directed at me.

"Hello? Is this a good time to talk?" Francine pressed.

"'Course. Just focused on the road at the moment."

"Where are you?" she asked.

"You'll never guess."

"California?"

"Far from it."

"Aw."

"I'm in Canada, babe!"

"Canada?"

"CANADA!!"

"That's cool."

"Isn't it?"

"How'd you end up there?"

"I persuaded a man at the company and he let me go."

"Cool, babe."

"Yeah."

"Is it different than everywhere else you've been?"

"Don't know yet. Haven't explored."

"Are you going to explore?"

"Gonna try," I said.

"Cool."

"Yeah."

Juliette leaned in, trying to listen to the conversation.

"So babe," Francine went on, "There's something important I need to talk to you about."

"Oh yeah? Well, I'm driving at the moment. Can it wait?"

"I really think we should discuss it now."

"Okay."

Juliette leaned in again. I shooed her away.

"You know," Francine mumbled, "this whole thing isn't working."

"Okay."

"The distance is too much. I'm lonely here in this crazy city and, well, I miss you. You can understand that, right?"

"Sure."

The road was black and squiggly. A pure night. Bobbing along, straddling eastern Ontario, scraping Quebec.

"I just don't want to keep missing you," she said. "It hurts. Every time you leave, it hurts."

"I know, babe. It's not easy for me either."

"Then why are you still out there?"

Juliette leaned in.

"Because it's my adventure and it's not over."

"How will you know when it's over?"

Pure night. Almost.

"I don't know," I answered. "I really don't."

"Then it's over between us, at least."

"Listen. Let's talk about this when I return to LA. I'll be back in three weeks."

"Three weeks."

"You can wait three weeks, right?"

Silence.

"Right?"

Silence.

I looked down at my phone and saw that I had once again lost reception during a critical moment. "Dammit," I muttered, tossing my phone into a cup holder. When I looked up, I met with Juliette's sacred eyes, lost in the umbra of our cramped cab. Deep, black pool eyes. Elegant, welcome-to-my-abyss eyes. And boy she had 'em. They grew big. Bigger. BIGGER. And suddenly Juliette was grasping and pointing at the windshield—"LOOK OUT!!"

—

IT HAPPENED as two distinct bumps. Strange how we remember things. Despite having seven sets of tires, I only recalled a double-thud. Juliette and I stood on the highway, staring at a blood smear at least forty feet long. My truck's shiny chrome grill had turned concave. Its headlights sprouted hair. I felt bad. Never killed anything this large before. Insects, yes. Some the size of my palm. But never an animal equivalent to the modern day house pet.

"It's okay," said Juliette. "You think you're the first trucker to smash a deer?"

"Could have been prevented," I responded, eyes to blood.

"Maybe. Maybe not. Everything has a time, place, and reason."

Her jacket flapped in the wind.

"I don't want anything to do with this anymore," I said, not knowing what I meant.

"What do you mean?" asked Juliette.

"I don't know," I said.

"You say that a lot."

"What?"

"'I don't know.' Heard you on the phone with your wife."

"She's not my wife."

"You shouldn't say I don't know," she reiterated. "It promotes doubt and insecurity."

"I just feel sorry."

"Don't say sorry either."

"So then, what exactly does one say in these situations?"

Juliette shrugged. "Oops."

Traffic whooshed by and she kept glowing and flapping.

"I've got to file a claim with my employer about this," I said. "Then we'll be on our way. Unless you want to hitch another ride. It'll take me awhile to make the call."

"I can wait," she said.

—

AFTER PANNING a flashlight underneath the trailer to ensure the bumper wasn't the only thing dragging, Juliette and I were back on our way, and soon we arrived in the small northern town. My delivery wasn't due 'til three p.m. the next day, and regardless of my sour mood, I still planned on spending the night under the stars. Parked at a rest area with Juliette, I looked over and realized she had fallen asleep somewhere between our crime scene and New Liskeard.

"Hey," I nudged. "Wake up."

She stirred. For a minute or two, at the risk of appearing a total creep, I watched her in the high lamplight. How many other beings on earth exist like her, I wondered. How much beauty on our pebble? What am I missing, O God, what am I missing? I saw myself in her. The circles. The dream. The getaway. She was on the run from something, *to something*; to her maddening music show and beyond. Where would she land? What was left to be found?

"Hey," I persisted. "Wake up, we're here."

The deer ordeal had clearly taken a toll.

"Hey!" I shouted.

She jumped up.

"We're here," I said, lowering my voice. "I mean, almost. We're in a parking lot at a rest stop."

Juliette rubbed her eyes and looked around the asphalt as though it were Mars.

"Where are we?"

"New Liskeard. You wanted to come here, remember? Music show?"

"Ahhh yes," she said, perking up suddenly. "Guess I was more tired than I thought."

"Apparently."

She yawned and stretched, and I couldn't help but follow her breasts as they heaved forward.

"Where are you staying tonight?" I asked.

"Oh, I'll find a place. Maybe pitch a cot or cop a couch."

"Do you know anyone in the area?"

"Nah. But I'm a butterfly. I make friends. Where are *you* going to sleep?"

"Normally I sleep here in the truck, right behind you. But tonight I'm gonna book a motel room, seeing as it's my first time in Canada."

"First time in Canada deserves a hotel room for sure," Juliette agreed. "Where ya comin' from anyway? Never told me much about yourself."

"Lots of places. Maryland originally, but I've lived in LA for the past three years."

"Three years? How'd you manage that?"

"I'm here, aren't I?"

—

She had no place to go, and I had no one to share those stars with.

—

THE SWEET OLD LADY at the front desk owned the motel and was swift in getting us the keys to a cozy room. Looking around the lobby, I could tell that she took pride in every detail, from the Bavarian-style tablecloths to dust-free chandeliers. In the morning, she would tell me and Juliette that she was German and missed Germany but loved the lake. She'd tell us that she used to work as a wedding photographer and that she used to have a husband. She'd tell us that sausage was on the way and sorry for the wait.

—

BUT LET ME back up.

Juliette had no place to go, and between the deer death and foreign land, I didn't want to be alone. Besides, she was interesting and pretty to look at.

"You don't have to do this," she said. "I'm a born camper. No, really, I was born on a campground."

Her stories were feature-film material, and as with Tecate, she inspired my journey forward. I thought maybe that's all I needed to revitalize the whole thing: new experiences to feed the dream and more love to feed the experience.

The dream was hungry, dammit!

Hot damn hot dream.

"The room has two beds," I said. "It's perfectly fine."

We dropped our stuff in the motel room and by then it was already ten p.m. I was jamming yawns back into my mouth; stale coffee, wine. The wine was Juliette's idea. So was the pot. She had a dime bag in her backpack and told me that she didn't want to waste it on "some random dude" at the festival, and that she'd much prefer to get high with some random trucker. Why not. This was my big adventure, and the adventure was not the adventure without the adventure.

She got up to close the blinds and I watched her ass wiggle across the room. Her chestnut-colored hair was down, pulled to one side, and it fell across her shoulders in layers. An apt roller of blunts, Juliette wrapped one up in about sixty seconds. It was clean and commercial-looking.

"You could sell that in retail stores," I told her.

She laughed and lit up.

"No, really," I said, taking a healthy drag and passing it back. "It's a skill. It should be valued like any other."

"You gonna be my manager or what?" she asked.

"Hm. Do I get a cut or am I just here for immoral support?"

"You get unlimited smoke sessions with me," she smiled, still passing the burning night.

Our TV was set to a channel with French-speaking soap opera stars, and suddenly I was reminded of the ones I came to see in the first place.

"Let's go outside," I said.

Juliette walked across the parking lot without shoes or socks, dodging broken glass and cigarette butts with her toes. She seemed not to mind anything, and I wondered if it was because she was still young. And I wondered if I cared so much because I was finally getting old.

"You're not old," she said.

"What?"

"Too many people worry about age. You're not old and you'll never be old, and you can always do anything you want."

We stopped at the edge of a lake.

"How are you doing this?" I asked.

"Doing what?"

"Reading my mind."

She laughed—"Whaaat? Dude, you're *high*"—and jumped into a small rowboat.

"What are you doing? We can't steal a boat!"

"Relax. We'll bring it right back. They rent these out to the public anyway. It's a Canadian outdoors-thing. I should know."

Reluctantly, I climbed in, still feeling wary for my age; more aware than ever of the great timeline. The boat creaked and bounced as I sat down on its plastic seat. Juliette untied it from the dock and we both grabbed paddles and started rowing onto the lake.

Nothing else needed to be said.

We listened to the slosh of water—each stroke sending a thousand notes to my eardrums. It's surface dancing. Legs pale and steady.

"Maybe we should stop here," I suggested.

"Why do you continue to use these words?" asked Juliette.

"What words? What are you talking about?"

"Maybe, sorry, I don't know."

"I don't know, I just—"

"You did it again!"

"Hm. You know," I said, "You're the first person to point these things out as unusual."

She kept rowing.

"How far are we going anyway?"

She kept rowing.

"Juliette?"

Loser! No one wants to fuck a loser!

"See what I mean?" she asked.

"Hm?"

"I bet you panicked when I didn't respond."

Juliette's body began moving through the air.

"Where are you going?" I asked, watching her hover.

"I'm coming over to sit with you," she said, walking across the boat. "Chill. We're far enough, remember?"

The crickets grew louder and I distinctly heard them chanting, "KISSher, KISSher, KISSher." But the boat was drifting, and I thought of the load that needed delivered, and Francine, and the boat—SHIT! The boat was stolen and "Where will we end up?" I asked, looking past hazel eyes.

"Anywhere but here, right?"

"You can't say these things," I told her. "It makes me want to, like, disappear or something."

"If you could go anywhere, where would you go? Right now. Five seconds to answer!"

"Five seconds?"

"Just lost one. Four, three . . ."

"Hm."

"Two."

"Here."

"You'd go here?" she chuckled. "Out of all the places in the universe?"

"In the *unnniiivveerrrrsseeee?*"

When I said the word, it seemed to carry forbidden weight. Universe. Uni-verse. Uni. Verse. Union. Unified. U . . . You . . . Her . . . crickets . . . boat . . . load . . . home . . . toad . . . toast . . . moon . . .

"That poor deer," I said.

"Kiss me," she said.

No, it was the crickets.

"Kiss me."

"Kiss you?"

"Sure, why not?" she replied.

I reached my hand around her neck and we dropped straight onto the boat's floor. And maybe it was the pot, but I noticed that her lips were like fish—slimier than usual, wonderfully pleasant—and I didn't want to let go. Juliette's hair, full in my fingers, and her legs, smooth against mine. Every sensation, everywhere her hand fell, was felt, as we drifted across our liquid void begging for permanent pause.

summer

26

JUNE 18TH ENTRY

"Two weeks and already missing her. Them! Francine and Juliette and everyone I've ever met. Confusing as hell. Sometimes I think I only miss one of 'em. Well. Don't know. How can I know? I only knew Juliette for a night. She'd tell me not to say "I don't know" anyway. Fuck. Maybe I am just a sorry sap. Tiiirrrrreeeed!!! Sick of all this driving. Everything is boring. How did it become so boring? Why do I keep asking that? Why am I whining? Aren't I allowed to whine? When do I get to cry like a baby? When do I get to

WAAAAAAAHHHHHH
WAAAAAAAAAAAHHHH – AH – AH – A –
AAAAAAAA"

Get it together, Johan.

—

THE MAIN QUESTION, really, was "What the hell am I gonna do back in LA?" Because that's where I felt I was headed. Surely my eight thousand dollars would not take me far around the world; although one morning while nestled in the back of my cab at an Arizona paper factory (during warm sunrise), I came across a media job located in the UK. I didn't really want the job. It looked stuffy. What I was fixated on, however, was the idea of Europe because it was the first continent on my list and I couldn't kick the idea. Furthermore, I left Juliette with a note that read:

TO EAST AND BEYOND WE'LL GO!
DON'T WAIT FOR ME, BUT WAIT FOR ME.

253

I REALLY DIDN'T think she'd take it seriously. But that was the nature of our one-night relationship: jokes and smokes. I probably could have gone on that way for a while. Maybe we'd live in the woods with wolves and berries. Maybe we'd be nude all the time and fuck like rabbits, and fuck alongside rabbits, and smoke joints afterwards and watch the stars. Maybe we'd forget about TV and clocks and age, and we wouldn't know how old we were or what was lacking because there'd be nothing to remind us. Maybe that sounds like a fantasy, however entirely possible. But what would we do for money? That was often the final hurdle: How would we eat if we couldn't walk into the grocery store and buy pre-packaged meals and hair conditioner?

The road snapped me present.

Rumble rumble
Rumble onward, young road!
Take me to your destiny
Take me to your ocean of promise
Take me *back* to your ocean of promise
Take me to big screen
Take me to UK
Take me to Francine
Take me to money
Take me to Juliette
Take me to myself

Or just let me dream
just let me scream
for one more minute
then I'll be done
promise

—

BREAKING OUT of a shell is never easy.

What I mean is that I was sitting in my truck, somewhere between Arizona and Colorado; between the Me of the past twenty-six years and the Me that was yet to begin. I was effectively killing all that was, and what had instigated this transformation was the great trucking adventure. I knew that I could not return to LA because it was tied to the Old Me. It would be a mess. Francine and I would not last. The days would pass, and I'd feel remorse and itches gone unscratched. Yes, I already knew these things. But I had a polished screenplay to sell. It was the key motivating factor for my return. Although I could use my savings to visit unknown places, I would not have access to the vast and powerful Hollywood network.

Still, something was off.

I didn't care to sell the screenplay.

Didn't care to make movies. That, too, was tied to the Old Me—the old shell—which had been left somewhere on Old 66. Maybe some new traveler would come along and try it on and find inspiration in its broken stitching. He or she would trove the world, and I'd receive postcards signed "Old Me," and frame them and show my grandkids.

—

STOPPED TO LOAD UP in Denver. Kleenex.
I did not cry.
I will not cry for you, Denver.
I will not cry for me.
I will not cry for free.
Free cries for me.

—

BUGS. EVERYWHERE. Stuck to my windshield. Stuck to the side mirrors and bumper. Smacking against glass and metal each night—clink, clink, splat, WHACK! Some of them left behind large smudges of bodily fluids, and when I stepped outside of the truck I could smell death in the air. It was like a graveyard, that windshield, and sometimes I marveled at the spectacle of it. Wings and antennae and stick legs.

I didn't bother to hose her down, as I was in Denver again, and this time I parked and caught a bus straight into downtown, where I wandered into a grocery store looking for a snack to bum around with. Peanut butter. Protein. That's good. Find some bread to go with it. But there's an old man blocking my path to the PB. What's he want? Looks at me. Shakes a bony finger. "You oughta check that peanut butter."

"Excuse me?" I asked.

"Twist off the lid and make sure it's not poisoned."

"Why would it be poisoned?"

"I was poisoned once," he lamented with watery eyes. "'Cause I forgot to check the seal. You oughta check the seal."

"Okay."

I followed his advice and twisted off the lid to find the seal intact. The man shrugged—"You just never know"—shuffling away.

Peanut butter. Protein.

The man returned.

"You a Christian?"

"Hm?"

"I said 'Are you a *Christian*?'"

"Raised Catholic. Why?"

"Well, I'll pray for you. And when you become a Christian, you can pray for me, too."

Peanut butter. Protein. Bread to go with it.

Then outside to walk some more.

I was ready to walk. My legs had grown soft in the truck. Your whole body grows soft in the truck. I saw three-hundred-pound men step out of Freightliners with slack jaws and slouched knees. Seen 'em waddle like ducklings. They started building gyms inside the truckstops but nobody used them. Dusty machines on display, just so the industry could boost morale with a shiny pamphlet. You got to get outside, man! Some of these guys are smart. Collapsible scooters and bicycles. It wasn't really a question of size. I was skinny as porch railing and still felt as though I couldn't pull my weight without cracking a few joints along the way.

Long explanation short: it felt good to take a jaunt around Denver. I watched all the women and trendy twentysomethings sit outside cafes, donning Ray Bans and drinking mimosas. This was a young town with young faces—golden and rosy—and everything exciting! The weather, the music, the alcohol, the politics, the shoes, the countries, the venues, the jobs, the marriages, the hopes, the technology, the rent, the words, the Zen, the sex. Was it good? Oh but wouldn't you like to know?

For a moment I thought back to the previous July, watching all the sandy bodies on the beach, surfers and freckles, and paused to consider how I was still in the same situation—standing on the outside, looking in. How far had I come since then? What did I really desire? Did I want my corner table and mimosa? Did I want my wakeboard and blunt? Or was I happy with truck and grease? How about cabin and Francine?

Something seemed off about it all.

I caught glimpse of my reflection in a furniture shop window as I passed, and saw the Me that I had dreamt one year before: cowboy hat and loose-fitting clothes, backpack, boots, and give-no-fucks expression. It was the portrait of a young explorer on an adventure, ready for more, but afraid to start all over. Starting over always meant an encore tango with fear. It meant cutting ties with all that's familiar (or in my case, what had become familiar)—*We adapt, see?*

I was happy with who I saw in the window.

In fact, I was jubilant. Redeemed. I had achieved the dream and sought the next. Next, next, next. Next, next,

next. Next, next, next. Next, next, next. Next, next, next.
Next, next, next. Next, next, next. Next, next, next. Next,
next, next. Next, next, next. Next, next, next. Next, next,
next. Next, next, next. Next, next, next. Next, next, next.
Next, next, next. Next, next, next. Next, next, next. Next,
next.

—

I HAD ACHIEVED the dream, and it looked a little unkempt
but pretty damn good. Suddenly I found myself questioning
why I was abandoning it and had forgotten all the reasons. It
seemed that there was indeed a way out of the lull; of the pit
I started to sink into. Movement itself would again show me
the way. Only by moving did I uncover clues of new thought
and feeling. It's true—trucking was dead—but movement
was not. I had simply milked the experience, drank the milk,
and gone thirsty again. Long live the truck-heifer! Long live
the milk of life! Long live Denver!

—

JULIETTE WAS STUCK on the roof of my brain and I could
sense her lounging up there while I continued to kick about.
It kept me from thinking of LA—another milk bottle that I
was soon to return to and sit at its dry depths.

But back to the moment.

I wandered into a Hard Rock Cafe because what I was
really thirsty for was a beer, and there was a sign outside that
read COLD BEER HERE. The server was a black chick with
dreadlocks and bleached teeth. "What'll it be?" And I told
her I wanted the Cold Beer Special, which of course opened
up a cornucopia of options—Heineken, Bud, Guinness,
Tecate—"Scratch that," I say. "Scratch that. Instead, I'll
take some liquor. Something easy on the stomach."

"How 'bout some bitters?" she says.

"Never had it."

"Never had bitters?!"

"Nope. What is it?"

"How do you explain bitters?" she asks a pudgy co-worker.

"Bitters," he says. "Never had bitters?"

"Nope."

"It's good," he says.

"I'll take it."

While I waited for the mixing—dreadlocks flying, whistling, K.I.S.S. overhead—I noticed an old couple seated next to me in the otherwise empty bar. They were curious, looking for conversation, and I really didn't think I had any because I could barely order a drink with the radiant bartender. Sure enough, we got to talking, and I learned that the kind folks were visiting from the Czech Republic. They told me all about their land of hills, churches, and beers. Come sometime, they said. But I'm a trucker. Come anyway! Bring the truck! Said I couldn't but that I was quitting and maybe I'd see them the following spring.

"I'm sure it's a beautiful place. What are you two doing here in the US anyway?"

"Oh, we travel by RV," said the woman. "We rent one and do a different route each year. It's suuuuuuuuch a big country!!"

"That it is. Hey, maybe we can switch places. You stay in the US for awhile and I stay at your lovely house in Europe."

They laughed.

I didn't.

"I have Slovakian heritage, you know. We're ancestral neighbors."

They laughed.

They were good people. They liked to laugh.

—

I DIDN'T STAY much longer in Denver. After I said goodbye to Dreadlocks and Czechs, I was back on my way to Strike terminal and truck via bus.

And the weary urbanites

And the kid with headphones looking down at his shoes
And you
Where were you?

—

REALLY, the question I should've been asking was "Where is Francine? And why hasn't she called? Why haven't I called her? Why am I not making more money?" Those were the *right questions*, right? But I felt as though when I asked the other questions such as "Where were you?" what I really meant to ask was "Where is the world and its spirit?"

You see, that's sort of where this whole adventure ended. Questions like that, when mulled over in the sleeper berth at eleven p.m., drew me into the abyss of What If; where all possibilities—shrewd and precarious—appeared as a series of colored doors in the great big circus of life. I stood in that harlequin hall with those options and my youth—all those OPTIONS!—and tried my best to imagine the scroll that would unfold from each door. The scenes that I would surf to death, or perhaps hop, skip, and jump to the next. My aim was crystal clear: I had to choose something or risk the Abyss. I had to *choose* something. Had to *move*.

27

THERAPIST: TELL ME AGAIN, why did you leave LA?

Me: I was looking for experience.

Therapist: And Francine, how did that make you feel?

Francine: Well at first I was shocked, really sad. But then I kind of understood it. But definitely sad for a long time. And confused.

Therapist: And Johan, how did that make you feel?

Me: Didn't feel like I had a choice anymore.

Therapist: I see. So, in making that choice, did you consider Francine and her feelings?

Me: I did.

Francine: But he kind of told me last-minute.

Therapist: And why did you do that, Johan?

Me: I knew that she would—

Therapist: To Francine. Explain it to Francine, if you could.

Me: What are you here for then?

Therapist: I'm a facilitator. Please, just follow my rules.

Me: Okay. Francine, the reason I waited to tell you is because I worried that you would react, uh, unfavorably to my wanting to drive an eighteen-wheeler. And I didn't want to lose you, but also knew that it was something I had to do.

Therapist: You were afraid.

Me: Am I talking to you again or . . . ?

Therapist: I'm a facilitator. You're talking to Francine.

Francine: You were afraid.

Me: Yeah, babe. I didn't want to lose you.

Francine: I didn't want to lose you either. I'm glad you're back.

Me: It's nice to be back.

Francine: I love you.

Me: Love you, too.

Therapist: And so...the question now becomes "What's next?" Are you here to stay, Johan? Francine has expressed her need to *know* these things. She needs you to become a more effective and open communicator. Are you prepared to meet those needs moving forward?

Me: Sure. That's why we're here, right? To strengthen our communication? Isn't this therapy session a good first step?

Therapist: It's an excellent first step. But I need a resounding YES from you. Are you prepared to meet her needs moving forward?

Me: YES.

Therapist: And Francine, do you understand and agree to Johan's needs as well?

Francine: I'm sorry, can you just repeat what they are?

Therapist: He's right there. Ask him.

Francine: What are your needs, babe?

Me: Hm. Never thought about it much. Maybe that's part of the problem. I don't know what they are. Certainly need my space. I think that's what drove me to the truck in the first place . . . I was kind of suffocating—

Francine: But don't I give you enough space, babe?

Therapist: Let him talk, Francine.

Me: Yeah. You do. But I need more space, you know. Buckets of it sometimes.

Francine: Buckets? How much is a *bucket*?

Therapist: *Francine*.

Me: Weeks, maybe.

Francine: Weeks? How do you expect to maintain a healthy relationship like that?

Me: Ha! Good question. That's what I mean: I don't know.

Therapist: Seems to me like you *do know*. Let me ask you something, Johan. What was it that drew you into this trucking experience?

Me: Maps, trucks, bathrobes.

Therapist: Bathrobes?

Me: Assholes. I don't know.

Therapist: Refrain from "I don't know." You do know.

Me: Yes. I do know. It was curiosity. When I looked at those maps and saw the colored squares—one of the states, like Arizona or New Mexico—I really wanted to know what the state looked like. Really wanted to *know*; to see the place for myself.

Therapist: Why was that so important to you?

Me: Because it was the idea of truth. Lifting the veil.

Therapist: Was it the truth of America or your own truth that you sought?

Me: Both.

Therapist: Would you say that you found it?

Me: I don't . . . I'm . . .

Therapist: Hm?

Me: Not quite sure.

—

I DRAINED my bank account during the following weeks.

Eight grand splintered into rent, furniture, and a Mazda sedan with leaky sunroof. My spiffy Honda was long-gone, sold earlier in the year to pay off its debt. I missed it. The Mazda smelled like a bag o' dust, and knobs fell off when I tried to adjust the radio volume, temperature, etc. But she ran hard and it was nice to glance up and see the sky. Miss

Mazda embodied the way I felt. Paint still glimmering in parts, jerking around with an angry kind of torque, revving loudly but invisible to the rest of the world—a silent scream brushing pine needles as I pulled into the parking lot of my neighborhood cafe.

I would write my way out, I thought
I'd write my way out of all of this
Write what I couldn't say to the therapist
What I couldn't say to Francine

Choose a seat somewhere in the back. Yes, that one. Next to the pale fellow with long hair and trench coat. Next to the pool table and couch with wooden arms. It's loud and messy here, but so is everything else. Live with it.

Get it together, Johan
You've got it together, Johan

Break open that laptop. Sip that coffee. Stare at that girl. Stare at the wall. Think of numbers, days, ways. Tastes like confusion. Tastes like youth—fleeting perhaps, but dying the death of a burning brick. She won't look back, will she? It's that nervous leg syndrome you've got. Paco'd tell you it's the diesel-blood. Maybe you've got a diesel-heart. Maybe she can smell it. Maybe coffee's too strong. Maybe you shouldn't have left that cowboy hat on the dashboard.

"What are you working on?" asked the man in trench coat.

"Same thing as everyone else in here."

"Hm?"

"I'm joking," I said. "It's a screenplay for a feature film. Just making some edits."

"What's it about?"

"Oh. It's, uh, about truck drivers. Eighteen-wheelers. The main character has a fatal disease, accepts an offer to drive a truck. Then he gets involved in a love triangle with his boss's wife, and a cat-and-mouse chase ensues across the country."

"Sounds good."

"Thanks. Something you'd pay twelve bucks to see?"

"Yes, of course. But can I ask just one question?"

"Sure."

"I'm from Russia, yeah? And in Russia we don't write for movies as much. When I moved here and saw these technical writing styles, it gave me deeper appreciation for literature. So with your story, why not prose?"

"Hmm. Always considered myself as a filmmaker," I replied, a bit shaken.

"But it could make great story, no? Storytelling is storytelling."

"Sure. But I like film. It gives me a broader license to lie. Especially here in Hollywood."

"Ha," he laughed, tossing thin hair, "but you don't look like a liar to me."

"Are you saying I don't belong in Hollywood? Or that I'm not a filmmaker?"

"I'm just saying," he went on, "why not prose?"

Then he slowly got up, trying to be stealthy but failing—it was clear that he was going to the bathroom or something. He was trying to appear mysterious and it wasn't necessary because I had already thought of him as a long lost sibling. But I didn't see him for a long time afterwards and thought that he really must've been stealthy because there was only one exit to the place, and my eyes were fixed on the front door all along, considering his query. I was sure we'd met before, just like Simon and Juliette, Paco and Professor Jake, and Fabio. And all the crestfallen people of the road. Even the ones who smiled as they went about their business, wiping tables and cranking wrenches in the dusty daylight and roadside motels. The maids right now, vacuuming, and the drivers, shifting through exit ramps with swelling bladders. And wild Tecate reborn for a new life in the desert—a place I was sure everyone must've lived at some point or another; thinking about colorful doors in their own dark beds after refrigerators are closed up, switches flipped, coffee gone cold, and Russians sent back to their homeland because of expired visas—who knows. The scroll unfolds for all, screenplay or prose; written or unwritten. It's all there is and will be, and as long as I kept living I would keep writing, and that's what I knew.

The Russian returned.
"Forgot my coat."
I smiled and handed it to him.
"Why not?" he said.

about the author

Steve Nahaj's work is based on his travels, which include exploring the US via semi-truck and mingling with bohemians in Paris. Although his second novel, this story serves as a prequel to his debut, *Welcome to the Abyss*. Steve lives in Berlin, Germany with his wife and a large monstera plant named Fran.

connect

Social: @nahajguy
Website: runawaypoets.com

acknowledgments

I offer gratitude to everyone involved in the publishing process and experiences that helped shape this book. My family, thank you for supporting me in the myriad ways that you do. Nothing goes unnoticed. Susanne, *danke für alles*. You continue to be a source of warmth and inspiration that makes me a very happy human. The Spoken Word and Paris Lit Up poetry communities: for allowing me to ramble on-stage, and for your applause at the end. To my friends far and wide, I appreciate your words of encouragement and am grateful to have such an eclectic network to shake the snow globe with. Lastly, I want to recognize the drivers, servers, cashiers, mechanics, clerks, managers, janitors, instructors, loaders, construction crews, patrolmen, patrolwomen, medical teams, and all other workers contributing to safer highways and the transportation of nearly everything we consume. Thank you.

www.ingramcontent.com/pod-product-compliance
Lightning Source LLC
Chambersburg PA
CBHW031025260626
47153CB00017B/2113